Aristotle & Sons

SET 'EM UP

The debtor is in

By A.N.G. Reynolds

Printed in the United States of America
First Printing, 2018

ISBN 978-0-9600207-1-3 (print)
ISBN 978-0-9600207-0-6 (ebook)

www.ang-reynolds.net

Cover design and formatting by
www.ebooklaunch.com

Foreword

G reetings, my dear reader! I hope you are having a lovely week (it must not be too bad, since you currently have a book in your hands).

I started writing this foreword shortly after receiving the edited version of this book from my amazing editor. Usually, forewords are the most boring part of the book, second only to the appendices. I believe Tolkien was the only author in the history of authors to actually make appendices interesting.

To that end, I abhorred the idea of subjecting you, my dear reader, to either of those. My editor, however, made me realize that if I didn't at least explain why some of the things in my book are the way they are, I'll probably do more harm than good.

Fear not, however, this will be an entirely spoiler-free foreword/reference; it will only give backstory to the universe I have created, sidestepping any important plot details of either this first *Aristotle & Sons* book or the next one. And if you feel that even *that* is too fraught with spoilerage, then feel free to stop here and dive straight into Chapter 1 of this book.

The first thing to clarify is that this book does not take place in the near future. Or, to some degree, even the far future. Instead, this is set roughly — I haven't actually done the calculations yet — 1.23 billion years into the future. Yes, that's with a "b"; may you never say I lack a forward-thinking mind.

Due to this a lot has changed. Humanity has risen and fallen a countless number of times technologically, culturally, and in geographic dominance. To this end, if you read a reference of a "few centuries ago" or a "few millennia in the past", rest assured that that past is just as foreign to you and I as the book's current present.

The other important thing to note is that the Solar system we call home is currently enveloped inside a massive, yellowish-green nebula, similar in color to the cover of the book. The cause of that nebula is currently shrouded in mystery, but the important thing to note is that it is as murky as a foggy London night and twice as thick, making travel and communication through space a sluggish endeavor.

Yes, I am aware that nebulae are not thick enough to be "murky" and that they technically aren't supposed to be green or visible to the naked eye, but for my book, both of those lovely scientific truths were thrown completely out the window. Like the multitude of scientific impossibilities lurking within all other space operas, sometimes style must be chosen over fact.

I like to think that where I lacked in astronomical precision, I made up for in biological correctness. My nebulae may be green, but my ecosystems are well-balanced.

The final — and perhaps most *irksome* — clarification is why I chose not to use the typical naval lingo when describing the story's main living ship's (the *Lilstar*) interior features (i.e. "bathroom" instead of "head"; "kitchenette" instead of "mess").

Setting aside my arguments against naval elitists who feel sci-fi should adopt naval parlance and attributes solely because we happen to call the interstellar vehicles star*ships* — need I remind anyone that the U.S. Air Force has had more members launched into space to the current date than the Navy has? — my reasoning for using more plebian terms is quite simple: the *Lilstar* was never really a ship.

While I do call her a ship throughout the story simply for ease of understanding, in my mind she was little more than a recreational vehicle designed for an adorable retiree couple to go sight-seeing across the solar system. The *Lilstar* is definitely not formal enough to use stuffy naval terminology on. Other ships in this universe — much larger and more "navy-like" — will probably get the "proper" terminology, but rest assured even that it will also be under severe protest.

I believe those are the most important facts you must know before reading this book. Of course, I'm sure many of you have skipped this foreword purely out of habit and are now tumbling through my story, lost and bewildered, wondering exactly where you went wrong. Alas, I cannot be held accountable for such an impulsive and reckless action.

With that, dear reader, I bid you happy reading.

- A.N.G. Reynolds

Skiptracing (verb):

The process of tracking down a debtor or fugitive who has fled and whose location is currently unknown, most often by following their *paper trail*. A *paper trail* may consist of receipts, tax data, credit card information, or other kinds of information left by the fugitive. It is used in a variety of occupations for various situations but may stand as an independent profession.

Skiptrace (noun):
A person who engages in *skiptracing* as a profession. (Archaic: *skiptracer*)

ONE

The wall wasn't kind as I bounced off it. For a moment all I did was lie on the floor, inhaling the warmed-over wheat smell of the organic deck material. I hurt all over and caring about the skiptrace took more effort than I was willing to put into it.

And yes, the fight was my fault.

Blood seeped from my forehead, leg, and a thousand other little cuts onto the deck. Who brings a knife to a fistfight, anyway? The greenish, fibrous floor began to absorb the thick red liquid, providing plenty of evidence of my being here. I tried to move to prevent too much evidence from escaping, but found myself quite unable. I was sure more than just a rib was broken. That gigantic shadow of a man stalked toward me. I went limp, or at least, limper.

"You need to learn some manners," he said as he dragged me to my feet, snarling. The skiptrace held on to only my upper arms. My side felt like it was splitting open and my insides were threatening to fall out at any moment. I kicked my toe trying to find the floor again.

"You wouldn't," I sputtered, trying not to spit out a mouthful of blood all over the skiptrace. Since it wasn't as though the station authorities couldn't identify me now, I just had to be careful not to offend my overbearing target. "You wouldn't hit a woman, would you?"

The brute paused for a moment, looking me up and down. If nothing else, my disguise worked. He laughed like a crow with chest congestion.

"Yeah. I think I might," he decided. His breath alone should have killed me. He heaved, trying to throw me into the wall or down the hall, I couldn't tell which one. I caught hold of his suspenders and, although that didn't stop me from flailing in the air like a drunk monkey, he wasn't expecting my weight to snap back toward him. He fell backwards. I flipped over his bulk, landing head-to-head with him across the floor.

For a second I stared up at the bioluminescent lighting that ran along the sort of greenish beige ceiling. Drops of nutrient-rich ooze splattered my face from a ruptured vein and I noticed some bruising along the nearby wall. Poor space station. I hadn't meant for you to get hurt during my fight. With that thought, I vowed to end it quickly.

"You are a jerk," I said simply. Scrambling to my feet, I kicked the skiptrace's head twice. He didn't thrash very much, still gasping from where the wind had been knocked out of him. Before he could regain any sort of traction with his next movements, I wrapped a long piece of fibered material around his pudgy wrists. The organic material I had carefully peeled from another part of the station fused with the deck and tightened horribly, trying to be whole again with its assigned being. It would eventually stop tightening, long before the skiptrace suffered serious damage to the circulation in his hands, as it formed a suitable amount of nerve and nutrient ooze connections with its host being. I gingerly lifted the license out of the immobile skiptrace's pocket.

"Good luck getting another one," I said, standing up. I dodged his thrashing legs and limped from the scene. Curses and swearwords were my wretched, but only, followers.

As much as I tried to focus on my next step, a sense of relief washed over me. After spending the last few years chasing after this poor excuse for a skiptrace, I'd finally managed to make sure he'd never be able to take another legal bounty. It was entirely possible for him to find another company to hire him, but getting your license taken away from you was an automatic blackball. Nobody wanted to turn over a valuable skiptrace license to someone who would so easily let it be stolen, since most employers were legally bound to let the stealer of the license keep it for at least one bounty. Plus, I'd checked his record; he was only successful in just over sixty percent of the missions his employer sent him on, which was as close to the low side as any reputable skiptracing business would want...and he'd had a license stolen before. Another strike and the Skiptrace Alliance would blacklist him from ever receiving a skiptrace license again.

Take that, jerk.

I made it to the populated part of the station slowly. You could tell you were getting closer to the population by how many tattoos the walls had.

A poor or practicing graffiti artist used an undetectable paint that could be scrubbed off. A good artist, who didn't want his or her work so easily erased, used a speed-gun with an extra wide needle. Of course, the station usually didn't appreciate it. How would you like it if someone doodled inappropriate words all over your innards? Not very much, I would imagine. However, the nerve endings along the heavy traffic areas of the station had been dulled purposely, leaving the main hallways relatively numb and easy to tattoo without setting off any alarms. Provided you weren't caught by station patrols, you could finish a whole, full-sized garden scene without so much as making the station twitch. I passed a pair of station crew currently trying to laser-remove a particularly crass phrase from the walls as I made my way toward the docking area.

I counted my injuries as I walked, all 34 cuts and bruises total, thankfully I discovered my ribs were merely bruised, not entirely broken. I rested temporarily in a more or less empty hallway to bandage the ones that bled most. Whoever said revenge was sweet never had to take on someone bigger than they were. I ached in places I didn't know were possible and as much as I would have liked to pass out or go to a doctor, that would have been too easy. No, getting off the station was still my plan.

Though, of course, that wasn't a very legal operation. Sneaking aboard the craft would be easy enough, but making sure the ship didn't see you was more difficult.

Well, the ships really didn't see you as much as feel or smell you. If you were lucky and onboard an undisciplined or lazy ship, it would most likely ignore you. A young ship was usually too quick to judge: you get caught, you get thrown out an airlock. I grew up on horror stories like that—ships sensing intruders and venting the compartment into space without a word to captain or crew. That's why you have to scout about, pick just the right ship. Right age, right route, right crew. Really old ships on mundane routes were best; usually most of their senses were too dulled to detect one small stowaway. The crew on such dinosaurs were usually an odd conglomeration of young and old and very bored; they really weren't paid enough to care about illegals.

I read through the list of departing ships. I knew most by name; the ones I didn't belonged to the Reichen Concern. Not that they were any different from any other company, but they dealt mostly with the Centauri and therefore none of their ships ever had routes to Earth.

Earth. Home sweet home.

Of course everything would have been easier if I had had the money to buy passage on a ship. But that wouldn't happen until I turned in the skiptrace's license. The cost to launch a formal complaint against the man drained me dry. Some days, when I was lying in bed staring at the ceiling too hungry to move, I wondered if it was worth it. Then I would roll over, seeing my brother's face forever young in a stupid photograph. I'd get angry and sad, roll back over, and tighten my belt one more notch. Yeah, of course it was worth it.

The company gave me the standard ultimatum. Find the skiptrace, take away his license, and return it. The reward being either to be the man's replacement or to receive a lump of cash. They hardly let me leave the office before they started cackling.

Fools. I'll take the cash.

U.O.S. Meramec. That seemed the best. It still had an Organic Ship title making it about fifty or sixty years old. Not *very* old, unfortunately. But it was going to Earth and the route it took was enormously complex to avoid the ever-prevalent helium pockets. The ship would probably be too distracted navigating to check its holds regularly.

And the cargo selected was greasy engine parts for locomotives. Of course, *I* would have to put up with the smell. Grease and metal never bothered me as much as it did some of the old timers. Anyone over eighty is sure to tell you about the good old days before the return of steam-powered transportation. The only thing I hated about trains were the whistles; I can't tell you how many banshee nightmares that blasted shriek gave me as a kid.

The ship wouldn't depart for a few hours, so that gave me plenty of time to pack my provisions and sneak onboard. As if on cue, my stomach grumbled loudly, and I figured it was about time for me to refuel.

I can't say I ever liked stealing food or supplies, and I know that my brother was probably looking down on me with some measure of disappointment, but it couldn't be helped. I was beyond poor and on a mission.

I had discovered relatively quickly that I was a horrible pickpocket. My clumsy hands and poor reflexes only made for some very awkward situations. Rescued time and time again only by my innate knowledge of the station, I switched to a much more devious approach. After a few weeks on the station, you could hear the station shopkeepers mutter about 'that bloody phantom.' What can I say? Those people should really upgrade their security system to include those new-fangled Centauri optical *cameras* on top of the easily fooled organic olfactory and auditory sensors. While the organic sensors worked great a few decades ago, new and largely illegal Centauri technology like voice recorders made them much easier to fool. I had gotten my hands on a fairly sub-par but functional recorder that recorded only the important frequencies needed to fool the door. The olfactory sensor was even easier to fool because all you needed was an old hat or piece of clothing from the shop owner. Of course, sometimes neither trick worked; I passed by the bakery nearly every day to stare at the fresh bread forlornly.

I made my way to the old corner I used as a hideout. It wasn't a very pleasant place, sticky from the station's wastes, smelly from the air filtration system, and relatively cold and mildly radioactive from the weakened, space-side walls. As far as I can tell, it suffered a massive asteroid strike a few decades ago. While the station had repaired itself as best it could, the residual scarring meant radiation from space seeped in and, unless the station was on one of its sunnier orbits, the ambient heat seeped out. I was secure in the knowledge that my cash prize returning the skiptrace's license would allow me proper radiation treatment if it became necessary. The good news was that this area of the station was completely numb, since all of the implanted nerve endings had been fried when this compartment depressurized. In essence, I could hide as many supplies as I wanted without the station ever catching on.

I stuffed as many of the more-important supplies as I could into an old toolbag. I couldn't carry very much onto the *Meramec* since the extra weight could very well alert the ship to my presence. I also coated the bag in a layer of slimy, ship-temperature goo that felt like lotion and made the scratchy canvas virtually undetectable to the ship's nerve endings. I carried a small bottle of the stuff with me to apply to my shoes later. I wouldn't make it very far wandering around the station with contraband goo all over my shoes, could I? The toolbag I could hide under my long coat.

Setting aside my packing for a moment, I tried to attend my wounds again. This time my wrist was beginning to stiffen horribly and I had lost feeling in half my leg. A doozy of a headache danced itself across my forehead. Carefully moving to sit on one of the thrumming pipes that made up the ship's respiratory system, I used the faint glow of decaying, bioluminescent lights to rebandage the wounds that were still bleeding and apply a brace to my wrist. I tugged at the sleeve of my jacket to hide the brace and pulled my hat down a little farther on my forehead, hiding the dermal patch that covered the three-inch slice above my left eyebrow. By now someone had probably found the skiptrace, with all that hollering he had been doing when I left.

For a moment I found myself sitting, waiting until it was close enough to the *Meramec*'s departure that I could sneak aboard. So I worked to take off my disguise. The hat was smelly and I wouldn't miss it, along with the cargo pants that were itchy beyond measure. Those were both replaced with a hooded jacket and a pair of dark-colored capris, the only thing I had managed to steal in my size. The only remnant I kept on was the oversized shirt. It reminded me of the kind of thing my brother used to wear when he wasn't working, plus it was nice and warm.

After a quick snack of mashed plant fibers and lichen, I dug into the portfolio of maps and schematics I had accrued over the years. Though I knew the layout of every ship in dock, a once-over of the *Meramec*'s design wouldn't hurt. I thumbed through the manuals I had until I found the correct one: *United-Consortium Organic Ship Schematics: Rewritten Lightweight Military Cargo Ships*. I opened it up to the "Cargo Hold & Loading/Offloading" chapter and reviewed the basic schematics.

You see, organic ships aren't as easy to remodel as the ancient all-metallic designs were. Organic ships had to be bombarded with different frequencies of radiation to shift their genetic facsimiles to hold whatever configuration was wanted. Without it, the ship would continue to repair itself using its original design, following its pseudo-genetic rulebook to the letter. While rewriting a ship was easier than building a new one from scratch, it was still an incredibly expensive operation. The only people who could afford, or would want to spend the money redesigning a perfectly good ship for the sake of distancing itself from the military, was the United-Consortium.

I really didn't like that company. It was big enough to qualify as its own nation and had enough devoted fanatics to be its own religion. The company had its fingers into everything from major ship overhaul to fine jewelry and design to groceries and pharmaceuticals. The goods it sold were either cheaply made or ridiculously expensive—if not both—and it had cornered pretty much every market. You couldn't fling a pudding pie without hitting one of its blasted advertisements, subtly boring into your mind and demanding you buy from the only company that offers free credits back after your hundred and fiftieth purchase from the store* (*offer only valid to 0.1% U.C. Credits back per purchase. U.C. Credits can only be used in licensed U.C. stores and cannot be redeemed for actual credits. U.C. Credits back must be used within four days of initial purchase. Not valid in all states and territories. Not valid in United-Consortium Proxima Centauri Branch stores.). Perhaps I was just bitter at being so poor, but I was sick of those blasted bioluminescent signs flashing in my face night and day. If I want something, I will go out and buy it. If I don't want it, you can't make me.

In any event, I wasted the last hour before departure poring over the blueprints of the United-Consortium's well-guarded schematics for a rewritten light military cargo vessel. Of course, the blueprints didn't tell me the whole story; the U.C. wasn't stupid enough to post the entirety of their refit plans out in the open for public use. They posted just enough to keep face with their "Re-Purpose After War: Giving broken and neglected organic ships a new home" campaign. I could sing the jingle before I learned to walk.

Pulling every last string my brother had had and spending entirely too much of my money on bribes, I was able to piece together a roughly complete picture of what the ship actually looked like inside.

They hadn't changed the design too much from the light military cargo vessel it had been. Even if they were trying to distance themselves from anything war-related, they admired the military's ability to design ships that actually work. In the long run, the *Meramec* had only suffered slight changes, moving a wall here, switching where the central human command was, and of course, adding the gaudy blue and gold symbol of the U.C. Unlike most other shipping companies that relied on a tattoo system to decorate the ships, the U.C. actually included the symbol into the ship's genetic facsimile. This really didn't mean much beyond the fact that if the ship took damage there, it would heal with the symbol more or less intact.

Assured I had my plan memorized perfectly, along with the layout of the ship, I made my way to the docking area. Once I had reached the bay, I covered the soles of my shoes with as little contraband goo as I could get away with. No sense in wasting it all, especially considering I might need more once I was on the ship. No sense in having shiny, goo-covered shoes, either—that was a fast way to get caught with all of the security prowling around the docking areas of the station.

Stepping past security was no big deal, considering there wasn't any. The U.C. prided itself in only hiring the best, most capable crewmen for long voyages, meaning that extra security was unnecessary. Plus it was also more cost-effective to replace cargo than it was to hire more bodies. I found a place to wait unnoticed behind the cargo of a neighboring ship until they finished loading the last of their Centauri-made locomotive parts through the ten-foot by ten-foot cargo door. Once they had, I waited a second longer for the door to begin to close. The crewmen were already deep inside the ship, letting it close its own hatches.

All I had to do was trick it.

Striding quietly up to the hatch, I reached with my left hand through the door, resting my arm on the ever-closing iris. I took my right hand and, adjusting it so that my fingers were pointed downward, pinkie to the left, I gripped hold of the outside of the hatch and waited anxiously as the iris closed down around my left arm. It didn't hurt, but it was a long moment before the ship decided it knew what was going on.

It, being the good little organic ship it was, assumed that my arms, awkward as they were, belonged to one of the crewmen on the inside of the ship. Of course, no crewman was stupid enough to get their arm stuck in such a slowly-closing hatch, but the ship wasn't aware of that. After a moment, it decided to open up further, just enough for me to wiggle my underfed body through. I breathed a sigh of relief as soon as I touched the ship's decking. Home stretch.

Within a few days, I would finally complete my plan of revenge and let my brother rest. Though, knowing him, he probably was getting as much rest as he wanted, wherever he was. I moved gingerly around the hold to find a spot to hide. I knew roughly where I wanted to be after memorizing the blueprints, but what those prints couldn't tell me was what cargo was where. The hold was massive enough to fit an entire, eighty-foot-long train engine inside with room left to walk comfortably around it and clearance to keep from bruising the ceiling. Fortunately it just had train parts, the boxes of which provided a much better place to hide. It was unlikely the crew would be back here at any time, but I would feel much better having a hidey-hole to dive into if needed.

It didn't take me long to find the perfect spot. It was far enough from the hatch that I would have plenty of warning should the ship decide to vent the hold, but tucked behind just enough boxes to make the chances of a crewman spotting me unlikely.

The only problem was that I wasn't the only person who had found the spot and its glorious positioning.

"Ayh!" called the high voice in almost the same moment I stepped on her ankle.

"Shhh!" I cried out quickly, bending down to shut the fellow stowaway up, should she decide to cry out again. She looked up at me with a pain-stricken panic.

"Who—" she used a choice word, "—are you?"

"Obviously not crew, slinking around the hold like this!" I said defensively. "Same could be said for you, I imagine."

"Yes," the girl said with a voice that was close to pouting. "You can't hide here, though, it's my spot."

"If they find me, they find you. How's that for your spot?" I gestured to an empty area next to her. With a scowl, she finally nodded.

For a moment, we didn't say anything. I was too busy trying to find something to sit on. I couldn't very well place my keister on the deck itself since the ship would sense my body heat, so I had to have a buffer, preferably one made of the same material as the cargo containers. After a moment of watching me search aimlessly, the girl sighed and handed me a spare piece of broken container. I accepted it and sat down carefully. I started to ache all over again.

"So, what're you doing here?" the girl asked. I glanced at her, throwing my hood back and fluffing up my hair a little. The more I looked at the other stowaway, the more grimy and unfeminine I felt. She should have been a princess, with a thousand elegant curls coming off her head in endless directions. She had a natural pout to her face that made her seem even more immaculate and, compared to me and the greasy engine parts, she was downright clean. I'm not sure how she had managed to keep her light-colored pants and tastefully ruffled top. Equally tasteful were the smattering of mostly geometric tattoos across her arms and the backs of her hands. I didn't see any gang tattoos, so at least I didn't have to worry about having any angry tribe members coming after me in retribution for her bruised ankle. The bracelets and earrings she wore looked like solid metal, cheap but still beautiful.

"Earth," I said simply. She rolled her eyes at me.

"Duh, genius," she raised an eyebrow just a twitch to cast me a condescending look. "I mean, why are you stowing away?"

"Because I'm secretly the Queen of Everything but my favorite minion forgot to buy my ticket on a luxury liner," I snapped back a reply, feeling a little sick.

"I hope your minion murders you while you sleep," the girl retorted.

"Yeah," I said glumly and feeling sicker. "So do I."

For a moment neither of us said anything. I realized how lightheaded I was feeling. During my spat with the other stowaway, I hadn't noticed the ship undocking and building speed. Now that everything was quiet, I could hear the steady noises of the ship's muscles, spreading few and efficient organic sails to catch the solar currents. For as long as I could, I focused only on those sounds, trying to ease away whatever was ailing me.

"I'm sorry," the girl finally said. "I didn't mean to be rude."

"I didn't mean to be either," I replied.

"I'm just such a curious person. Sometimes I blurt out questions without meaning to," she rubbed her sore ankle. I reached into my toolbag for some salve.

"Here, sorry I stepped on it," I said, and handed her the small can. She smiled gratefully.

"How about names?" she said, putting on the salve. "Mine's Ariadne King."

"Marcie Dunn," I said, bombarded by another wave of sickness. This time, however, I almost threw up.

"Are you okay?" Ariadne asked. I looked toward her. The fuzziness of her hair seemed to spread to her entire body. I blinked before I realized it was my eyesight, not her becoming some kind of were-beast.

"Actually..." I said through enormously thick thoughts; I suddenly felt warm, and panicked. Why was the ship spinning like that? "I...don't think so."

"Neither do I," Ariadne said, moving a bit closer. My vision started to distort, on top of being blurry, and before I could recognize her giant face standing over mine, I blacked out.

I think my head banged against something too.

TWO

I felt terrible. Not I-just-went-four-rounds-with-a-smelly-mammoth terrible either. This was far worse. Like an itchy flu on steroids. I spent a disproportional amount of time semi-conscious, that much I know. I heard a lot of voices and obnoxious pacing. But mostly I tried to drift back into the void I'd been thrown into. I avenged my brother adequately, hadn't I? The skiptrace couldn't go back to work after losing his license.

The part of me that wasn't interested in the void sighed. No, that wouldn't do. After all, those men had laughed you all the way out of the office. You *have* to turn that license in.

I sighed again and woke up.

That bright light definitely wasn't helping my headache any. Nor was it helping my nausea or the fact my skin felt like it was on fire. I blinked a few times to see if it would go away.

"Mphm," I think I said. Someone else sighed.

"Fine. I'll turn it off," the huffy voice, coming from my right, reached up and turned off the light. I tried to breathe a little easier. It didn't work, of course, because my lungs were burning too.

"Owie," was the only thing I thought to say. I tried looking around to see where I was. This didn't feel like a ship, needless to say. No, this was definitely on solid ground. It wasn't a space station either; the walls were too square and covered in beneficial molds. This was definitely a hospital, by the almost overwhelmingly musky smell that came from all the infection-preventing microorganisms and free-floating antibodies. Hospitals were a completely different creature from normal organic buildings. Their immune systems were up to four times as active as their counterparts and that allowed them to withstand most diseases, especially the kinds that could be transferred from person to buildings, like leprosy and some forms of colds. What the hospital buildings itself couldn't cover, other organisms like molds and mosses were introduced and kept in just the right balance.

"What hurts?" the huffy voice asked. I tried to spin my head around and look toward it. That was a horrible idea, given how much pain shot through me. Why couldn't someone have just killed me? I couldn't see who was speaking, however, given how much my vision was blurring again.

"Everything, genius," I said in a tone snippy from the pain.

"Good," the voice was now angry. After a moment it sounded repentant. "No, I'm sorry. You're in pain, that's not good. I'm just so angry at you."

Oh. The voice became recognizable. What was the girl's name?

I looked toward Ariadne carefully. She sat primly in a seat, with an expression that was somewhere between man-eating-bear angry and worried mother. Her big eyes stared solidly, not necessarily boring through my soul, but they were unmoving in their expression.

"Why are you angry at me?" I asked feebly. She blinked a few times as if I was stupid.

"Nothing, never mind. Just get better, we'll deal with everything later," she waved me off, turning back to the book she was reading. The light was kind of low for that.

"You can turn the light back on," I said, turning my head away from the bioluminescent source. "I think I'm going to try to sleep some more."

"That'd be a good idea. The doctors said you'd need it," Ariadne said without much venom.

I closed my eyes for a second. The light from her reading lamp seemed to ignore my eyelids, but I was used to sleeping with a bright light. I was pretty much used to sleeping anywhere. On trains, on park benches, in the middle of a space station, and even as a stowaway on board a ship.

Any*when* however, is a different matter.

"What happened on the ship?" I had to ask. I knew it was probably a bad idea, given that I was now in a hospital bed, but my overactive, if slow, brain wasn't about to let me sleep wondering.

"Chaos," Ariadne said glumly.

"Please?" I asked politely, turning to look at her sideways.

19

"You fell and hit your head, knocked over a container of locomotive parts, sent the ship into a panic, brought the crew down on our necks, and nearly died of radiation poisoning," Ariadne said without actually closing her book. I frowned, thinking over the plausibility of what she said. Given the fact I was no longer on the *Meramec*, it seemed to make sense. Given the fact my arms were covered in lesions, it continued to make sense.

"Where...?" I asked with an inkling of the answer.

"Earth," Ariadne said.

"Okay," I commented, processing. My brain seemed to be running exceptionally slow at the moment. "How did...?"

"The crewmembers took pity on us. Besides, I'm well-connected enough that they couldn't risk venting me into space without an investigation happening." Ariadne finally closed her book.

"Oh. So why am I here?"

"It was the cheapest place I could afford," the glum-ish tone creeped back into her voice. I processed what that meant.

"Why did you do that?" I asked, looking at her again. "I can't pay you back yet."

"Yeah, I noticed," she said, holding up the skip-trace's license. "We'll have to figure something out. I had had plans for that money."

"I'm sorry," I said.

"Just don't do that, okay?" Ariadne seized up in a frustrated motion. "Don't apologize, just stay alive and we can make a deal."

"Fine," I said curtly. I would have bit off my tongue if I thought that wouldn't make me hurt even more.

"You…" Ariadne's anger came back. She stood up so fast she almost knocked over the char. Gripping the skiptrace's license in one hand and her book in another, she continued her fuming. "Are the single most inconvenient stranger I have ever met!"

"What were you going to do with the money?" I asked quietly.

She stopped being angry for one moment.

"I was going to buy a ship," she stood the chair back up and sat down in it with almost a singular, graceful motion. Maybe someday I could be that elegant.

"Oh," I said. "What kind of ship?"

"Just a little one," Ariadne smiled more to herself than to me. "I was going to start a messenger business, for high-priority parcels you know. I had all of my runs planned, from here to the stations to Baltia to Myrkheim to Bjarmaland, when it's in-system, of course."

A sinkhole opened itself up in my chest. I felt horrible beyond the radiation sickness. I had never imposed myself on anyone like this, not the point where their dreams were in jeopardy. She could have told me I'd stepped on her favorite pet and I would have felt about the same amount of guilt.

"I'll make it up to you, I promise," I said sincerely. "Once we turn that license in, I'll pay you back for the radiation treatment."

Ariadne held my gaze for a moment as if she was one of those human lie detectors. After a while she must have decided I wasn't lying.

"Sounds like a deal."

I held out my least lesioned hand as a gesture of friendship. She took it very gently and gave it one small pat and smiled. Gosh even her teeth were perfect.

• • •

The treatment went well and within a week, I was up and about. I still had ever-fading scars from the lesions, but I wasn't dead.

The only problem came when we discovered that the hospital I'd been treated at was on the wrong side of the planet from the skiptrace's home office. I was still broke and since the office wouldn't just take my word I'd bested their giant over communications, we were faced with one option: use more of Ariadne's money. I felt terrible every time she charged that account, promising continuously that I would repay her. Each time she merely smiled and said she knew.

It cost something of a small fortune to finally arrive on the right side of Earth, a place currently called Dinium. We boarded a real, steam-powered locomotive and made a beeline toward the skiptrace's home office. Ariadne seemed right at home on the train, where she chatted up the ticket master ad infinitum about exactly how the train was designed, which factory on Proxima Centauri was responsible, and some of the finer points of maintenance. I mostly stared at the window, marveling at how fast the landscape was speeding by. The murky light that filtered through from the sun brought a sort of yellowish tinge to the whole planet, washing out most colors and, if you weren't looking closely, making the wheat fields look just like the corn fields which camouflaged the low, rounded shapes of organic houses. From orbit it was almost impossible to tell city from farmland unless you were on the night side of the planet. Some pockets of inorganic buildings, mostly made of stone or concrete, still existed, but they were few and far between.

Even with the sunlight handicap, Dinium's buildings gradually began to look familiar and after we disembarked from the train, I led the way to the skiptrace employer. The building was like any other on the street: outside it was a brownish kind of organic structure they hadn't bothered to paint, and it had a façade littered with odd-sized windows. Richer buildings often had more uniform windows and some even had falsebone siding to make it a bit squarer and more old-fashioned looking.

This was definitely not one of those buildings. To be fair, it wasn't rotted completely through and the pulmonary system still seemed to run just fine, if a bit noisy. The building had an old heart, that was to be sure and its thrumming could be heard a block away. Overall the building was sagging with age and use and the once-fancy "Aristotle & Sons, Law & Licensing Ltd." sign was hanging even more crooked than it had been when I first visited the office a few months ago. Aristotle would be lucky if he got another year's worth of living out of the building before it disintegrated completely and he'd have to relocate.

The inside of the office was little different, though the rooms and ceilings were lined with completely numb falsebone to give the interior a more rectangular structure and provide a place to hang paintings and put up shelves. Like the outside of the building, however, no one had bothered to paint any of the surfaces, leaving the offices a sort of moldy brown color to add to the murky atmosphere. At least the floor was carpeted.

I strode up to the door marked, "Aristotle Simon, Lawyer and Skiptrace Commissioner," and opened it after a muffled, "C'me in," answered my knock. The rotund, red-haired man looked up at me over spectacles with first condescension, then surprise. I moved to stand directly in front of his desk and gaping mouth, Ariadne following close behind.

"You seem surprised," I said flatly, but gloating more than enough on the inside. I had the opportunity to make him eat his laughter and it felt amazing.

"Ah," he finally said, "not really, all you've done is show up in my office with a new friend."

"Oh," I blinked briefly, my satisfaction melting somewhat, "let me fix that."

I spent more than an embarrassing amount of time searching the various pockets of my outfit before I noticed Ariadne handing the skiptrace's license to Aristotle. I had insisted that she carry it as collateral for the money she'd spent to get me this far. Plus I was somewhat afraid my still-addled brain would leave it somewhere accidentally.

"I took that from your skiptrace, as per our agreement," I said as the lawyer read over the slightly crumpled document. He looked over it at me and Ariadne in surprise.

"This is a fake," he said in a tone that was more questioning than actually accusatory.

I shook my head. "I took it from your guy myself."

The lawyer sighed wearily and swore just a little.

"Well, if he could be beaten by two sprites such as yourself, I don't want him on my payroll anyhow," Aristotle tucked the license into a drawer of his desk and pulled out an all-metal money safe. He unlocked it and began to count out the woven metal credits one by one. Ariadne shifted somewhat as she watched the lawyer finish.

"Is that it?" she asked as I reached for the credits. I looked at the leaflets in my hand, trying to count how much it was. It had been nearly a fortnight since I woke up with radiation poisoning and my brain was still very slow.

"Should be, that's better than the standard rate for returning a license," Aristotle said with a shrug.

"What's the matter?" I said. I had somewhat reached Ariadne's conclusion, but I needed to verify.

"That's not enough to cover all the expenses." she said with a concerned frown. I frowned with her and tried to count the money against the amount we had spent on treatment and transportation. In the end I didn't have an exact number, but even my figures showed that the money in my hand wouldn't be enough to repay Ariadne.

"Are you sure that's it?" she asked the lawyer with concern. The man nodded with assurance. It was the sum I had agreed on when I first set out to discredit his skiptrace. At that point, it had been more than enough to get me to a city where I could find a job and an apartment. Of course, I couldn't see into the future and predict that I'd be up to my neck in debt to a fellow stowaway.

I glanced at Ariadne. Her face was now more than a little defeated. I looked at the credits in my hand. This wasn't enough to pay for her ship. She met my eyes with a sad gaze but didn't say anything.

"Crap," I said out loud and handed the money back to the lawyer. "Give me the license back. I'll be your new skiptrace until I pay her back."

"I don't think so. You might've bested that brute but you're no good as a long-term investment," Aristotle said. I slammed my hands on to his desk to surprise him and I leaned in real close to his face.

"Our agreement was money or a job, my choice as to which one. Mr. Carver can verify," I spoke without much in the way of leniency. Aristotle looked more concerned than actually intimidated, but he nodded. And muttered under his breath again.

"Fine, fine. Fine!" He made more than a few exasperated gestures and ripped the credits from my hands. Eventually, he replaced them with the license.

"But you work for me now, understand? I only have to keep you for sixty days and if I don't like what you do, you're out," Aristotle said. I shook his outstretched hand solemnly. To his credit, he didn't glare at me too much.

"Return here in two days. By then I will have everything legal sorted out," Aristotle said, grumbling. I nodded and strode with Ariadne out the door into the sickly daylight.

"You didn't have to do that!" the ingrate hissed at me.

"Oh would you just shut up!" I said to her in a more than irate tone, stomping down the sidewalk ahead of her. "Go find yourself some place to stay and open an account where I can deposit the money I owe you."

"I can't just wait around for you to pay me the money back," Ariadne spoke as she caught up with me. She was pouting, I could hear it in her voice.

"Well you can't come with me, that's for sure!" I shouted the words without thinking them through fully. It would actually be useful to have a partner in this endeavor.

"Wait...that's a brilliant idea..." Ariadne pulled me to a stop. I glared at her, although secretly thankful she'd caught on to my idea. "We can work together and earn the money back."

"Didn't I just say I don't want you with me?" I asked, trying to fight it. No, it was not practical to bring Ariadne with me, considering I barely knew her and she didn't seem to have any experience as a skiptrace. I could do this on my own. Ariadne dismissed that idea with a wave of her hand.

"I don't care what you want or don't want. You are definitely not capable of tackling wanted criminals as a skiptrace. Not by yourself." The stubborn girl didn't cross her arms or even give my anger any attention.

"I am more than capable of handling whatever comes my way! You should have seen the guy I took this from," I waved the license in her face. She plucked it from my hands with two fingers.

"Well I didn't see that guy, and the only person I know you as is a Class A klutz who's still wobbly from her brush with radiation poisoning," she said, before turning on her heels primly and striding down the street toward the main highway. I stuck my tongue out at her retreating backside before following. I snatched back the license once I had caught up with her.

"All right." I gave into the idea of a partner. "At least until I pay you back, you can come along. But I'm the one with the skiptracing experience."

"Got it, boss," Ariadne said with a smile.

"Let's go find somewhere to stay," I said, walking toward the center of town.

"Who Mr. Carver?" Ariadne asked suddenly.

"Didn't you see him sitting there?" I said without really look at the princess. She made a strange sort of confused noise.

● ● ●

We spent the two free days twiddling our thumbs anxiously in the cheapest hotel we could find close to Aristotle's office. It hadn't taken an exhaustive search to find one. We definitely weren't rich enough to be living it up any, so we spent the first day calculating how much I owed Ariadne, plus some interest I insisted on, and the day after that tearing apart old magazines and folding paper creatures in our dingy hotel room. My creatures were always far more anatomically correct than hers were, but hers always had some sort of secret mechanical component that made them move.

We didn't talk all that much during those days; I'm not certain why. Perhaps we were both too busy trying to analyze all that had happened. Perhaps we were just being entirely too polite with one another. By the end of the second day, I was fairly well sick of it.

"Where are you from?" I asked, folding my next paper whale, trying to position the eye of the model from the magazine where the whale's eye would be.

"Merge, Theopa, but my family moved around a lot. What about you?" the princess asked without looking up from her…whatever that was she was folding.

"I think I was born somewhere in Olds I, but my family moved to Dinium when I was young," I said. Ariadne nodded, and continued to work on her ambiguous paper beast. More silence. I sighed as I put the last fold in my rhino and set him with the other fifteen creatures I'd folded into existence.

I leaned back on the couch.

"Tell me about your parcel business," I said.

"I was thinking about calling it King Shipping; that has a nice ring to it," the princess said, her coffee-colored eyes lighting up with the idea. I wished I had that much passion about something. Even skiptracing had a more or less functional purpose and I doubted I'd be in the field much longer than it took to pay back Ariadne.

"Why parcels?" I asked.

"First, I get to fly around in my own ship. Second, you never know where those packages are going or who they are going to. What if it's a wedding present from an uncle that missed the wedding? What if it's important evidence for a system-spanning trial?" She stared off into the distance a little, mind probably racing with more and hopeful scenarios. The princess finally looked back at me and asked, "What about you? Why skiptracing?"

"Revenge," I said easily. I didn't really want to spill my entire life's story in that moment, or ever if I was going to be honest. Unfortunately, that would be unfair since Ariadne had already told me her plans.

I fiddled with the rhino in my hand until its horn was bent out of shape.

"My brother got caught up in the system. I got the license from the skiptrace that mistakenly put him behind bars," I tried not to mutter. Ariadne nodded solemnly.

"I have a brother too," she finally said. We sat in silence with our papercraft for a minute. I wasn't entirely sure I'd make it any further in the conversation without losing it, but Ariadne seemed to understand.

"I'm hungry, want a pizza?" she finally said.

"Five-kind mushroom with black olives?" I asked.

"Green ones, extra whites," she grinned and made for the door.

I decided I could grow to like Ariadne King.

• • •

Aristotle seemed no happier to see us again the next morning, but he outlined everything official without muttering under his breath too much.

"I give my employees all the regular holidays off, though you won't be working here long enough to have to worry about that. You work 24/7 until you catch whomever I send you to find and then you get between three days and a full week off afterwards, depending on how long it took you to catch the quarry. If I send you after a criminal, you take him to the local police and collect the reward, which I split with you. If he's a debtor or someone of that mostly harmless ilk, you bring him here or to one of my branch offices. Got all that?" the lawyer said and looked from me to Ariadne.

"Got it," we spoke at nearly the same time.

"I can't issue two licenses, so you'll have to share. Only the person holding the license can make a legal arrest," he looked from me to Ariadne again and I nodded impatiently. "Once you sign this, it's yours until you lose it or I take it from you."

I snatched a pen off his desk and scribbled my name on the license under the half-dozen names of owners that had come before me. I put my signature under the name of the skiptrace I had beat up and with a great deal of satisfaction drew a lovely "x" over his signature. I handed the pen to Ariadne and watched as she flawlessly signed her name with great loops and swirls. I noted the new seal of the Sodality of Skiptraces stacked on top of the outdated ones. The Sodality updated their official seal for skiptrace licenses every year to help cut down on counterfeiting. It didn't help much, but since they are technically the only entity legally allowed to approve the licenses, it made them feel better to keep things new. At least Aristotle hadn't run into trouble getting our license approved.

Ariadne handed the license to the lawyer for his approval. He blew slightly on the paper to make the ink dry quicker and gave me one last concerned look. I took my new livelihood in my hands as he finally gave the document up.

"My first case for you isn't an easy one, but I'm also not sending you after a mass murderer," Aristotle said, reaching for a new sort of folder. "Open it later. You start your hunt tomorrow and I want weekly updates until you catch him."

I nodded solemnly and turned with Ariadne to walk out the door.

"So what's our assignment?" she said almost as soon as our sneakered feet hit the sidewalk.

"I don't know, I haven't opened the file yet." I cast Ariadne a sideways glance before flipping the cover over. In the process, I managed to nearly spill its paltry contents across the mildewy sidewalk. I made a disparaging noise as I caught the few pictures and what looked like an old hotel receipt with the insides of my elbows.

Ariadne made some kind of soft comment but didn't grab for anything. I sorted the loose papers as best I could before handing the mugshot to my new, and temporary, partner.

"Not too tough, though he looks like someone forced him to swallow a whole, raw sardine," Ariadne crinkled her elegant nose as she observed the picture.

"His name is Ottoman Lee." I frowned a little as I spoke the words. "He's not wanted for anything more than petty theft, but he's knee-deep in debt. No outstanding warrants by the look of it."

"This must have been the last hotel he stayed at. It's here in the city, so we should go check it out." Ariadne handed me back all of the papers and then helped me adjust them properly in the file. I kept the mugshot out of the folder and held it up for a better look.

The man was narrow and less scowling than he was glassy-eyed. He had fewer tattoos and piercings than I had first thought, aside from the rather hideous scrawl of "LOSER" on his left cheek. I wondered if that had been a conscious or drunken decision and how much he regretted it. Not that it was any consequence to me. All I had to do was drag his sorry hind-end to Aristotle & Sons and impress that lawyer into keeping me for long enough to pay off Ariadne.

It's not like I had anything better to do.

Ariadne and I made our way to Ottoman's last known hotel address, making good time by taking an engine-powered cab, rather than a train. The cab sputtered and choked a bit, probably struggling from all the residue and sludge organic cities produced, but it seemed to function well enough. We were already running up an expensive tab to catch this guy, but Ariadne insisted that the train would take too long. I abdicated my position as my head started to spin, probably residual effects from the radiation poisoning. At least cabs were far quieter and less jarring than their train counterparts.

Ariadne was out of the vehicle almost the instant the driver announced our arrival at Ottoman's hotel.

"Wait!" I called after her, not running up the moderate building's slippery steps. The falsebone sheets that had once run across the tops of the steps for traction and structure were beginning to be absorbed by the building's organic compounds, meaning the only thing left was slimy epidermis.

"What? We don't have all day, Marcie!" Ariadne stamped her foot slightly as she turned to face me. Ringlets of her hair bounced in agitation.

"This isn't a nice hotel," I said, though it did smell somewhat less than Aristotle's building and it wasn't sagging quite as much either. "But I doubt the owner knows that. We have to be a little more like women on an official mission and less like ditzes who just happen to have a skiptrace license."

Ariadne looked at me with a pained pinch of her eyebrows. I shrugged her off and walked into the hotel's terrible lobby.

It wasn't that the organic structuring of the lobby was suffering any serious damage, but someone had covered every inch of the expensive falsebone lining with metal and designs. The carpet was something of an ornate tartan which was almost completely faded, aside from the metallic strands that ran through it. Those were corroded horribly. The walls were covered with more of the metal, except the corrosion only covered the top three feet, near the ceiling. The rest was half-heartedly polished, almost like they made a short person do all of their wall cleaning. The design itself was something akin to an old Greek pattern with lots of leaves and what could be taken for clusters of grapes. The entire room was also painfully orange, even faded as it was. I strode into the nightmarish room without fear, however, and reached the front desk before a pouting Ariadne.

"May I help you?" the long-fingered clerk asked me. I tried to see the eyes that I knew hid behind her thick glasses, but gave up quickly. I settled on talking to her nose.

"Yes, we're looking for this man." I showed Ottoman's mugshot to the spectacled woman.

"One moment," she said, reaching into her bosom for another pair of glasses. For a moment I thought that she would replace the ones she was currently wearing with the new pair. She didn't, instead placing the new, albeit smaller, pair on her nose in front of the other pair.

"I recall a man somewhat like him in the hotel a few days ago. I could never read his tattoo right; I always wondered why he had the word LOVER placed so conspicuously," the clerk said, looking at me and Ariadne from behind two pairs of glasses. "What do you gentlemen want with him?"

I could hear Ariadne sigh even if the clerk couldn't.

"Our lawyer wants him for something, looks like a debt. Do you know where he is?" Ariadne asked and tapped her foot at the same time.

"No," the clerk said slowly. I gazed into her double-spectacled eyes. Somehow the second pair of lenses made it easier to see what they actually looked like. They would have been pretty and grey if they weren't so distorted.

"Ariadne," I said, not taking my eyes off the clerk. "Got any credits?"

"Why should we have to pay her for information?" the impatient princess demanded. I scowled in her general direction.

"Because that is what she wants," I said helplessly. "Just play the game, we're good."

Ariadne seemed to keep her grumblings to herself and produced two fine, 10-mark credits. I plucked them from her fingertips and ostentatiously felt their metallic fibers in front of the clerk's glasses. She looked from me to Ariadne one last time.

"He muttered something about catching the next flight to Meropis-C," the clerk said, placing a tired hand palm-upward toward me. I placed the credits dutifully into her fingers and led Ariadne out the door.

The princess muttered curses accordingly.

• • •

"Meropis!" she spat at the slippery, organic steps. "Where is it this time of year, anyway?"

"The South Pole, I think? We'll have to look at an Orbit-Time book to be sure." I slumped on to the steps, trying to calculate how expensive a trip to the station would be. More than likely we'd have to make a jump to one of the geostationary hubs and then catch a flight to the ever-moving Meropis-C. That is, of course, after we booked a ride to take us into low orbit. It would be expensive, that much I could figure out. I began to work on alternatives as Ariadne sat beside me.

"What if... Never mind," Ariadne started after a moment of thinking. I glanced at her, who then looked at me a little sheepishly. "It's a selfish idea, don't worry about it."

"Will it get us off the planet?" I asked. Ariadne chewed her lip as she refused to make eye contact and nodded. "Then what harm could it do us?"

"A whole debt of harm," she sighed. "I was thinking maybe we could take out a loan and get my ship. Then we could go anywhere without having to worry about catching flights. We could work to repay the loan with these bounties."

I gave her idea a good mulling before I reached a conclusion. It sounded like a reasonable way to solve our problem, though I was already indebted to someone and I didn't relish owing a bank more money. If we had a ship, however, things might be a bit easier on the skiptrace front too. She wasn't wrong about a ship making everything easier.

"How quickly could we get our hands on a loan and a ship?" I asked.

"I already have someone who is holding a ship for me in Theopa until I collect enough money to officially buy it," Ariadne shrugged with a sort of fake indifference. "All we'd have to do is get a loan."

"Who would hold a ship for you?" I asked quizzically. Ships were expensive, especially ones that could take you into orbit. Ariadne merely scowled at me. It looked almost cute on her, like a growl on a kitten, but I ignored it.

"Where can we get a quick loan?" Ariadne asked.

"We can either go ask Aristotle his recommendation of banks, or we can scour the newspaper for ads on the topic," I said, standing. Ariadne followed suit, taking a moment to think over the options I had given her. "Or I can contact this bank I know. I'm not a great credit risk, but my brother was once owed a favor by a guy."

"I like that last option best," Ariadne said, and I nodded wholeheartedly.

As it turned out, the guy that owed a favor to my brother didn't work at the bank anymore, but he was owed a favor by the lady who replaced him at the bank, so in some round-about way Ariadne and I managed to get hold of the bank manager's ear. She was none too pleased to offer a loan to a couple of half-employed misfits such as the princess and myself, but after a bit of coercion, and the understanding that if we didn't pay up she'd send skiptraces of her own after us, we secured ourselves a loan. I swore when I realized the interest alone would kill us, but Ariadne assured me that that was her problem. Once I'd paid her for the radiation therapy, she'd be free to set up her parcel business and work off the loan. It would have been much easier if banks offered loans for medical procedures, which meant I could have paid off Ariadne directly without the whole skiptracing thing, but the U.C. made sure its health insurance plans were the only possible way to pay off medical bills short of directly paying the hospital or arranging for some sort of hazard pay.

I still felt like a spider spinning a web that would later come back to haunt it. There wasn't a thing to be done about it now.

The next step for Ariadne and I was to pick up her ship in Theopa. It wasn't a long trip, though it set us back a few more pretty pennies. Ariadne was bouncing in her seat the entire train ride. She didn't seem to care a stitch about how far we were in debt, so I kept my mouth shut. She didn't do me the same courtesy, of course, going on and on and on about her ship and parcel runs and so forth. I tried to stay awake for most of her ramblings, but once or twice she would wake me up to remind me of something exciting she had remembered. If we weren't so far in debt, and our only means of employment were not hanging on whether or not we could catch someone who was impossibly more down on their luck than we were, I probably would have been a little infected by her bubbliness.

Almost the moment our feet touched the ground in Theopa, Ariadne was off and running toward the nearest engine-powered cab. We could have taken the public shuttle or even walked, as I pointed out to her, given the fact the train station and shipyard were only a half mile from each other, but she tossed her head indifferently and paid the cab driver entirely too much. I frowned and wondered how easy it would be to get that extra ten-credit back from the driver.

"Look, look, look!" Ariadne said, jamming her finger against the cab's window as the shipyard came into view. I couldn't tell which of the many ships she was pointing at. They all looked like boring and stationary blobs of bulbous organic material, little different than the buildings among which we had spent the last few weeks. Some were pulsing with a bit of life, their antennae twitching or color-shifting scales going through the entire spectrum, but it was still kind of like watching a cat while it's sleeping. Dozens of shipyard workers and ship owners milled about, inspecting the ships applying antibiotics with massive, wheeled syringes or tending to small wounds. I watched with understanding for a minute, but then got bored and turned to Ariadne.

"Which one's yours?" I asked.

"That one, the *Lilstar*," Ariadne said, ramming her finger even more into the glass. I looked at the ship she was indicating and tried not to throw up a little.

It looked like an excellent ship, if a bit used. I couldn't tell its age or maker, and it didn't have any real markings to designate it as something special, aside from the "*Lilstar*" tattooed across its bow. The problem was that it was a two-person craft, not designed to haul anything more than a pair of people and all the provisions they would need.

"How are we supposed to bring Ottoman back in *that*?" I gazed at the princess almost accusingly.

Ariadne looked at me with hurt surprise. I couldn't tell if she hadn't thought of the situation before or if she had and I was now insulting her intelligence. In either event I was somewhat directly insulting her ship and thus her.

"We could..." she said, looking back at the craft. By the time we had entered the shipyard and were walking to the office of the man holding the *Lilstar*, she still hadn't come up with a solution or even finished her thought.

"James!" Ariadne shouted as she bounded across the meager distance between us and the office. The man who answered her call looked more than a little startled, but I didn't get a good look at him right away. I was busy giving the *Lilstar* a better inspection.

It was undeniably a healthy ship, only scarred enough to mark it as moderately used. Every ship has seen its fair share of asteroid hits, infections, rashes, and I'd heard that some ships even got acne. All of this just made each ship a little tougher.

The overall outside design of the ship was a green, elongated blob, kind of like all those single-celled organisms you see through a microscope. Of course, it was about a million or so times bigger than most of those organisms, but that was beside the point. The top of the ship stood about twelve or so feet high with its six legs extended. The legs would tuck back under the ship to give it a more aerodynamic shape during launch and would extend again during landing, stretching out the webbing that was connected between each of the three legs on both sides. This webbing acted like a parachute and, coupled with an extremely shallow angle of descent, allowed the ship to glide to planetfall in a more or less gentle manner.

Organic ship landings were not nearly as precise as their metallic counterparts.

I kicked at the webbing gently, testing its elasticity and checking for any holes or scars that could cause it to rip while entering atmosphere. Like the rest of the ship, it was healthy and free from any kind of damage that I could see. I moved to the back of the ship to check the engines before I crawled underneath to look at the ship's underbelly. The engines were embedded into the ship itself and, from the outside, kind of looked like giant ear canals. Deeper inside the canal would be a bladder of sorts which stored up the gaseous byproducts that were a result of the ship's innate photosynthetic respirations and expelled it as a form of propulsion. Basically, the

Lilstar sighed a lot to get from Point A to Point B. I could also see part of a Centauri-made screw embedded in the walls of the canal, which allowed the ship to travel even faster than if it was merely traveling on sighs alone.

It wasn't a particularly fast method of travel, but for jumping around the solar system, it was entirely adequate. Now, if you wanted to travel out of system, that required a Centauri-designed faster-than-light drive and a metallic ship. Organic ships were not, by any stretch of the imagination, designed to go faster than light. Faster than sound? Sure, that was almost easy for some of the sleeker ships, but there was no way to shore up an organic structure to handle anything faster than about Mach 20 or so, which could only be accomplished by utilizing a planet's gravity as a kind of slingshot to build up speed.

My next step was to crawl into the ship's underbelly. It was actually pretty roomy underneath, especially for someone as petite as I was. Everything seemed to look fine: the epidermis was calloused and thick, like an elephant's foot, and the faint outlines of the inorganic Pseudo-Gravity system could be seen a couple layers up. The system, like most organic implants with a mechanical or electrical component, was, of course, Centauri in origin. Our nearest neighbor seemed to be tapped into a whole wealth of inorganic scientific knowledge, but I guess that's what it takes to survive on a rogue planet.

I had only one last test to perform before I deemed the ship acceptably healthy. I walked over to a more or less insensate part of the ship and took my knife out to test the epidermis' reactiveness. The slight cut I made sealed up within a few seconds. Of course, the ship's epidermis would harden in space given how cold and dry the vacuum is, creating a near-impenetrable shell. The knife test was to ensure the ship could heal itself quickly if that shell ever took a direct hit from something.

I was muttering things to myself about trying to squeeze three people into the *Lilstar's* tiny compartments, until Ariadne's shrill voice alarmed me. She was utilizing a loud, emotive tone and I wasn't sure whether it was directed to the frustrated-looking James or something from the conversation I had missed. Either way, James and I let her finish a decent rant before trying to communicate with the princess.

In that time, I gave James a better once-over. He had to be of Ariadne's kin, given the fact he had the whole "royalty-among-rags" thing going for him. His hair was a lot shorter than the princess's, but his overall features were just as refined. If I hadn't spent my late teens on a break or bust quest for revenge, I might have developed the ability to swoon over cute guys. Unfortunately, I was the girl out for revenge, not a date, so encountering James meant little in the way of attraction for me.

I thought over whether or not I should fix that when I'd paid off my debt to Ariadne. I mean, any human person *should* think about dating at some point, right?

"I'm Marcie Dunn," I said, introducing myself to James, who hadn't acknowledged my presence with much.

"Ariadne's partner with the skiptrace thing?" James said.

"Technically I'm the skiptrace, she just won't let me do it by myself," I commented. James nodded as if he were familiar with that kind of behavior.

"That's because you are still suffering from radiation poisoning," Ariadne said. She seemed to have moved beyond her swear-fest and into pouting.

"Actually I'm suffering from the *effects* of radiation poisoning, and at this point I'm almost as healthy as that ship back there. What's the matter now?" I asked the princess.

"James says he has to report me to the Ship Commission Board for my questionable transit choices on the ride back here. Plus he doesn't want me to get involved with the whole skiptrace thing." Ariadne scowled greatly. James didn't even try to act indifferent.

"Your little stowaway stunt is entirely your fault! And no, I'd rather not have to tell Mother you're out chasing down who-knows-what scum of the universe for a living," James said. For a moment I looked between the two. Ariadne had a brother and he was not so unlike mine. Suddenly I was thrown into the past, remembering that same sort of terse tone in my own brother's voice whenever I was about to do something stupid. Of course, Ariadne was neck-deep in stupid with me and there wasn't a thing to be done about it to protect James from it now.

"Look, James, the guy we're going after right now is just a debtor. He's not even that deep into debt anyway, so I doubt he'll put up a great fight. Besides, all I need is for Ariadne to drive the ship; I'll get the guy myself," I said, trying to smooth everything over. I stuck a hand in Ariadne's face as she tried to speak up. I wasn't finished yet. "And you're bluffing about the SCB issue. Ariadne and I were on board a United-Consortium ship and they'll sue your little behind to Proxima Centauri and back for exposing information pertaining to a stowaway incident. Unless of course you are after the settlement they'd grant you for keeping your mouth shut."

"James, how dare you—" Ariadne started to accuse. I spun her to face me and put a finger in her face.

"Shut up," I said simply, not giving Ariadne's shocked expression much merit. I turned back to James, who was sporting just about the same expression.

"Who is this?" James pointed an accusing hand in my direction. Ariadne made some sort of undefined shrugging motion.

"Does it matter?" I asked. "I owe your sister my life and she's not going to let me pay up without help. So you may as well assist us for the time being. I'll keep Ariadne out of trouble until I've paid her back."

For a moment, each of the Kings looked at me in some kind of strange and mutual emotion I couldn't figure out. They weren't wholly disgusted with me, that much I could tell, but they were a bit perturbed, which I didn't mind. It united them somewhat and kept down the squabbling.

"I'll go get the paperwork for the ship," James finally said, raising his hands in resignation. I nodded in affirmation and turned to Ariadne.

"Ow!" I exclaimed as she punched me in the arm, hard.

"Don't ever insinuate my brother would use my position to get underhanded money like that," she hissed. If she had been the princess I assumed her to be, with the weight of an entire nation behind her, I might have been intimidated. As it was, I was more touched by her loyalty to her brother.

"Okay," I said, shrugging with faux indifference. So far I really liked the Kings.

THREE

I could almost physically measure the room's emotional dynamic as Ariadne signed the title for the *Lilstar*. At first James was a bit tense, but as long as he held on to the ship's paperwork, Ariadne couldn't go anywhere. Ariadne, on the other hand, was tight as a fiddle string until she put her mark on the paperwork. Before the ink even had a moment to dry, she began to bounce with indescribable glee, nearly knocking me over into a vat of used ship antiseptic. I watched James as he grew more and more solemn and displeased, but he could only manage that for so long. Before Ariadne even had a chance to inspect her new ship, James was breaking out some very expensive soft drinks to toast his sister's new purchase.

"May the *Lilstar* always bring you home!" James led the very solemn toast. I tried not to gulp my bubbled delight too quickly, but it had been more than a year since I'd had my last one. This one seemed to be more bitter than what I'd remembered, but that was due to the fact the expiration date on the bottle was close to a few months past. I drank the whole thing anyway.

Ariadne had taken two sips before she made the hundred-yard dash to her new ship, squealing as she inspected it. The ship was then given our scent and fingerprints, both of which gave us access to its entire systems. I followed Ariadne into the ship's tight quarters.

There was as little to the inside of the ship as there had been to the outside. All of the controls were shoved in an ease-of-access fashion to the right with two chairs, one for the pilot and one for the copilot. The controls involved sensory nodes that sent signals throughout the ship when pressed, controlling the ship's organic structure. Some areas were made up of color-shifting scales that acted like an organic read-out, signaling the pilot about the ship's status. The controls also had two metal and plastic control panels embedded in the control area that operated the Pseudo-Gravity system and the engine's screw.

The living quarters, incredibly cramped I might add, were closed off by an archway to the left. The arch created pockets on either side of a small hallway and those pockets housed the small kitchenette to the right with a small inorganic stove and lots of stowage for space rations. The left had more stowage, but this was mostly for clothes and other non-food items. Above the kitchenette and consumables stowage were small alcoves that made up the bunks, each with a narrow step built into the stowage's falsebone doors, which locked securely into place with a pair of metallic hinges. I'd hate to roll out of one since it sat almost a whole four feet off the ground.

Beyond the living area was the bathroom which surprised me because it managed to squeeze an almost-full-sized bath into such a small space. It was an entirely efficient space, much like the rest of the ship. Directly across from the bathroom was a cargo... closet. It was hardly big enough to carry enough provisions for extended flights, which made sense for how much of a runabout it was. A step left from the bathroom was the small accessway to the ship's bowels. The organs sat to the left, fitted into the last few feet of the ship's frame and walled off from the living compartments by a semi-opaque membrane. The ship was kind of built like an inflated pufferfish. It had a relatively small body compared to the big, cavernous space it created. A falsebone ribcage, complete with a spine that ran along the entire body of the ship, provided stability to the living quarters and protection to the ship's organs.

Overall I though the *Lilstar* was a lovely ship. For two people. And only two people.

The problem was the same as before: I wholly doubted that this ship could carry three people and all their provisions to or from Meropis-C. That being said, there was little we could do about it now. I began calculating how much we'd have to starve Ottoman in order to get him back to Aristotle.

There was no way I was skipping meals for a debtor.

Farther back into the ship was the access to its key organs. While these were sealed off to prevent infection, the dermis was relatively thin allowing for easy access for topical medicines, injections, ard even surgery if the ship needed a transplant. Hopefully the company was still growing or willing to grow spare organs for the *Lilstar*'s model.

Overall the *Lilstar* was just as healthy on the inside as she appeared to be on the outside, with a strong pulse and good coloring. The ship didn't smell quite like the warmed-over-wheat of normal organic buildings and ships, instead having an almost lavender-like scent that was at its strongest in the living area. The temperature was also a lot cooler than what would be expected for a ship this size sitting underneath direct sunlight. The *Lilstar* must have an excellent temperature-regulation system. I wondered how that would fare whenever the Centauri-made micro-stovetop was turned on. I fiddled with the device that sat in the kitchenette just below one of the bunks. While it would be a handy thing to have, I wondered about whether or not it would heat up the whole cabin or burn the *Lilstar*. I thought about asking Ariadne about it, but decided against it. She seemed focused on something at the pilot's seat.

Ultimately I decided this ship would make a great runabout.

For *two* people.

"When can we lift off?" I asked, leaning against the command chair in which Ariadne was sitting. She was pressing buttons that didn't seem to do anything but light up. I assumed the ship was in some sort of diagnostic mode.

"Lift off?" she asked without really looking up at me.

"Yeah, you know, Meropis-C, Ottoman the Debtor, being an astronomical amount of credits in debt ourselves?" I kept adding things to the question until she finally gave me her full attention.

"A few hours maybe. I have to finish my inspection of the ship, then we have to hire a Boot and clear the launch with one of the Slings, all after we plot a course to Meropis," Ariadne said with something of a shrug. I glanced at the ship uncertainly.

"What do you want me to do?" I asked. Ariadne looked at me like I was a flat tire. In a word: completely useless.

"Uhmm…." She looked around the ship much like I had a moment ago.

"I'll go call Aristotle and then figure out where Meropis-C is this time of year," I said with a sigh and wandered back out to the hangar.

I made it into the hangar, which was filled up with all kinds of skin grafts and falsebone splints, ready and waiting to patch up any broken ship that might come along. Like human bones, falsebones sometimes broke and more often than not it was impossible to put a cast on an organic ship. This meant that other ways to stabilize the bones were used, such as metal splints or mesh sleeves, depending on which bone was broken and what type of break had occurred. Rarely was a ship ever decommissioned from a broken bone, but there had been some cases of old ships retired because their falsebone had degraded too much to handle. From what I could tell, the *Lilstar* had close to a century before retirement. Most organic ships outlived their owners by decades or more, especially when they were well-cared for.

"Are you Marcie?" Someone who was not James startled me as I rummaged through the hangar, looking for the telephone. I knew I had seen one earlier. While not a wide-spread technology, surprisingly not a Centauri import but rather the result of a U.C. funded communications project, most companies had a phoneline.

"Uh, yeah, who are you?" I blurted out to the slick-haired woman. She smiled from ear to ear and it unsettled me just a bit. While Ariadne was in a good mood because she finally got her ship, I caught the impression that smiling was this woman's natural setting.

"Sasha, I'm James' girl." She kept smiling. "I hear you and Ariadne are going into business together."

"I sort of owe her for some medical bills," I said. Sasha nodded as if she understood the entire story. A moment passed, and I could feel her trying to pry into my soul and judge me. At least that was what her stormy eyes seemed to indicate. Two can play at that game, sister, I thought. Except she was a lot better at hiding herself than I was. All I could read on her was a wall of nothing. Fine, if I can't read you, then I won't give you the luxury, I concluded. I shrugged off her bemused expression with some annoyance. "Isn't there a phone around here? And an Orbit-Time book?"

"Sure! Phone's right there and I'll go scrounge up an O.T." Sasha said with a disarming smile. Just like that, she turned from creepy soul-seeking judge to a smiley, normal-looking woman. I glanced at her with a frown as I started mashing the nearby telephone's buttons. Sasha was undoubtedly the kind of girl who lurked in corners at parties. Not saying anything to anyone, not joining the chaos, just lurking. Watching everyone. Smiling.

Aristotle was none too pleased with Ariadne and I's late start to Meropis which he made clear as soon as the phone finally went through. He made the matter even more obvious as he outlined the rough time estimates involved in finding a suitable Sling to launch us into orbit, then the undoubtedly long queue at a Light Atmosphere ReHy station before we could come back to Earth. After he finished lecturing me about the fact that his company could cover some of the transportation expenses, however, he didn't seem too angry with the whole affair. I could hear him sigh and resign to the idea that his two newest skiptraces were little better off financially than their quarry. Angry employers were something I actively avoided, but annoyed was easy enough to handle.

"Just bring back that debtor," he said finally.

Of course I left out the part where Ariadne's ship could only hold two people.

No need to worry him.

Sasha had returned with an O.T. book as soon as I hung up. I was a bit more than relieved to find the book was from the last 5 years, though I didn't know why; this was a *shipyard* after all. Having an up-to-date O.T. book was a fundamental requirement.

"Where are you headed?" Sasha asked, looking over my shoulder just a little.

"Meropis-C," I said simply, kind of wishing for her to leave.

"Ah," I could hear the frown or concern on her face before I actually looked up and saw it. "How big's your knife?"

After a quick moment to verify that I understood what she was asking, I pulled out the little folding knife. It was kind of dull and what had been a white ceramic blade was a bit stained from use. Sasha plucked it from my hands and fiddled with it. Her frown deepened. With a motion that had no warning, she flicked it across the hangar into the hangar's organic wall. The knife embedded itself perfectly straight into the thick epidermis. I gave her a wide-eyed expression as I processed how easy she made that look. Sure, I could throw a knife with some accuracy, but nowadays, who couldn't? She was downright talented.

I watched as she plucked my knife from the epidermis, inspected the unbleeding wound, and walked back toward me.

"Let me sharpen this. You'll need something a bit more impressive on the Merse," she said simply. I shivered slightly before returning to the Orbit-Time book I'd forgotten was in my hands.

I quickly found Meropis-C's relative location to Earth this time of year. Unfortunately, its orbit was built for ice and water exportation, so it spent most of its time above either Pole or any of the oceans. This made it great for a booming trade with ice and water freighters specially designed to simply fly upward. The freighters weren't made for even shallow space travel, just barely climbing above the atmosphere, and didn't have to go through the lengthy wait at a Sling or ReHy station. This meant Meropis just needed to be over a targeted loading site like the ocean.

What this meant for other kinds of ships, the kind that had to use Slings or ReHies, is that you had to launch into orbit somewhere not underneath the station's ocean-polar orbit and then cut across high atmosphere or shallow space to get to it. This used up a tremendous quantity of time and fuel, meaning money. Of course, if I really wanted to, I could probably figure out how to smuggle myself aboard one of the ice or water freighters. That was never fun to do unless you had a liquid pod, of course, to dampen the massive quantity of G's the ships pulled to exit and enter the atmosphere.

I sighed loudly as I began to calculate how much everything was going to cost us. I rubbed my forehead when I realized this was all for the idea that Ottoman the Debtor was even still on Meropis-C. He could be halfway to Proxima Centauri by now.

"B or C?" I asked Sasha as she reappeared with my knife. The ceramic blade was now polished and sharp enough to scare me. I tossed it to the epidermis for fun. My technique definitely wasn't as elegant as Sasha's, but I hit the center without too much error.

"B," she said with just a hint of unease. I didn't blame her. I'd only spent a collective few months on any station and didn't envy the livelihood. I couldn't help but ask, though. "I've tried to kick the habit of calling them Merse, but it's tough."

Sasha's stormy eyes let down one iota of her guard. I nodded with an understanding smile. Then I realized she wasn't the kind of person to accidentally let a slip of the tongue reveal her entire life. People who lived on the stations were tough like rawhide. People who grew up on one were either broken or impenetrable. All I knew is that I wouldn't want to face Sasha in a fight on top of not wanting to face her at a party.

"I also found this for you," she said, slapping a flat disk into my hand. I yelped as it shocked me terribly before retreating almost magically back to her hand. My entire arm tingled and seized up before falling completely limp. "Like it?"

"You little jerk," I cursed. Sasha only smiled a little more.

"It doesn't have a name, and it's very contraband, but if you use it on someone, they're out like a light for a few minutes. The nice part is that it comes back." The sadist showed off the device. It was a little bigger than someone's palm and was made largely of tough plastics I knew weren't biodegradable. It had two removable disks from what I could tell, each one capable of delivering a great shock to a person, or ship, and returning magnetically to the core device.

I looked at Sasha with some measure of uncertainty before I took the device. It was heavier than I expected, but I definitely wouldn't find that a problem if I needed to use it.

"Merse-B was bad enough, I'd hate to think of what C is like," Sasha said in all seriousness and I realized part of what my mission would be: bring Ariadne back home in one piece. Even to Sasha, I was the stranger that got her caught up in this mess. I pocketed the device right as the princess bounded into the hangar.

"So did you find Meropis?" Ariadne asked in a bubbly yet unyielding demand.

"Yes, yes," I said waving the Orbit-Time book with my good hand. The other was beginning to regain some sensation, but it still tingled like I'd sat on it for a week.

"Good, where is it?" Ariadne commanded, not even attempting to shrug off the arm Sasha had draped across her shoulders.

"At apogee, dead center above the ocean," I said, showing Ariadne the map. The princess crinkled her nose in irritation.

"That means we either have to shoot from the local Sling and cross nearly the whole planet to intersect it, or pay to have a Boot come and drag us to a Sling across the continent and launch from there." Ariadne chewed her lip in thought. I watched as she completely phased out of the hangar for a moment, trying to figure out the best, and hopefully cheapest, route we could take.

"I have it on good authority that your brother was going to treat you to a launch once you got your ship," Sasha said in low tones and without making eye contact with anyone.

"Why would he do that?" Ariadne said, and although her tone was accusing, she perked up a bit.

So did I, in fact. Finally, life had a little hope.

Sasha just nodded, still leaning on the princess's shoulder.

"I'll go ask," Ariadne said, freeing herself of Sasha and then dashing across the hangar until she was swallowed up by it.

"Oops," Sasha shrugged without any real remorse.

I looked at the station girl for a moment, trying to decide if I actually wanted to press her for more information on the Merses or not. Fortunately, she decided to read my brain at that moment and said, "There's not much to tell about the stations. The company that runs them makes the United-Consortium look like a church. Back when I was really little, they were shy of outsiders, a murderous kind of shy, but the company finally realized that was a bad habit to kick," Sasha said. I nodded. "I suggest you don't even try to blend in."

"That's good. I'm pretty sure buying another outfit would completely ruin my credit as it is," I said with some speck of humor, which Sasha caught and laughed a little louder than was comfortable.

"I think Ariadne is in good hands," she finally said, apparently over her laughing fit. I shook her offered hand and Ariadne magically reappeared.

"Sasha!" James cried out pathetically, being dragged by his currently effervescent sister. The offending station girl shrugged apathetically.

"You made the offer, I'm just here to remind you of it," Sasha said, catching her love at the waist.

"Ahh, fine," James relented, snaking a hand around Sasha and pulling her a little closer. "Yes, I did say that I would pay for a launch once you finally bought the *Lilstar*. I can always save it for another day, of course."

"Oh no," I said with a brief shake of my head. "I think we need it now."

"She's right," Ariadne said, batting some long eyelashes at her brother. "We could really use it now."

"All right," James nodded. "Just tell me which Sling you want and if you'll need a Boot."

"I'm thinking a Boot that'll take us to the Sling at Aban," the princess snatched up a map from the table. "That way we only have to cross shallow space for a few hundred miles to intersect with Meropis-C."

"Sounds good to me. You make all the calls, put me down as the creditor for the Boot and the Sling, but not the ReHy station, you hear me?" James warned his little sister. She nodded with childlike solemnity.

"I hate to be a bother, but is there a couch I could crash on until you guys get everything sorted out?" I suddenly asked. I hadn't realized how tightly wound I was until that moment.

"The only one we have around here is somewhat infested; it'd probably be safer to sleep on the *Lilstar*," Sasha commented. I nodded in agreement.

Besides, sleeping on the ship would give it a better chance to recognize me. Good ships were like cancer-sniffing dogs, even capable of judging its occupant's health to some degree. This was mostly a safety feature; if the pilot was unable to send an SOS, the ship could. Of course, it wasn't as though the *Lilstar* and I weren't going to get to know each other over the next few weeks.

"Which bunk do you want, Ariadne?" I asked as I started toward the ship. The princess looked from me to the ship for a few brief seconds.

"It's your mission, you can pick the bunk," Ariadne smiled genuinely.

I picked the bunk to the right coming in the compartment door. It gave me a good vantage point to the ship's main hatch.

Four

I slept nearly the entire boring process of hiring a Boot and putting our bid in the Sling. In fact, I didn't wake up until Ariadne slapped my face, telling me to buckle up, the Boot had arrived.

I groggily made my way to the copilot's chair and fumbled with the straps until Ariadne had to reach over and help me. I scowled in her general direction but kept my mouth shut as she coordinated things with the Boot operator and waved goodbye to her brother and his girl. I waved too, but I knew they couldn't see us through the semi-opaque membrane of the cockpit. In space, the membrane would lift to reveal a delicate and transparent window, but in-atmosphere the risk of damage to it by fine particles and moisture was great enough that the eyelid stayed shut.

My stomach did a single flop as the Boot lifted the ship. To be honest, I have no idea why they are called Boots. The big, 75-feet tall, insect-like walkers hardly looked like a boot, but that's how everyone knows them.

The good news about the *Lilstar*'s small size was that the Boot could just walk over us and lift us straight off the ground. I had seen pictures of a thousand Boots lifting up a single, massive luxury liner, the U.C.S. *Excelsior*. Crawling at a snail's pace, those first Boots had to be beyond tough, inching their way underneath the ship to lift it enough for another row of Boots to crawl underneath. The process was repeated over a few days until every row of Boots was under the ship, lifting it only a few dozen feet into the air. It was like watching ants carry a cucumber as they slowly made it to the only Sling on Earth that could cope with the ship's enormous size.

Unfortunately, the whole launch ended in disaster when it turned out that the Sling couldn't take the weight of the *Excelsior* and one of the town-sized springs burst, tearing an unfixable hole into the side of it. Within moments the *Excelsior* was completely dead. The carcass of the ship would take millennia to rot out and could still be smelled across the entire planet. The Sling was a total waste with all hard metal components corroded or warped beyond repair. So the site sat, rotting away, with clean-up being way more expensive than letting nature take its course. Some advocates called for the whole thing to be burned to the ground, shaving decades off the natural processes at work. Unfortunately, that would require a fire large enough to create a continent-spanning ash cloud that would carry all sorts of rotting smells and toxic fumes for hundreds if not thousands of miles. The best option was just to wait out however long it would take for the ship to disintegrate and then try to salvage whatever could be salvaged from the Sling. It was still unlikely that anything could be done about the Sling itself; all that could be salvaged was the gigantic hole in the dirt in which it sat. At least the liner and the Sling had both been United-Consortium property, meaning that the economy took no great hit, although stock in luxury liners plummeted for a few months after the accident.

Overall, I had many reasons to be pleased at the *Lilstar's* insignificant size.

For now.

I waited patiently for the Boot to lift the ship completely in the air, secure it to its underbelly, and begin the moderate walk to the Sling at Aban. It was a quiet but very jostling trip as each of the Boot's four legs took turns taking one step after the other. The *Lilstar* swayed slowly with the motions, but remained secure. Although pleasant, I realized how wholly boring this was going to be. I cursed myself slightly for leaving my book and schematics on my bunk. Fortunately, before I knew it, I was dozing peacefully in my chair. Of course, I was still paying some measure of attention to what was going on around me. Like when Ariadne sighed, loudly. I noticed that. I also successfully ignored it until she sighed again.

"Yes?" I asked.

"What?" she wondered in what sounded like genuine confusion.

"You keep sighing," I said.

"Oh, yeah probably," she said. I opened one eye and peeked at her. She was looking at me suspiciously.

I glared at her with my one eyeball until she finally gave in.

"What happened?"

"Use whole sentences."

"Fine. What happened to your brother? What did the system do to him?" she finally asked.

I swallowed painfully before rolling my eye back into my head.

"Just be glad that the skiptrace I took the license from is no longer in the field," I finally offered.

"That's it?" Ariadne asked. I cursed mentally. Why did she have to ask? I'd be much happier if she didn't.

"Basically," I said.

"What do you mean by 'basically'?" she queried further. I contemplated using the fancy shocking device Sasha gave me on her. Of course, if it had any adverse effects on the princess, I would be at a dead-end. I sighed myself.

"Just fly the ship," I said.

"We're strapped to a Boot," she said.

"That's not what I meant!" I spat slightly.

"D'oh," the princess said with a hint of condescension. I glared at her until she began to giggle.

"What's so funny?" I demanded.

"You are genuinely terrifying. And only about five-foot-three," Ariadne giggled further.

"For the record I am 5'5", ma'am. I'm sure you are a lot more vertically challenged without those springs you've got all over your head," I spat back, pouting deeper into my chair. The ship seemed to be adjusting it to the way I was sitting.

"Oh, don't you mock this," Ariadne said, gesturing to her near-perfect mane of bouncing curls. To be quite honest, I almost didn't have the heart to mock it. My own hair was definitely not as lively, nor had it ever been. That had been a problem living with only an older brother; I was a bit behind on hair-care. Once, we even agreed to take me to his barber to cut my hair super-short in an attempt to save some time and effort and keep the snarls at bay. Even though I was capable of some rudimentary styles and was more than adept at keeping it tangle-free, I'd never forgotten about being proud to walk around with a short-but-stillshaggy hairdo that looked like my brother's.

"I can if I want to." I stuck my tongue out at her. She stuck hers out farther than I had, and I moved to slap her jaw. She batted my hand away without much thought and slapped my forehead.

"Ahh!" I cried, trying to reach over as far as I could while still strapped into my chair. The princess leaned back as far as she could, at first swatting my hands and then dissolving into laughter that was doubling her over.

I was laughing too; so much so that my ribs began to throb.

We continued our inane gigglefest until I was in too much pain to continue and Ariadne was wiping tears from her eyes. We tried not to look at each other in fear of bursting into laughter again. I felt better than I had in a very long time. Perhaps the whole being-a-skiptrace with Ariadne thing would be good for me. I'd never really had a job or a friend before. Being out for revenge really puts a damper on both employment and a social life.

"What's that?" I suddenly asked, noticing something odd. The ship was still swaying to the Boot's rhythm, but there was a different motion, one which I could just barely pick up. It seemed to be slowing down.

Ariadne stopped her laughter cold to look over the ship's controls. I looked at my own panel; though I was much less skilled than the princess, I saw nothing that appeared to be weird.

"The ship's endorphins are slightly elevated; I guess we made her laugh," Ariadne decided.

"Ships can do that?" I asked in a tone that hopefully contained more surprise than fear.

"Some ships," Ariadne said with an easy shrug. "Smaller ships use the same genetic facsimile base as the larger ones, but since the Over-Code that makes their bodies are smaller, everything is a little more concentrated. Usually a ship has just enough endorphins to take the edge off its pain if it's injured, but sometimes the smaller ones produce extra."

"I knew that," I said, still a little bewildered. "But I didn't know ships could *laugh*."

"Only the small ones," the princess flashed me a grin. "Besides, the *Lilstar* was a custom job, so her facsimile is a little more refined than most."

"Oh," I ended the conversation. I wasn't wholly convinced a laughing ship was something useful.

The rest of the Boot's trip lasted for nearly ever, compounded by the fact that Ariadne and I had exhausted our conversation for the day. I had also used up as much napping as I had, so my options were either to familiarize myself with the ship's panels that were in front of me or fiddle with any loose object I could get my hands on. That object happened to be the fancy shock device Sasha had given me. While I understood the biology behind organic ships and buildings, I was no pilot by any stretch of the imagination.

I messed with it quietly and carefully, trying not to catch Ariadne's curiosity too much. It's not that I didn't want her to see it, it's that I didn't feel like explaining what it was, where I had gotten it, and how deep in trouble we would be in if someone caught us with it. Thankfully, the princess was more interested in reviewing her ship for what was probably the fortieth time.

The device was just big enough that my hand couldn't hide it fully. It fit into my palm well enough, but it stuck out beyond my thumb and pinkie finger about an inch in each direction. I carefully removed one of its electroshock discs and replaced it. I ran my fingers along the seams until I found the tab to open the semi-secret compartment it had. No great treasure fell out, much to my chagrin, but the compartment did reveal the device's settings and power level.

If I was reading it correctly, the power was self-regenerating, although I didn't know how. The device also had three settings, described accurately with small pictograms indicating what you could incapacitate at each level and how many discs you would have to use at once. The lowest with only one disc had a picture of a mining mite, a foot-long and tick-like creature that could scour and store minerals from almost any inhospitable environment. Aside from blatant thievery of property or raw ores, there really was no reason to stun one of the beasts. With two discs at the lowest setting, you could stun a small, generic dog-like creature—going by the picture, anyway.

The next setting had a generic picture of a human at the one-disc use and a generic picture of a short-yet-athletic Centauri at the two-disc level. Again, I had no idea why anyone would want to stun a Centauri. It's not like they were responsible for our war, although they insisted on supplying each side with some pretty high-grade weaponry. Overall, they were a boring species which humans couldn't really interact with, given the dichotomy between our natural and preferred atmospheres. Trade between our two peoples was an incredible industry for anyone lucky enough to participate, but that was as far as our relationship with our nearest neighbor went. They had the faster-than-light drive needed to cross the great gulf that existed between our two planets, and we had the organic ships they needed to navigate the nebula, done and done.

The final level had a picture of a Boot at the one-disc slot and a small, *Lilstar*-sized ship at the two-disc slot. I mused over how much damage the palm-sized device could actually do. It felt more and more like a doomsday weapon the longer I held it. Given its materials, I'd bet it was a Centauri weapon too. They preferred old-school plastics and wiring to the more organic options. Another reason our two species had little contact other than economically.

Of course, I still thanked Sasha for the device. Ariadne was right, I don't have the height to pull off intimidating.

"There's the Sling!" the princess squealed in a shrill voice. She bounced up and down in her seat as she peered through the still-lidded eye of the ship. I followed suit, pocketing the device, with somewhat less enthusiasm. Of course, I'd used a Sling before, although it wasn't my own ship. I swallowed, mentally preparing myself for a heck of a ride.

The Boot carefully set the *Lilstar* on a conveyor belt some few miles away from the Sling itself. For the moment, the belt was halted, waiting dutifully until the Sling had launched its current ship into the atmosphere.

The Sling itself looked like little more than a giant, gaping hole in the earth, with three concentric circles inside of it and a trio of tines that stuck up straight into the atmosphere for a few thousand feet. Perfect for three different sizes of ship. The three spires that stuck out were placed equally around the outside of the Sling's biggest circle, adding some extra height for whatever idiot company would decide it needed to launch a superliner again. These tines could also be fitted with a giant rubber band of sorts to help guide the ships into orbit, kind of like a ginormous slingshot. That was only used when the weather was inclement, however, and today was as calm as a tomb.

I waited tensely, seeing what little I could through the ship's eyelid. Since the Sling had a gaping, medium-sized hole in its center, it was preparing to launch a ship at escape velocity. I could just make out the broadcast countdown through the *Lilstar*'s hull.

Although it was difficult to make out the loud *thump* the middlemost springs made as they were released and flung the medium-sized cargo ship into the atmosphere at great speeds, I still winced slightly when it happened. The medium and small concentr c circles of the Sling bounced up out of their ground-level frames for a second as if they were trying to follow the ship into space, but settled down in a moment. Portable chocks used to position the ships properly on the Sling's platform leapt up several hundred feet into the air before crashing down cn the empty plain that surrounded the Sling. I watched as one crashed down a few yards from the ship and prayed it wouldn't bounce or roll and hit the *Lilstar*'s hull. It didn't, thankfully.

The conveyor belt on which the *Lilstar* rested slowly began to move toward the Sling, giving more than enough time for the crew and machinery to reset the contraption. My stomach churned just a bit. Sure, I had been slung into outer space before, but the idea of being launched forcibly into a vacuum of infinite directions without any sort of initial guidance was still a little unsettling. Plus I could never quite get rid of the whole rotting and mangled superliner image that was stuck in my head.

The giddiness Ariadne had been sporting since we first touched down in Theopa was replaced by some quiet determination as she began to check all the ship's systems and prepare for the Sling. I knew if

I put on the headphones above me, I could hear both sides of the conversation she was having with the Sling's control station, but my anxiety-riddled brain wasn't all that interested in listening to a conversation that I probably wouldn't understand. Pilots practically had their own language and I doubted not knowing what Ariadne was saying to the Sling operators would help my nerves any.

The conveyor belt briefly halted just outside the Sling's largest circle and a troupe of crewmen walked over to the *Lilstar* to give it a final inspection before launch. I chewed my lip as the ship was doused with a deep violet goo that had two purposes. The first purpose was to check for atmosphere leaks, and the second to check hull integrity. The goo briefly weakened the ship's hull and the crewmen climbed all over her, taping the sides loudly and jumping up and down on the roof a few times to make sure there weren't any weak spots. I watched Ariadne wince after a particularly loud blow to the *Lilstar*'s port flank.

After the goo was washed off and we waited required 20-minutes for the ship's hull to regain its strength, the conveyor turned on once again, inching us through the Sling's outer circle and toward the center of its smallest. Ariadne now kept up a running conversation of repeated "yep" and "roger that" with the control station, and I put on my headphones for the sake of making sure my eardrums didn't burst with the sound of the springs releasing.

The *Lilstar* was slowly aligned and tilted nose-up with the help of crewmen, cranes, and a miniature

Boot. Before long, I was sitting with my back to gravity, staring up at the clear sky above, waiting to be lowered into the Sling's smallest hole. As soon as the platform was cleared of men and equipment, the whole contraption began to vibrate, and I could feel the *Lilstar* sinking into the Sling as gears inched the platform downward against the four springs that rested underneath it.

I could feel the tension increasing on so much metal and I marveled at how uncomfortable I felt. Nothing like a small ship to remind you what a stupid idea the Slings were. There were so many things that could go wrong. A spring could break. A platform malfunction could bruise the *Lilstar* or even break its falsebone skeleton. Our launch angle could be off and we would end up belly-flopping some few hundred miles from here. I glanced out the still-covered window at the hole I was now deep inside. I could see the springs for the medium-sized circle easily and remembered how a Sling three times that size had ripped through the ship and platform above it. Even Ariadne was quiet at this point.

For one tense moment, the ship stopped moving backward, sitting helplessly on top of four springs larger in diameter than the average human's head. Then, with a loud thump that was felt more than heard, the Sling released the platform and the *Lilstar* shot upward, into space too quickly for gravity to pull it back down. I tried not to scream aloud as we smoothly sailed through the atmosphere until the whole visible universe was murky brown with nebulous gasses and speckled with only the brightest stars. The nebula that engulfed the solar system was usually comforting to me, like some kind of inter-stellar blanket, but at the moment, I was too focused on other problems. I'm not certain how many G's the ship pulled; fewer than the unmanned water-cargo ships for certain, but definitely more than the freighter I had used nearly a year ago. It felt like my brain was being sloshed backwards into my skull and my innards turned to mush.

Ariadne and I were breathing hard by the time we finally made it to space. I could feel gravity slacken somewhat before the ship's P-G system kicked in. Pseudo-Gravity was not a decent replacement for what was missing in space, but it was much better than nothing. I took big, gasping breaths as I waited for everything to stabilize.

And then I unbuckled and ran to the bathroom.

Five

The trip to Meropis-C when launching from Aban at this time of year supposedly only took a few days. It took Ariadne and I nearly a three full days until we finally made contact with the stupid place. If you ask her, it was because I had read the Orbit-Time book wrong. If you ask me, it was because Ariadne couldn't find her way out of a United-Consortium mini-market, much less figure out where to pilot a ship in the infinite possibilities of space. We argued about whose fault it was until the proximity alarm went off and the station nearly ran into us full-speed.

Turns out, we were just a little early.

"Why didn't it see us?" I demanded after our narrow escape. "Isn't the transponder on?"

"What rock did you grow up under? A ship the size of the *Lilstar* doesn't have a transponder, that's just for cargo ships or superliners," the princess declared. She refused to let me finish the argument by starting up a conversation with the station's flight controller.

"...Cleared to dock, *Lilstar*," the flight controller said over the radio link as I put on my headphones and opened up my side of the conversation. It used to be that ships communicated solely through bioluminescence, which, while excellent to identify ships and convey brief messages back and forth, it was a terrible way to communicate complicated ideas across large distances. So humanity eventually invested in the Centauri radio system. It was always garbled in-system as the nebula's gases interfered, but it was still more effective than bioluminescent communication. "Once you have docked, prepare for immediate boarding and inspection per Article 45 of the Meropis-C Docking and Cargo Regulation Handbook."

"Pardon me, the what—" Ariadne began until the headmaster cut her off again.

"All contraband items will be removed and destroyed per Sub-Paragraph L of the Meropis-C Freight and Personal Item Regulatory Mandate. Visitors will be given copies of these documents as required reading for anyone staying on board Meropis-C or remaining docked with the station for more than fifteen minutes. Please familiarize yourself with our regulations and have a pleasant stay with us," the headmaster cut off the transmission as soon as she was finished.

Ariadne and I looked at each other with a decent amount of horror and confusion.

"Where's your smuggler's hold?" I asked quietly. The princess blinked at me for a moment before springing into action without any sort of question. I followed her back into the bowels of the ship.

Not even the purest or most innocent of ships were without a decent smuggler's hold. Some people preferred the term "valuables chest," but I'd rather call it as I see it. The *Lilstar* was no exception to this trend and, thankfully, Ariadne knew exactly where it was.

"What is that and where did you get it?" the princess asked as she peeled back a thick layer of epidermis along a little fold near the membrane that separated the ship's bowels from the rest of the compartments. It was a great place for a smuggler's hold, being almost impossible to locate from a distance because it existed along a natural seam in the ship's epidermis. It wasn't a very big hold, not much larger than a magazine, but it could easily hold any small contraband one would wish to hide. A bag of jewels, a weapon, drugs, and even the very-contraband shock device, which I had to shove deep into the hold to keep its dark plastic from showing through the epidermis. Eventually, however, I managed to get it in there and replaced the flap, which sealed to become almost invisible.

"It's a shock device and Sasha gave it to me," I said simply, returning to my seat as the ship began its docking procedures.

"*Sasha* gave you that?" the princess asked with an expression so surprised it was almost disgusted.

"Yep," I said simply and with what I hoped was a conversation-ending tone. It apparently was.

Or maybe Ariadne was simply too focused on preparing for boarding.

That was the more likely answer.

The jackbooted thugs that entered the *Lilstar* after the docking procedure was complete were about as far from what I had been expecting as they could get. Instead of the greasy, malnourished and thieving station rats I was familiar with from past encounters, these men wore crisp uniforms, took themselves seriously, and didn't even loot Ariadne and my stuff as they opened up cabinets and poked at the contents with metal sticks. I swallowed as the guy in charge requested we step outside the ship for a briefing as the rest of the crew continued their ship-wide search. These guys might actually have known what they were doing in terms of finding smuggler's holds.

They seemed intolerably efficient.

Not that there was anything I could do about it now. I couldn't very well eject the shock-device into space at this point. So I followed Ariadne meekly out the *Lilstar*'s hatch and stepped into the reprocessed air of Meropis-C.

The inhabitants here had obviously been doing some remodeling to fit their new, rule-abundant lifestyle. Although the airlock was little more than nine feet long by ten wide, they had installed chairs along one of the walls. I didn't understand the need until the lead searcher stepped out and gestured the princess and me to the chairs and handed each of us a bound paper copy of both the Meropis-C Freight and Personal Item Regulatory Mandate and the Meropis-C Docking and Cargo Regulation Handbook in both their technical forms and a bright, easy-to-read kids' version. After that came the oral lecture of what each manual/mandate had inside of it.

The leader of the searchers, a man who announced himself with a straight face as First Segen

Samuel Sykes, gave the welcome-to-the-station-here-is-how-not-to-get-arrested speech with a remarkable amount of talent. He spoke with a strange sort of lilt that can only be found among space-born citizens and made the entire half-hour lecture somewhat less ponderous than it should have been. Plus, he wasn't too hard on the eyes; his grey uniform washed out the pair of liquid blue eyes he had to the color of a thunderstorm.

My only consolation, however, was that it didn't take his men the *entire* half-hour to search the *Lilstar* and, since they didn't interrupt the segen's lecture, I assumed they hadn't found the valuables chest.

"...And that concludes your official briefing on the basics of Meropis-C's cargo and personnel legislature," Sykes said. I heard Ariadne sigh loudly and I kicked her slightly in the foot, ignoring her scowl afterwards. "If you have any questions about anything at all, please feel free to ask."

"We're good—" Ariadne began.

"Actually we do," I said, taking advantage of an opportunity. "You see, we are skiptraces from back on Earth and I was wondering if you could help us locate a person of interest."

"Who is it you are looking for?" Segen Sykes asked with a slight tilt of his head.

I forced back an odd and slightly nervous smile as I pulled out the papers we had on Ottoman. I showed the segen the picture of the debtor and told the station officer the meager information we had on him.

"Let us check with the Meropis-C Passenger and Traffic Recording Office," Sykes said, beginning to lead the way down the hall.

"Just a moment, I need my bag," Ariadne said, dashing back to the *Lilstar*. I rocked back and forth on my feet as I waited with the segen.

"You seemed surprised when we first greeted you," Sykes said in a dull tone, waiting at some sort of at ease.

"I wasn't expecting such officiality," I said honestly.

"Ah, yes, this is somewhat new to the station. We only implemented these rules two years and change ago. It often catches people off guard," Sykes said easily. I tried not to get lost in his eyes.

"Yeah. I have a friend from B who warned me that things would be rough here," I said.

"They are not incorrect about Meropis-B. It is atrocious and should be evacuated and destroyed," Sykes said without flinching...or any real emotion. I chuckled somewhat anyway. "Our controlling company, however, was displeased with the state of the station and insisted on the changes."

"I thought all the Meropis stations were controlled by the same company?" I asked.

"No," Sykes said simply. The longer I talked to him, the more I realized he only went as deep as his eyes. I didn't say anything more until Ariadne returned with her bag. We followed the segen farther into Meropis-C.

Although it was the same basic brownish color as every other station I had ever been on, Meropis-C seemed to actually make an effort to be well-lit and tattoo-free, aside from the periodic location markings and simplified maps. Its natural, wheat-like smell was made even fresher with some light, spring-like tones that made the whole station smell like a meadow.

Even the people seemed to hold to this standard, usually well-dressed, well-groomed, and in no fear of being caught dawdling. If I had known the station was so formal, I probably would have dressed a bit more nicely, though I was far from slovenly in my wrinkled-but-stain-free shirt and clean pants. My hair was even brushed and done up properly. Ariadne, of course, looked like she had just come back from a luxury spa. Even after a week of living with her, I had no idea how she was able to keep so neat.

Overall Meropis-C was clean to nearly a fault. There were no parasites, no molds, not even a speck or two of lichens to ruin the pristine walls. In fact, the deeper the segen took me into the station, the more it smelled of disinfectant and natural oils. Whoever was running this particular station had no idea what they were doing. Keeping an organic structure healthy, be it a small ship or an entire city, was an artform. Kill too much good bacteria and you invite infection. Don't kill enough bad bacteria and the same thing is bound to happen. It was better to look at organic vehicles and buildings like they were their own ecosystems, not just one singular organism.

Despite this, I had little room to judge: Meropis-C seemed to be parasite and infection free, although I was willing to bet that its immune system was significantly weaker than a normal station of this size. All this sterilization could still cause a superbug down the road, costing the station up to millions in antibiotics and production delays; it was not as though people could still inhabit a sick organic structure without the risk of the virus or bacteria becoming zoonotic.

Segen Sykes took us all the way to the station's official center, called, unimaginatively, 'Meropis-C Station and Administrative Center.' There, he took us past the main waiting room and two long-lined desks entitled *Station Help* staffed with what appeared to be very overworked and dull-eyed personnel. Down the hall two more doors, a left, two rights, and what was left of the soles of my shoes, we finally made it to the Passenger and Traffic Recording Office.

"If you need anything, please feel free to inquire at the Station Help Desks," Segen Sykes said blandly before bowing stiffly and walking off. Ariadne and I looked at each other as we strode into the Recording Office's waiting room.

"So, did you get his number?" the princess demanded with a stupid grin on her face as she cautiously handed me the shock device. "I saw how you looked at him when he gave the speech."

"Nah, he's dead on the inside," I said plainly, pocketing the shock device and striding up to the closed window of the office, beginning to knock against the thin falsebone door.

"Actually, I have this one handled," Ariadne said, beating me to the knock.

Someone rustled papers inside and it wasn't a moment before an ancient man slid the door back. His nametag read "Frederick," which I thought was fitting.

"Yes?" he said around a sagging nose.

"We need help finding a person of interest; would you be able to oblige us?" The princess delivered her lines smoothly and with just the right amount of flirtation to keep any man a little off balance. It was immediately after that that she made the fatal mistake. Well, perhaps fatal is an exaggeration, but with any other person aside from Frederick, it would have been.

"Are you trying to bribe me, young lady?" the ancient clerk asked, eyes shifting from the credit mark in Ariadne's hand to a random corner near the ceiling. I rudely leaned over to see what he was looking at carefully. There it was, a station eyeball. Nowhere near as sophisticated as a human eyeball, being more of a mechanical sensor than a biological one, it was nonetheless a useful tool in ensuring that one's clerks and station workers were seated well within the law. I plucked the credit obviously from Ariadne's hand, waved it in front of the eye, and then shoved it down the front of my shirt. I hoped that was enough to get Frederick off the hook. With his sigh, I assumed it was.

"No sir, she was not trying to bribe you, that's for our lunch and she just happened to have it in her hand," I said smoothly. I pitied Ariadne somewhat as her face flushed with embarrassment and she backed away from the desk in apology. At least she hadn't been thrown in jail overnight like I was, after the first bribing mistake I made.

"We are looking for this guy," I said confidently, showing the picture of Ottoman to Frederick, keeping the paper well away from the other side of the falsebone door. It wouldn't do to make the station heads believe we were trying to bribe the ancient clerk more subtly now.

"Name of this...artfully tattooed fellow?" Frederick said, already thumbing through some files.

"Ottoman Lee," Ariadne piped up over my shoulder; she seemed resolute to make amends.

"Humph, no wonder he got the tattoo," Frederick commented as he thumbed through the station's new files with an amount of dexterity no one could possibly expect from his wrinkled hands.

I yawned as we waited for Frederick to finish sorting the files. Ariadne tapped her toe, arms still crossed with embarrassment. I tried to smile at her, a gesture she returned rather weakly.

"Ah, ha!" Frederick finally coughed in triumph. I tried to peer over the file he held and see what had turned his victory expression into one of confusion. "Well, at least, that's his name. The picture is all wrong, though."

A beyond-wrinkled hand presented me with an image that made me more uncomfortable than I had been in a long time. Although both pictures looked incredibly alike, the man whose picture sat in Ottoman Lee's Meropis-C file had the word "LOVER" tattooed along the right side of his face instead of "LOSER" being tattooed down the left side of his face like Aristotle's file. My jaw dropped somewhat as I tried to figure out what in the world was going on.

"Aahhmm..." I said in confusion. "Maybe this is the wrong file? Or the wrong Ottoman Lee?"

"Tell me, darling, how many Ottoman Lees do you think there are in existence, much less have visited Meropis-C in the past three weeks?" Frederick had a more than sound point.

"Can we have a copy of this?" Ariadne said. Frederick shrugged, stood up, and disappeared into the back of the office with the picture.

"Maybe Aristotle set us an old picture. Ottoman could have had his LOSER tattoo removed and the new one put in," I suggested. Ariadne simply made a confused gesture.

"I guess we'll just have to show both pictures around until someone says they've seen him," the princess said. I agreed, but something didn't smell right.

"That fellow," Frederick pointed to the guy with the LOVER tattoo. "checked in to the station about two weeks ago and just left about four days ago."

"Anyone know where he went?" I asked, my stomach turning just a bit. I had two weeks to catch this guy before Aristotle got angry and I'd never be able to pay off Ariadne.

"His file says he boarded a U.C. transport bound for the Asteroids, by way of Myrkheim," the ancient clerk shrugged. "You can check with Station Security, though."

I perked up a little at this information. If the princess and I were very lucky, and more than a little quick, we could make it to Myrkheim and its near-perpetual darkness in a week. Then we would have some padding to catch Ottoman. Of course, that would leave us very little time to make it back to Aristotle's, but the man never did say that bringing him back within the month was part of the bargain. In fact, he only said that I had to *catch* Ottoman before the time was up.

Of course, Aristotle was the lawyer between the two of us. I'm sure he would have an excellent counterargument for that idea of mine. But, as long as I held the skiptrace license, I was legally able to do anything a skiptrace could, and there was no real remote deactivation of a license, especially given that the cross-system communications was crap even with the Centauri radio systems. It's hard to communicate through the equivalent of space pea soup. That was why couriers and parcelmen were so popular.

"We need to leave about now," I turned to Ariadne.

"After we resupply; Myrkheim is kind of far," the princess determined with a nod, and almost began to dash toward the door. She stopped and turned back to Frederick with some confusion.

"Map's at the end of the hall. You'll want to speak to the Resupply and Provisions Department," the ancient clerk said. With a nod, Ariadne dashed off again. I turned to give Frederick a thank you, but he stopped me first. "Are you sure you gals need to be looking for this Lee fellow?"

"Why?" I asked, suddenly suspicious. Frederick had a dark expression hiding under his wrinkles. He reached out a hand as if to grab my arm, but thought better of it. I could see old tattoos and scars peeking out from under his sleeve.

"Just, well, make sure you are prepared for anything," Frederick said, pursing his lips. I nodded carefully and finally thanked him.

Crap.

Six

It took Ariadne and me about four days to reach Myrkheim, mostly because half of the trip was spent in the nebula's empty pocket. Though we hadn't truly escaped the gaseous soup and wouldn't for about ten light years in the forward direction, the sky was clear enough of brightly ionized particles to see a handful of stars. I spent a good hour after we reached the Corridor simply staring at the little points of light. They made me feel very empty and uncomfortably small, but it was a good kind of feeling. Sometimes it's okay to feel just a little insignificant, as long as you don't let it swallow you whole.

In this quiet and relatively bump-free region of space, Ariadne and I also took the time to inventory the *Lilstar's* supplies. We'd gone through most of the foodstuffs and would undoubtedly need a refill before we returned to Earth. Especially if we were carrying an extra passenger like Ottoman Lee. I still hadn't quite figured out how we were going to go about traveling with an extra passenger in a two-person ship. I supposed we could just stash Ottoman on one of the bunks, establishing regular shifts to enable us to keep an eye on both him and pilot the ship.

Of course, I was no pilot, so Ariadne would need to be awakened in the event of an emergency anyway. If only the *Lilstar* had one extra bunk and the pantry space to match. Plus I still spent most of my days curled up trying not to let the turbulence on the outside of the ship reach my innards. I had grown to hate ionized hydrogen pockets as much as the *Lilstar* did. I think the ship was even sympathizing with me; my showers were always nice and warm.

Thankfully, Myrkheim at this time of decade was in a pocket of nothing. Pure, sweet space without the burden of brightly colored ions. Most of the time, ships used the asteroid station as a way to readjust their ships for travel outside the nebula. Proxima Centauri was more often than not outside the nebula our systems shared, but on occasion, its orbit carried it along the edge of the gases. This was called the Tepid Corridor, a rare moment when ships get to travel in open space back and forth between Earth and our far trade partners at more impressive speeds than normal. Haunting and beautiful as the omnipresent cloud could be, the nebula made space travel little faster than slogging through waist-deep and corrosive mud while wearing a pair of wool jodhpurs. The Centauri learned a while back that their metal-based ships did little good inside the nebula, wearing out more quickly than they should due to a bad reaction between their favorite metallic alloys and the nebula's highly-charged ions. This presented an excellent source of trade for our two peoples. They had the metallic ground-based transports we needed, and we had the organic, spacefaring ships they needed.

Myrkheim itself was a smash colony embedded along the inside of the asteroid. Once the massive organic structure had reached maturity, it was flung at high speeds utilizing gravity toward the face of an asteroid, embedding itself deep into the craterous surface with eight long, vise-like pincers. These were reinforced by a rhizoid system, similar to that used by mosses on Earth, that would grow into the crater over time. This kept the colony from flailing around whenever the asteroid got hit by another and began to tumble end over end - although that was a rare and predicted occurrence, monitored closely by any company with a stake in Myrkheim's importance, which was mostly the U.C.

The colony was positively hopping by the time we reached it. Ships of all kinds, companies, and people were milling about its space. We almost ran into a few by accident and I could have sworn the *Lilstar* tried to go check out the cute little United-Consortium runabout that flew by at a leisurely pace. It took nearly a full day to finally reach a parking spot and after we finally had it, I knew we wouldn't leave Myrkheim unless it was an absolute and utter emergency.

Or we caught Ottoman.

Much unlike Meropis-C, Myrkheim avoided the omnipresent legislature and personal "welcome to the station" top-to-bottom contraband search. For that I was immensely thankful, although I surmised that it was probably because, if Myrkheim officials harassed every visitor to the colony, they wouldn't have time for any other duty. Ariadne and I stepped off the *Lilstar* without so much as a glance from the security guards patrolling the airlocks.

It took a good half-hour of walking to actually reach the main portion of the colony. The important thing to know about Mykheim was the fact that it was a real, honest-to-goodness city. It was not small or windowless like most of the stations in their various orbits around the solar system, and not cramped and crowded like the massive starliners that the U.C. is always boasting about. This was a trading post, a refueling stop, and most importantly, an entirely other world with its own unique culture and ecosystem. It was expensive to run but invaluable to this part of the human universe. It was a place nearly half a million souls called home and it was where Ariadne and I had to find our quarry.

Thankfully even with its size, Myrkheim made it easy to reach the center. Ariadne gasped a little as we finally rounded the corner.

The massive windows stood to the right-hand side if you were coming from the civilian docking sector. Almost a mile tall, they afforded the best view of starry space any Terran not wanting to leave the nebula could ask for. Held in place by the kindness of the Centauri who provided carbon-glass implants, the translucent epidermis that the colony produced naturally stretched upward. Of course, they still had to cover the windows with thicker epidermis whenever there was the threat of meteors or attack. It had been decades since they'd had to resort to that, however. Peace had been well-earned in this corner of the solar system.

The windows made for an impressive sight, sitting directly across from the living core of the colony. Myrkheim was a lot like a fox hunting in the snow, burrowing its specially-designed nose deep into the rock. The asteroid-side of the colony had nearly two hundred shelves of smaller organic buildings and walkways lining the walls. These shelves were at least twenty feet apart but each one, as a visitor moved upward was significantly smaller than the next, meaning that there was plenty of headspace on the lower levels. Once you'd reached the middle —— the narrowest shelves from the back wall —— the shelves began to expand once again until you reached the uppermost level. These top layers were mostly maintenance and miniature factories, along with a few important colony municipal centers. It was really the middle that held the most affluence.

"Ahhh…" Ariadne almost cooed, taking a deep breath of the colony's air. Unlike Meropis-C or any other station, the wheat smell had been completely replaced by a cacophony of a million other scents. Most were food-related as this lowest level we walked on was filled with shops and restaurants. There was even a Centauri bar where customers had to put on special breathing apparatuses to enter its argon-rich atmosphere. I've heard the food was good as the Centauri had several dishes on the menu that were blends of their own ethnic delicacies and human favorites.

Not that I ever had the credits to afford that kind of food.

Ariadne and I strode down the nearly-mile-long front boulevard for a while, simply taking in the enormity of what was of what surrounded us. The pseudo-gravity plating that overruled the asteroid's natural but meager gravitational field and kept the colony's patrons upright and perpendicular to the true center seemed to be turned down just a little. I felt bouncier than I had in the *Lilstar* and I vaguely began to wonder who had not adjusted the pseudo-gravity to normal. It wasn't as though a proper up and down existed in space.

"Well," Ariadne said, taking another deep breath. She already seemed to be truly enjoying herself and I envied her enthusiasm. I found it hard to be cheery with the prospect of searching the *whole, freaking city* for the only person who could secure our futures as skiptraces. "What do we do next?"

"I think we deserve a decent meal, no more space rations," I suggested. "Then and only then will we stop by the Transportation Agency and see if anyone has shown up on the station as Ottoman Lee."

"You don't hit the ground running, do you?" The princess cocked her head to one side almost mischievously.

"Oh no, we need to eat something that hasn't been overly processed," I said in an emphatic tone. "I mean, I don't mind sautéed canned meat but after a few weeks something fresher is just what I need.

Besides, finding a restaurant will give us the lay of the land."

"Alright," Ariadne nodded understandingly. "Let me go find a bank; we need real credits."

I nodded and strode toward a massive directory. I flipped the pages until it listed all the banks on the colony.

"There's one just over there," I pointed toward the United-Consortium Credit & Debit Exchequer.

"Mmm, no, I need a different branch," Ariadne said, looking over the directory in confusion.

"Like, U.C. Galaxy Bank? Bank of the Consortium? United Trust?" I kept suggesting, hoping one or more of those would strike her fancy.

"Do you only bank at U.C. banks?" the princess asked with puckered eyebrows.

"Only when I'm on a U.C. monopolized smash colony," I commented.

"Monopolized...?" Ariadne asked, looking like she'd just lost her appetite.

I nodded my head slowly.

"They bought this whole place about fifty years ago, so they control everything that is in here."

"Ahhhh..." the princess moaned loudly, setting her face on the directory.

"We have no money," I said plainly.

"Oh no," Ariadne said with a wry sort of laugh. "We have plenty of money. What we don't have is access to it."

"Can't your bank transfer to a U.C. owned bank?" I asked hopefully.

"Nope. That's why I bank there, no U.C. connections, no U.C. legislation," Ariadne said.

I perfectly understood her position. I would have kept my money in an independent bank had I known they existed. And had I had the money to actually put in a bank. The problem with U.C. is that they had unfettered rule over the entire human economy, meaning that they could rob you blind without any sort of government to stop them. Not that governments really had any real influence or jurisdiction any more. Law was a matter of perspective and mostly upheld by independent police forces and a healthy body of skiptraces. The U.C. was as close to godlike as any corporation had achieved to date; it basically controlled every aspect of your life whether or not you wanted it to.

I rubbed my face, hoping money would suddenly fall from my hands. Instead, my stomach growled and I grew nauseated thinking about canned meat.

And being stranded on a massive colony, flat broke.

Ariadne handled the situation little differently, looking through her pockets as if they would suddenly produce money. She finally raised her hand triumphantly. "Yay. A button. It doesn't even match my coat."

I had to sit down at that point. At least the ground was warm. This close to the epidermis floor, I could almost smell warmed-over wheat.

"I really didn't want to die here," the princess said, sitting down beside me.

"Me neither," I muttered. I should have left that skiptrace to the proper authorities, spent my inheritance on a nice apartment, and gotten a job at that biologic construction company that had an office just down the street from my childhood home. I probably knew just as much about organic structures and how to grow them as their favorite organic engineers. I mean, what kind of adventure would *that* be, but sometimes doing good work is just as good as slaying dragons. Besides, I probably would have a cold cellar filled with delicious food.

I'm not certain how long we'd sat there, underneath the directory, waiting for some miracle to happen. We probably looked like neatly-dressed hobos, lurking in the street. I sighed loudly, watching the people duck in and out of restaurants and shops. Spending money. Money I didn't have.

I could get used to this colony, with all of its unhurried bustle and movement. I wasn't fond of crowds, but I still liked people and wondering who they were and where they came from. My brother used to take me to a park not far from our house between his shifts and my school. It was filled with good old trees and grasses; unlike the mosses that coated rooftops and sidewalks, this was real grass. He would then tell me all about the people he had seen that day. Not going into the gruesomeness of their injuries or the illnesses he'd had to treat, of course, just who they were. The mother who held her small son's hand, the old man who sang opera to an emergency room full of sick and injured people, and the young woman with gang tattoos who gave up her seat for a limping man. The stories weren't always so sanitized or kind. Sometimes my brother would straight up tell me just how messed up humanity could be, or sometimes I could just infer it.

So I grew up people-watching. Trying to figure out what kind of life they'd led and why they were where they were. That man, for example, with the ridiculous looking leather vest. Where did he get that wicked scar across his arm? And was the vest a fashion choice or did he just not care? What about that old couple over there in their matching cardigans and shoes? Did they have a destination in mind or were they just out for a stroll? They seemed content, whichever option they had chosen, and I smiled a little. Maybe one day I'd grow old with some guy.

Of course, that would be very unlikely if I starved to death here on this colony.

I decided to continue my people-watching for just a while longer, trying to gauge exactly how this colony breathed, so to speak. Given the fact it was the dayshift, the people walking about were made up mostly of people who didn't feel safe at night; young women without a group, the rich, older people, families. I wondered what kind of rabble rousers plagued this colony during the night, if any did. I doubted places like Meropis-C had any trouble with nightcrawlers and bar-hopping noise makers, but this colony was much more like a city than a true station. It would be a lot more difficult to corral the highly varied inhabitants of Myrkheim.

A lost-looking young woman suddenly veered toward the directory Ariadne and I were sitting beneath. She looked business-y, but approachable, giving both the princess and I somewhat odd looks. I gave her a wry sort of smile, trying to not come across as someone really strange, sitting in the middle of a public place, staring at random people.

Let's face it, I was set up for failure on the not-a-creep count.

To continue down this looks-like-a-creep-but-isn't path, I decided to try something desperate.

"Would you like a button?" I asked the lady. Her face contorted into a nervous sort of expression with pinched eyebrows and an uncertain smile.

"Excuse me?" she asked.

"We're trapped on this colony with only a button that doesn't match either of our jackets. I was wondering if you'd like it in trade," I said very plainly, gesturing for Ariadne to present the button. Her expression was less nervous than the lady's but still confused. She complied, however, presenting the shiny and somewhat plain bluish button.

The lady looked at Ariadne and I in turn before picking up the button and inspecting it.

"It might make a nice replacement for my other suit..." she murmured, then looked apologetic. "I really didn't bring any loose money with me."

"I don't mean money," I explained, standing up. "I'll take anything of somewhat equal value to this button."

"Well," the lady quickly searched her pockets. "I have this single glove. I lost the other one somewhere on this level and I can't find it. It's a nice glove, just not very useful without the other."

"Sold," Ariadne said, taking the brown glove in her hands. It did look very nice and decently warm. "I know the brand; it'll still be worth something even as a single."

"Alright." The lady's smile was still tinged with some confusion, but she shook on the deal and Ariadne and I were now in possession of a singular but warm glove.

"Brilliant plan," the princess commented after the bewildered lady had left. She shoved the glove on to her hand and waved it at me.

"Oh, it's about to get much better," I said, and gave Ariadne the biggest, cheesiest grin I could. "Let's see if we can find a home for this."

As it turned out, it is much more difficult to peddle a single glove than it is a button, though the glove was undoubtedly much nicer than said button. Even with as cold as it was on this front strip, no one seemed interested in taking us up on our offer. Soon, Ariadne and I were back at the *Lilstar*, half-gloved and hungry, but not for space rations.

"Tell me again why I decided to be a skiptrace with your sorry—" — Ariadne started. Before she could finish, I yanked the glove out of her hand, hoping that maybe its mere presence would inspire a brilliant idea in me. It didn't. It was brown, soft, and insulated but not inspiring in any sort of fashion.

"Our problem is, most of the population doesn't want a single glove. There has to be someone, however, weird enough to just want one glove."

I said aloud, opening myself up for some commentary on my ability to state the obvious but also hoping for the triggering of a brilliant idea out of either of us.

Turns out, it was Ariadne's turn to be brilliant. Without a word, she leaped from her seat and snatched the glove back, disappearing into the bathroom and returning with a pair of scissors. She sat back down, carefully snipping off the tip of each finger and a large swatch out of the palm.

"Ah, good. You're butchering our only real bargaining chip besides this sludge bucket you call a—" — I said. Ariadne put the now-fingerless glove on and shoved a bare, disapproving finger in my face.

"I encourage you to stop what you are saying and revel in my brilliance before I have to forcibly remove you from *my* SHIP." Her gaze never wavered.

"I don't get it," I finally had to say. Even upon an up-close inspection of her new creation, I didn't see how it would help us.

"What sort of rock did you grow up under?" the princess wrinkled her nose in disapproval. "This is no longer a single glove: it's a fashion piece, and I know just the demographic who eats this kind of thing up."

"Those music-hating punk types?" I filled in the blank. Of course I was familiar with the movement, I'd just never crossed paths with one of them long enough to know the fashion trends.

Ariadne just grinned at me broadly.

"Well, if they are nightcrawlers they should be out and about by now," I commented.

"Are we sure we want to be out and about by now?" Ariadne asked in concern. I mused the thought over for a minute.

"It's either risk it or we scarf down what's left of the space rations," I said. The princess shrugged and we made for the airlock.

Myrkheim was not a supremely dark place to be during the nightshift. In fact, it was barely any darker than usual, although someone had cut the power to the electric lights running along the massive windows, making the few stars that could be seen and the chartreuse-colored nebula stand out as prominent features. I guess it did make everything seem a little more night-like, and pockets of nightclubs could be found where all the usually yellow lights were replaced by neon-colored signs, most of which were made of a bioluminescent material that had a natural, if faded, glow. The patches of nightclubs looked like black swaths of nothingness standing out against the rest of the lit buildings. The middlemost shelves of the colony were also dimmed, some even dark, since they were made mostly of living quarters. All the shops and factories, however, remained brightly-lit.

"Let's head toward that clump," Ariadne said, taking lead on this particular task. She gestured at the nearest nightclub grouping on this level. Of course, these were *nice* nightclubs, the exclusive kind the rich socialites always go to be seen publicly. Fame was not something that was for me, I had decided a long time ago.

I followed the princess in an effort that was just as futile as I'd first assumed. None of the nightclubs on this lowest level housed any kind of subculture we were looking for. It was all high fashion and overly-expensive champagne. So we ascended to the next level, which housed nightclubs that catered a little more to the common man. Still, it was an affluent common man. It wasn't until we had reached the second quarter of shelves that we found the kind of place we were looking for, and even then it wasn't until the fourth or fifth club that we found any sign of the punks.

Don't doubt the pain our feet were in as we finally approached the first gaggle of our target demographic at well past midnight.

"Hey, you," Ariadne said without finesse. I wasn't certain if it was a lack of sleep or food that was putting her on edge.

"You talking to *me*, shorty?" a chick with dazzlingly braided hair, almost no tattoos or piercings, and overly-shaped eyebrows asked in an accusing tone. I decided to wait this one out.

"Yeah *you*," Ariadne said in an equally abrasive tone. She presented the glove, however. "You look like the kind of gal who could use some fashion help. Luckily, I have this. I just need something in return."

"I'm not certain—" "I began to tell Ariadne as I looked at the chick's friends. They were all tattoo-less rebels without any kind of happy expression on their faces. The princess had made the right call with the glove, however, as more than one of these punks had a fingerless leather glove —— just one —— as some sort of statement I couldn't even begin to fathom.

"What does a squeak like you know about fashion?" the chick said. However, she still hadn't turned away from Ariadne.

"Puh-leeze, your boots aren't even a genuine *Maestro Martinez* pair. They're cheap Centauri knockoffs at best. What are you, new to the life?" the princess declared, crossing her arms and kicking out her hips in defiance. She was beginning to look more and more like these people. All she needed was to dress in black.

Whatever she was doing was effective, however, and the punk-chick looked more embarrassed than angry as all of her friends looked at her boots. Apparently she was new.

"Although, now that I notice, only that guy has the real deal," Ariadne said after scanning the rest of the group. The goateed fellow shrugged while everyone else looked self-consciously at their feet. "But my offer is with you. What do you say?"

The punk-chick took the glove and tried it on. It at least fit perfectly.

"What is this made of?" she said in excitement. It was still a nice glove, if dismembered.

"Trade you for it," Ariadne said.

"How about this belt?" The punk-chick gestured.

"Nope. Too difficult to peddle," Ariadne said. "Anything else?"

The punk-chick sighed and thought for a few moments.

"How about this? I don't even like coffee," the punk-chick-newbie dug through her pockets for a piece of somewhat crumpled paper. It was a voucher for a coffee house on the lower level. "My sister gave it to me but she thinks I'm some sort of bookworm."

"My brother thought I was a wrestling fanatic," I chimed in, remembering a birthday with ring-side seats to a local beat-em-up. Sure, I had thought Ignacio Sonata, three-time Sol System Champion, was cute from a poster when I was seven, but that didn't mean I was obsessed with wrestling. After that, he made sure to carefully observe my likes and dislikes and what I was *actually* into and what was a passing fancy.

All of the punks and Ariadne looked at me like I had grown another head.

Yep, definitely not my tribe.

Finally, the punk-chick gave me a quiet little chuckle and then Ariadne and I were on our way with a voucher for coffee. As I yawned loudly, I seriously considered cashing it in myself.

"Should we head back to the *Lilstar*? I'm dead on my feet," Ariadne said, shifting from the undercover punk she had been a minute ago into a tired-looking princess.

"May as well, I don't think the coffee shop'd be open today," I said.

"We're not cashing this in, are we?" the princess said, confused.

"No, but where else are we going to find some-one who will definitely be interested in free coffee from it?" I pointed out. Ariadne just shrugged in understanding.

Our slog back to the *Lilstar* took up the rest of the night and we decided that space rations just weren't on the menu for breakfast, so we slept most of the day and woke up hungry.

"This plan is getting us nowhere," Ariadne complained as we started toward the coffee shop.

"It will, we just need to keep trading upward," I said.

"Why don't we just take bounties? Aren't we skiptraces?" the princess suggested in a tone that implied I was an idiot for not thinking about that earlier.

"We are legally bound to Aristotle's company and can only take bounties from him or Mr. Carver," I sighed. "Otherwise I'd be looking over the local bounties right now."

Ariadne made a sound like the growl of a dying hippo and fell back a few steps to roll her head dramatically.

"Yep. That helped, I feel much better," I said wryly, sticking my tongue out for effect. The princess shot me a pouty glare and stomped on ahead of me toward the coffee shop.

It was a very nice establishment with a warm, brownish sort of atmosphere about it. The whole place was a riot of mostly coffee-type smells with various herbs and spices to make the average cup of joe ridiculously but deliciously complicated. I could never quite manage coffee; it was entirely too strong for my taste even when doused with copious amounts of cream and sugar. Of course, it wasn't technically *coffee* in this place, it was *café* and the people who dined here would be quick to judge you for using the wrong word. Although I didn't hang out with this crowd very much, I'd seen enough to know that they were generally good people, mostly poets, writers, and other artistic souls. Despite their outward glares, I highly doubted they were any kind of real threat.

That being said, I could feel my nose sticking up in the air the minute I walked through the door.

"I wonder what will get us kicked out faster, telling the proprietor of our plans or not telling him," I mused, looking toward the counter with what I hoped was not a suspicious glance.

"Getting kicked out wasn't part of the plan," Ariadne frowned in surprise.

"It was always something that could happen," I commented as I made my way toward the counter. May as well attempt the choice with decency first. Maybe the manager would take pity on us. I shot quietly back over my shoulder, "We could also go to jail."

The princess cringed visibly.

I walked up to the counter with a smile on my face.

"Hi,there. My friend and I are flat broke, so we were wondering if we could trade this voucher for something with your clients," the more words I said, the less inclined *I* felt to letting Ariadne and me try to trade the voucher.

Which was exactly how the proprietor felt. As it turns out, there was an option I hadn't thought of: getting thrown out and *then* arrested. Technically the arresting came after we spent hours lurking in the various corners of the colony trying to trade a piece of paper that represented one free coffee. Apparently we'd become a pair of suspicious-looking public nuisances and enough people complained to send a pair of cops after us. I really wasn't certain what I expected from our desperate plan, but it seemed reasonable looking at it from the outside in.

SEVEN

"How does this rank with space rations?" Ariadne commented pointedly, shoving bits of mashed...vegetable around her plate. I wasn't certain prison rations were worth more than the super-processed meat I had been eating three meals a day, but at least it was something different.

I cleaned my plate and what was left of the princess's in any event.

We'd really only been behind bars for a few hours, but the cops that had arrested us seemed nice enough. They'd gone somewhat out of their way to get us a meal hours before the actual lunchtime. That being said, we still were locked up without access to bail money and facing charges of at least scalping and loitering. Not *that* much, granted, but enough to set us back in our hunt for Ottoman Lee a fair bit. Besides, Aristotle might not like having his two newest skiptraces hold records on such an important colony. Heck, we might even end up with bounties on our heads.

"So, ladies..." one of the cops that had arrested us, Officer Remiel, came up to the jail cell. He leaned forward on the bars with a pitying expression on his face. "What are we going to do about you?"

"I apologize, officer," I said sincerely. "Ariadne and I are flat broke and I thought trading items would get us somewhere more easily than any other option."

"Why can't you just cash bounties? This checks out, you are definitely licensed to skiptrace on this colony," Officer Remiel said with a shrug, waving our license in the air.

"Legally we aren't allowed to cash bounties unless our employer directs us to them," I said glumly.

The cop nodded his head a few times in understanding.

"There has to be *something* you guys can do to earn some cash," Remiel said, stroking his chin. I wanted to say something a bit sarcastic, but that felt unnecessary. I mulled over nothing in particular, not really wishing to walk the dog on what I could do to earn quick money on this colony, until Officer Remiel snapped his fingers.

"I have an idea for you ladies. It's not great work but it should get you enough money or trades to get back on your feet. Plus it uses a lot of skiptracing techniques," the cop smiled broadly as he unlocked the cell.

"We can go?" Ariadne asked.

"If you promise to give my idea a shot and not creep around the center like you have been," Officer Remiel grinned.

"I think we can do all of that," I said enthusiastically and exited the cell, following Remiel as he led the way to the front offices. He gestured to some chairs and sat down behind a desk. "Now, here's the idea: this colony has some animal control but not enough to keep up with the ecosystem, so we usually have bounties up for animal capture for anyone willing to put in the effort. What do you think?"

"Sure!" Ariadne said without hesitation. I gave her a questioning look. It wasn't as though I was going to refuse this officer's entirely reasonable proposal, but she answered him without even a moment to think it over. She seemed to do a lot without hesitation.

"Okay, that sounds good," I finally agreed. The cop nodded in approval. "Do we need special permits or something?"

"Nah. If you can take on humans, we figure you're good for critters. Here's the address to the animal control facility that will set you up with traps and predators," Officer Remiel said, handing us a slip of paper. It was only a few streets over.

"Thank you," I said genuinely. The officer just smiled.

"Keep your noses clean, ladies," he said as Ariadne practically dragged me out of the police station.

We walked up two blocks and made a left, arriving at the nearly overcrowded animal control building. There wasn't exactly a line spilling out the door onto the streets, but the main office was packed with all sorts of colorful, skiptracing characters. They had to be skiptraces, because there was no way that this many rogues could have been there to adopt stray puppies. Plus, they were all staring up at the screens of color-changing scales that organized themselves into words and numbers and displayed the various critter bounties. These ranged from a trespassing neighbor's iguana to some missing miniature cows from a microfarm to an infestation of moths at a local factory. I sighed, thinking over my options. Infestations might be easy, since that would just involve setting out traps. Tracking down missing turtles? Much more difficult.

Ariadne and I finally made it to the front desk, where a harried but low-voice clerk looked at us blankly.

"Here to adopt?" he queried just as blankly.

"Actually we were sent over to help with animal control," I said, a little hesitantly.

The clerk actually blinked at us in slow surprise.

"Do you have your license on you? I have to register you in the database," he finally said. I produced the license and rocked back and forth on my feet.

"Am I reading this right?" the clerk said after a minute. "You two took down Big—"

"I did," I said sharply. My vendetta was old news and so was that pig whose license I stole.

"You're scary," the clerk said with enough respect for me to regret being snappish.

"Yeah, she also brushes her teeth with a child's toothbrush," Ariadne said, turning to watch my face. "It's powder blue with a little cartoon ship on it."

I jabbed her in the side with a pair of fingers as hard as I could. She didn't even wince.

"Hey, I don't judge. I have a whole set of Captain U.C. underwear," the clerk shrugged.

I didn't know what to say to that, and neither did Ariadne, so we let the moment pass in silence.

"All right, you're in the database, so you now have access to the animal control bounties," the clerk said. "Once you have chosen a bounty, you go to that desk over there and Mildred will outfit you with the necessary equipment. After you have completed your bounty, report back here for your compensation. Pets and pet-like animals are to be captured alive and brought to an animal control building. Pests and infestations are handled with the appropriate predators and traps for which you will be responsible from the time you request it until it is released at the site. Don't go coming back for more wolf spiders if you happen to drop the first ones. Do you understand?"

"Yes," Ariadne sand I said in the same, uncertain tone. The clerk didn't seem to notice the uncertainty, however, and gestured to the scalescreens.

Ariadne and I sidled up as close as we could to read off the available bounties.

"What are you thinking?" Ariadne asked.

"Infestations seem like the easiest to handle, but also pay the least," I said thoughtfully. "Maybe start with that?"

"Alright, which one?" Ariadne's brows furrowed a little.

"How about that one? 'slug infestation at restaurant *Jones'* Tier 3 Row 5 from the left; bonus available,'" I suggested.

"Yay, invertebrates," Ariadne sighed, but accepted the idea. We walked back to the clerk, declared our bounty, and walked over to Mildred. The overly short woman with white hair nodded. After a moment, she placed a carboard box and a bottle of beer on the counter in front of her.

"Slugs are a mess, especially in restaurants. What you'll want is some of these violet ground beetles; they clean up the area without leaving a mess and can't carry zoonotic diseases. Don't forget to tell the restaurant to shut down its kitchen for about a day; these guys are genetically modified and don't live much longer than 24 hours. After that, they can clean up and resume business." Mildred gestured to the surprisingly noisy box. The beetles were scraping up against every side, giving the box an almost writhing quality to it. I swallowed loudly.

"What's the beer for?" Ariadne asked, looking over the bottle.

"For attraction," Mildred said. "You pour the beer into choice areas around the infestation, which attracts the slugs, then you release the predators in those areas. It makes clean up easier."

I made a gesture to the cardboard box, which Ariadne flatly refused to pick up. Instead, she snatched the beer from the counter, leaving me the more unpleasant choice. I could almost feel the beetles crawling all over my skin after I picked up the box. But I imaged starving to death in a strange colony and held the box in a firm but gentle grip.

"Thanks," I said cautiously.

"Thank the beetles," Mildred replied. That wasn't going to happen.

Unless I got that bonus.

"Ugh, this isn't even the good stuff," Ariadne commented once we were out of animal control. She looked at the open bottle of beer in disgust.

"You really drank the slug-juice?" I accused her. She turned a little green around the edges.

"Well, don't put it like *that*," she muttered.

• • •

Ariadne and I made our way to the restaurant, *Jones',* which turned out to be much more like a nightclub with blacklights, loud music, and a mosh pit filled with writhing, bioluminescent-tattooed partygoers. It was barely even lunchtime, but I decided not to judge. I was the one bringing in a box of squirming beetles to take care of a slug problem.

I weaved my way up to the high bar to the left. It sat a few steps up from the dance floor and was incredibly well-stocked with both alcohols and flavorings, backlit by soft bioluminescent lights that were just bright enough to let you read the labels. The bar itself was topped with what appeared to be falsebone slab embedded into the epidermis. That's how you know when it's a high-class establishment, if it has an level bar. I walked up and glanced around for the bartender, rapping the bar a few times. I was finally greeted by an eye-patched bartender with a surprisingly pleasant smile and a nametag that read *Ylva*.

"What can I do for ye?" she asked.

"We're skiptraces from animal control, we've come about your slug problem," I said declared. Ylva nodded and curled a finger for us to follow her. It wasn't that easy, of course, given the fact that we had to wade through a very thick crowd while she got to walk a clear path behind the bar. I considered leaping over it, but that seemed uncouth.

Ariadne and I caught back up with Ylva at the end of the bar and she took us through the massive double doors of the kitchen.

"We dinnae have a problem until just this morning," the bartender said, leading us into the largely metallic kitchen. A lot of the appliances were obviously Centauri, not surprising given the fact that Myrkheim was *the* waystation between Proxima and Earth. But even with this inhospitable tech, there were enough organic components in the walls and falsebone floor to house a decent-sized infestation. "All of a sudden they overran us."

The two cooks looked at us a little suspiciously, but didn't stop their work. One did harrumph loudly as a hungry Ariadne poked her nose over a pot of something that was undoubtedly mushroom stew. It smelled earthy and warm. Unfortunately, I missed the expression she shot back at him.

Ylva had led us to another set of doors, gesturing to a half-eaten corner of the doorframe and leading us into what appeared to be an herb garden. I heard Ariadne make a small gagging noise as the slugs in the doorframe began to squirm as the door opened and closed. I swallowed again and entered the herb garden bravely.

Well, it mostly used to be an herb garden, being filled with plants looking little better than the doorframe. Slugs squirmed all over the place, chowing down on leaves and organic structure alike. I walked over to one of the low, table-like beds. The slugs were even disappearing underneath the layers of cloth that allowed the plants to root. There was no real dirt on the station; most gardens were either for water-based plants, fungi, lichens, or algae, none of which required soil, or used some form of dirt substitute for the plants to hold on to, like layers of cloth or paper. In a few places, the slugs were even eating away at the cloth itself.

I cringed.

This was my life for the moment: chief slug remover.

Of course, I was faring better than Ariadne, who had her hands pulled back into her sleeves, looking around cautiously at the slimed and dying plants. I tried picking out the worst areas, presuming that would be the best place to pour out the beer and release the beetles, but it all looked like the same, like a gooey nightmare.

"What areas have been the worst hit?" I finally asked Ylva.

"The thyme and rosemary were hit the hardest; but our seedlings are nae much better. The slugs haven't touched the mint," the barkeep said, leading Ariadne and I to the specified areas. She was right — the slugs hadn't touched the mint. The plants were a happy, optimistic oasis in the middle of a gooey, gooey apocalypse.

"Alright," I said, looking at Ariadne. She gave me a wide-eyed gaze.

"What?" she asked.

"The beer? You opened it and tasted it, so you get to pour it out," I said gesturing to the slimy pile of dead plant.

Ariadne didn't say anything, pouring a measured amount of the surprisingly sweet-smelling beer. She gestured as if to confirm that she did, in fact, fulfill her part of the bargain.

"You go to the other areas, and I'll start releasing the beetles," I said bravely. As it turns out, the easiest way to release a bunch of beetles is to open the box, let them crawl all over your hands, stifle a scream, and carefully walk over to each beer trap and shake off beetles, all the while cursing the day you were born. I swear Ylva sniggered at my beetle-covered hands.

"All done," I said, scraping the last purplish beetle from my hand. I could still feel them crawling all over my skin. Ariadne looked like she'd finished drinking the slug-beer. "You'll need to keep the kitchen locked for about 24 hours. The beetles will be dead by then and you can clean up."

"I figured as much," Ylva said, with an understanding nod.

I nodded and led the almost shell-shocked Ariadne out of the kitchen. Ylva followed, locking the doors as we went.

"Thank ye ladies very much!" she said with a smile. I smiled back at least a little. "I believe we advertised a bonus in the bounty, correct?"

Ariadne and I nodded in unison, which was a little embarrassing.

"Well, ye have a choice..." Ylva said.

"Can we come back for a meal?" Ariadne boldly asked.

"Really? After what you just saw in the kitchen?" I whispered fiercely.

"Yes. I want a guaranteed hot meal and I don't care where it's from," she said defiantly. I shrugged.

"A meal will work fine. The beetles will be dead in 24 hours, yes?" Ylva asked and I nodded. "Then come tomorrow, two hours from the time it is now. Mr. Jones will want the kitchen cleaned well."

"It's a deal," Ariadne said enthusiastically. We both shook Ylva's hand and made our way back to the animal control office.

For the next day, we dashed all around the colony, curing infestations and capturing strays. For the most part, we stuck with the light bounties, which didn't pay a lot, but working for 18 hours straight made us feel financially secure enough to eat a cheap meal and sleep it off in the *Lilstar*.

We also managed to make a brief stop at the Transportation Agency to see if we could pick up Ottoman's trail. Inexplicably, there were not one or two 'Ottoman Lees' on Myrkheim, but *four*. Thankfully it turned out that two of them could be ruled out immediately, one being a woman and the other being a six-month-old. Neither Ariadne nor I had enough time to continue following the paper trail of the other two, however. Trying to make enough money to survive was taking precedence.

The next morning was most of the same. We stopped by animal control, picked out our bounties and got talked at by Mildred regarding the specimen of predator or type of humane trap and bait we needed. It wasn't necessarily pleasant work, plus it made me feel like a Skiptrace Junior Edition, taking bounties on such things as singing, bioluminescent cockroaches rather than actual criminals, but at least I was working.

Exactly two hours past the 24-hour lockdown of *Jones'* kitchen, we arrived at the restaurant/nightclub. It was a little less busy, but not by much. Ylva, however, welcomed us to the best seats at the bar.

"How's the slug problem?" I asked.

"All gone, thanks to you lasses. The herbs should be bounding back in no time. What can I get for ye?" the eye-patched bartender said.

"I need food, so let's do..." the princess said, looking over the menu somewhat chaotically. "A grilled cheese and a water."

"And for you?" Ylva turned toward me. I glanced at the neat rows of liquors behind her, taking brief stock of each one. Then I sighed, gave Ylva a tired look, and just said, "I'll have the same." To which she chuckled understandingly.

I sat rubbing my temples as Ariadne began to groove to the music. I had to admit, it was nice to listen to, but she was on a whole other level of enjoyment.

"Do you dance?" she suddenly turned and asked me. I shrugged half-heartedly.

"Not really. You?" I sipped my water as Ylva brought our orders out. The princess shrugged, herself, as she crunched down on what smelled like a heavenly sandwich. Taking a bite of mine, I determined that assumption to be correct. There had to have been three or four different kinds of cheeses at least, all bringing together different notes and harmonizing with something that had to be oregano. Whoever was the creator of such a heavenly food was a genius.

"Nah, I just like music," Ariadne tore off a piece of her grilled cheese with her fingers and chewed it thoughtfully. "What do you like?"

"I dunno," I said, thinking over my options. I *had* used to like "things," music, jewelry, poetry, radio programs, brightly colored toys, and hair doo-dads, but that was an awfully long time ago. Revenge is an all-consuming business and I hadn't had enough time yet to switch from grieving avenger back to normal Marcie...if she still existed. I didn't really know what I liked anymore. "I guess I like putting bad guys in their place."

Ariadne nodded without any sort of judgement. In fact, she seemed to be contemplating my answer like it was something new to be explored. At least, that was what her expression said, though she may have just been enjoying her grilled cheese. I started to retreat into my glass of water, falling down a rabbit hole of self-analysis. I probably *should* figure out something to do with my life aside from catching bad guys. Especially since it could all end abruptly if we didn't catch Ottoman in time. I supposed I could go work at a factory somewhere. Or maybe get an internship with a real skiptrace. That seemed like a good option. I had quite a few of the basics down, chasing after my...well my predecessor. I could make a living off bounties. I'd even heard some skiptraces make up to—

"Hey, hey hey!" the princess suddenly got excited, interrupted my thoughts, and began to tap me repeatedly. She spun in her chair, finally looking away from the dancefloor. She whispered almost vainly: "Really cute guy at my 4 o'clock."

I, of course, threw subtlety out the window and stuck my face in the air to get a good look at him.

"Which one? The short guy with a lip piercing?" I asked, picking a random person out of the crowd. Of course I could spot which one was the "cute guy" Ariadne was cooing over, because he stood well above most of the other patrons. He was probably a station brat who grew up in the slightly lessened gravity of Myrkheim. He sported an immaculately fluffy Mohawk, artfully placed bioluminescent dots along his already elegant face, and at least two piercings in each ear. Even my un-refined man radar could tell that this guy, with his high cheekbones and easy smile, was a little above attractive.

"What? No, the tall one over there," Ariadne cast a furtive glance toward him.

"Huh, let's call him over here," I began to stand up to catch his attention, a feat I managed before the princess pulled me forcibly back down into my seat. The Mohawk waved back to me and started to move toward the bar. He passed through the crowd with ease, so I surmised he was at least a regular.

"Have you gone utterly bat-faced?" Ariadne asked with unspeakable horror on her face.

"You said you thought he was cute. I figured I may as well call him over so you can say hi," I said innocently. The princess simply sputtered and tried to hide within her grilled cheese as the cute guy slowly made his way over. To my surprise, he didn't greet us from this side of the bar, instead walking around to the other side, greeting Ylva with a friendly kiss to the cheek.

"Hello, ladies! You are the gals from the animal control, correct?" He smiled easily and his voice was rich as molasses. Ariadne continued to inspect her sandwich.

"Yes, we are," I said, refusing to be dazzled by this man.

"Apologies for not thanking you two earlier; it has been a busy few days." I swear this man could tell me he was a monkey's uncle and I'd believe it. Ariadne would believe it doubly.

"You're very welcome. Actually, I'll be honest, I called you over for my friend here, Ariadne King," I patted the princess' back as if to prevent her from the choking fit I knew would descend upon her. She probably would have glared me to death if not for Mr. Mohawk's disarming smile. His eyes almost disappeared in all the sunshine he was producing.

"Well, it is nice to meet you, Miss King," the smile persisted as he presented a hand to Ariadne. He kissed the back of hers when she finally gave up on the sandwich camouflage. "I am Leopold Jones, proprietor of this establishment."

"Oh, thank you — I mean, you have a lovely place here," the princess said, flustered, but I applauded her bravery.

Of course, she still came across as the height of graceful royalty, if immensely shy. She was working the whole flirty-head-tilt-and-batting-eyelash trick for all it was worth. Leopold seemed charmed, and not just as a proprietor trying to please his patrons.

"Thank you, Miss King. Please, never hesitate to ask if you need anything. I will be sure to handle it personally." His smile persisted. The two held hands for a few seconds longer than was actually necessary and Ylva and I exchanged a look that was part eye roll, part shrug. At least for this moment, Ariadne and Leopold were meant for each other.

"Oh, this is my friend and co-conspirator, Marcie Dunn," Ariadne suddenly said, finally removing her hand and gesturing to me. Leopold gave my hand the same kiss and excellent smile, but let go of it just a few seconds more quickly. I gave Ylva a second look, to which she chuckled.

"Technically I'm the conspirator, she is the pilot," I said, leaning on the bar flirtatiously, making Ariadne compete just a little. Not that I was the slightest bit interested in Leopold, but I had to make sure she put a whole foot into pursuing him. It worked, and after almost forcefully shoving her plate aside, the princess moved to lean even farther into the bar than I was. I kept the 'ah-ha!' part of my smile internal.

"Really? What are you ladies conspiring for? Or against?" Leopold said, gesturing to take Ylva's spot in mixing drinks so he could keep talking to us.

"Oh, we're in the skiptrace business. I own the ship and she knows how to find the bad guys," Ariadne let the words roll off her overly gentle demeanor. I realized that I should have been taking notes; I might be able to adapt her technique in the future. Of course, pulling off her level of grace was something at the very least improbable for anyone who was not a King.

"Skiptraces? That is an exciting line of work." I felt honored that Leopold took a moment to nod in my direction before returning his undivided attention to Ariadne.

"It's not so bad. We get to travel around quite a bit and see interesting places," the princess said, casually drawing invisible doodles in the bar.

Yes, I chided her internally, *almost three weeks from Earth to Myrheim via Meropis-C in a tiny, two-person ship.* It wasn't exactly a vacation on Eden-3, but I kept that to myself. Leopold gazed at her like she was a golden chalice filled with silver wine, something altogether too beautiful and too captivating to look away, so I didn't have the heart to ruin the moment using that particular method.

That didn't mean I wasn't wracking my brain trying to come up with a different way to break things off. A sudden slap of reality to fracture the encounter, leaving both Ariadne and Leopold with a cliffhanger; a reason for another rendezvous.

I gasped, looking frantically at the clock above the bar.

"What?" Ariadne asked, still mostly distracted by Leopold.

"We need to get to animal control before it closes," I explained, standing up and tugging Ariadne's arm gently.

"What? Now? It's midday, and they stay open all afternoon." She turned her whole attention to me.

"I know, but we want to catch it before it closes for lunch and we have to wait a whole hour or more before we can get our next bounty," I said. The princess looked at me almost sadly, so I added quietly: "If we don't get another bounty, we can't afford to eat here *and* restock the ship."

"Oh, all right," Ariadne finally acquiesced, looking back at Leopold. "I'll be back later."

"This seat will be waiting," he said smoothly, waving until we were out of sight.

Ariadne sighed dreamily.

I smiled triumphantly.

EIGHT

"**O**W!" I yelled as I banged my head against the falsebone beam. The kitten had decided to bite me, behavior I didn't necessarily agree with, but definitely understood. I was the one who had mysteriously whisked his mom and brother away and now threatened him and his remaining two siblings with my grabby little hands.

"Are you okay?" Ariadne called out from below. She held the humane box with the kitten's yowling mother and third sibling.

Somehow I had drawn the short straw and got to climb up into this home's crawlspace.

"Yep," I said, gently handing her the little biter. The mother cat didn't seem to be appeased at the fact that three out of four of her kittens were still missing. Of course, the three remaining in the attic continued to cry out to their mother pitifully, which was not helping matters. I managed to corral them into a corner and avoid their razor-sharp claws, handing one off to Ariadne before climbing carefully back down the ladder with both of the remaining kittens.

"All done," I sighed. Of course, the Centauri family couldn't understand what I was saying, so they merely nodded with concerned but curious faces. The little boy took a few steps toward the cat-filled box before his mother pulled him back. I waved in a friendly manner to them before Ariadne and I began our long walk back to animal control.

"Think the *Lilstar* has a mice problem?" I almost suggested hopefully. Kittens were my one true weakness. That and a good slice of nutty pie.

"Unfortunately, I'm not certain we want to be in a 300-square-foot ship with a cat," she said flatly.

"You have a point," I agreed with reluctance.

Although the animal control office was still as busy as always, Ariadne and I had made enough of an impression over the past week to be allowed to cut to the front of the line without any trouble.

Well, aside from the scowls of skiptraces that still had to wait in line like animal control peasants

"Here you go! Mysterious crying sound from above solved," I said as Ariadne presented the cat-box.

"What is this? Cats?" the clerk blinked in surprise.

"Yes?" I suggested.

"We can't take cats, they're not an established part of the ecosystem," the clerk's eyebrows pinched together painfully.

"So what are we supposed to do with them?" Ariadne asked.

"Well, I mean we can take them, but we can't... we'll have to...you know."

I nodded in understanding.

"No way!" Ariadne said, hugging the box defensively.

"I'm sorry, but if they get loose they might decimate the vole population and we'll have a massive yellowjacket hatch," the clerk shrugged hopelessly. "The voles already have enough predators."

"Can't you adopt them to people leaving the colony?" Ariadne asked.

"We could, but they're illegal to have on-site. They'll have to stay somewhere else," the clerk said.

I looked at Ariadne. She pursed her lips with the same realization I'd just had.

"Could they stay on a ship?" I asked.

"If you promise to keep them locked up," the clerk said.

"The *Lilstar* just got a lot smaller," Ariadne said wanly. I nodded, but ghosted a smile as I peeked into the cat-box. The littlest runt of a kitten batted at my fingers through one of the airholes.

"Let us know if you've got anybody who's looking to adopt," I shot back to the clerk, secretly hoping no one would ever claim these sweet faces.

"How much money have we made?" Ariadne asked as we trudged back to the *Lilstar*. I counted the credits in my hand carefully. It definitely wasn't much, and in fact it could be considered barely anything, but there was enough to keep us comfortably fed while we searched Myrkheim.

If our quarry hadn't decided to pack up and leave by now.

The good thing about working for animal control, however, was that we had a chance to get to know Myrkheim and its people a little better. We were developing contacts, something a well-respected skiptrace once taught me was more important than any paper trail a quarry could leave behind.

Of course, these contacts largely consisted of Centauri who don't have vocal chords and old ladies missing their prized potbelly pig, but it was better than being completely alone. Plus, we now had a regular place to get a good meal: *Jones'*.

"We could actually buy something off the middle shelf," I suggested, stowing the money into my pocket.

"We're really moving up in the world," Ariadne grumbled. Although the words sounded optimistic, Ariadne was decidedly not and hadn't been for a while. I was kind of hoping the kittens would cheer her up, but perhaps she was more of a canine person. "Plus we haven't made any real headway catching Ottoman. We haven't had time for it."

"Well, it's not like we have any other choice," I said. Originally, I had meant that as a more helpful our-situation-is-unavoidable-lets-make-the-best-of-it type of encouragement. That, apparently, was not how it came out.

"Well I'm sorry I bank at a non-U.C. bank and stranded us here," Ariadne huffed.

"I'm sorry," I said, looking at her strangely. "Geez, it's okay."

"No it's not! Marcie, we are up to our precious necks in debt, and the only chance we have to get out of it could be halfway to Proxima by now!" The princess stuck a finger in my face.

"Calm down," I said sharply. "We are going to be fine. I will figure this out and—"

"Yeah? You, figure this out? I don't care if you took that license off of the *Ethon Longma* itself, neither you nor I know what we're doing," Ariadne declared, then spun and stalked toward the *Lilstar*.

Unfortunately, she was probably right. No, I was not some great skiptrace. I never had formal training, I never apprenticed under anyone. All I had really done was track down one deadbeat who'd falsely put my brother behind bars. I was a one-time giant slayer and that didn't make me qualified to slay giants full-time.

But I was no idiot. I observed. I watched. And I learned. I had had help from the best of the best. I could do this.

I marched toward the *Lilstar* with new resolve.

I stopped dead in my tracks for a moment, staring up at the big, bold, bright and bioluminescent advertising board in front of me. It was currently showing a woman gently washing shampoo from her obviously genetically-tweaked hair, but between misleading advertisements for United-Consortium goods, there were skiptrace bounties. Most for hardened criminals, the dangerous or exciting ones more than a single party was interested in. Simple debtors, unless they were gambling debtors, usually did not make the cut.

Unless we added some misleading information. I made a dash for the nearest advertising company.

I was either a genius or stupid.

"What do you think?" I asked proudly, showing Ariadne the print-out. She turned from her chair at the *Lilstar*'s helm, looking over the receipt with a suspicious look in her eyes.

"This was your idea?" she finally asked, eyebrows puckered.

I stuck my bottom lip out, taking back the receipt. It was from the advertising company, describing just how much I'd paid for these words to be displayed in the Center's promenade, in plain font, once a day for the next five days:

WANTED, Information or Whereabouts

Name: Lee, Ottoman

Height: 5'7"

Weight: 135lbs

Eyes: Brown

Skin: Pale

Defining Marks: One or two facial tattoos with the words "LOVER" or "LOSER"

Wanted For: Grand Larceny, 2 counts; First Degree Murder, 3 counts; Ship Theft, 1 count; Sexual Harassment 5 counts; and $1.6mil in debt.

Contact: U.C. Myrkheim Advertisements Inc. for details.

It wasn't necessarily cheap, but I figured it was enough to get the ball rolling on the skiptracing part of this adventure.

"Sexual harassment? He's a freaking debtor and we're currently in more debt than he is!" Ariadne cried.

"What am I supposed to do? We can barely make enough to feed ourselves and those five cats we're fostering!" I raised my voice. It wasn't a perfect idea but I'd appreciate a little support given our current situation.

"I don't know. Do skiptracing or something, you're the flaming skiptrace!" Ariadne yelled.

"You said earlier that neither of us know what we're doing!" I shouted.

"Neither of us do know what we are doing but—" Ariadne flustered.

"But what?" I asked.

Ariadne scowled at me, an expression I returned.

"I'm going out. I have errands to run. Someone around here has to be *useful*," she said quietly. I barely gave her a nod as she stormed out of the *Lilstar*. I crumpled up the receipt and threw it as hard as I could against the wall. It sat there for a moment on the floor, shaming me, until I decided the kittens would have more fun with it and put it in the bathroom with them.

• • •

I was awake most of the night. I felt frustrated, particularly because Ariadne made good points about our inability to actually make headway in our mission. There had to be some reasonable alternative to our current plan that would make everyone happy. It's not like Ariadne ever wanted to be a skiptrace anyway. It's not like she needed to be here either.

I could always tell Ariadne to just leave me on the colony and chase after her parcel business. Ottoman Lee shouldn't be too much of a difficulty for me. He wasn't much taller than I was and unlikely to be some sort of dangerous psychopath. I also had the very contraband shock-device that Ariadne definitely wouldn't need running around the system delivering packages. The license didn't require both of us there to make the arrest anyhow, it just meant we both could.

I'll tell Ariadne in the morning, I mused, *and offer to stay behind.*

Of course, just as I was ready to drift off to sleep, she decided to return to the *Lilstar.* I caught her arm as she walked between the bunks.

"Have a minute to talk?" I asked, sliding off the bunk.

"No," she said thickly, tucking her head away from me. "I'm going to take a shower and go to bed."

"Did I make you cry?" I asked, a sinking feeling in my stomach. I held on to her arm.

"No, I just went out. I made us a few extra credits," she said.

"How? What did you do? Ariadne—" I began. I didn't finish, however, as she plucked my hand off her arm, grasped my thumb, and twisted my arm behind me. She didn't use a lot of force, but the idea of my thumb being bent completely backward made me compliant. She pushed me against the wall, pressing her free hand against the back of my neck. I panicked, a lot, slamming my foot against her knee. She had it braced, but I hit it enough to hurt and make her release me. I spun around quickly, fists up, staring at the monster that had hurt me. Ariadne had her hands in the air defensively.

"Stop it!" she cried out, lowering her hands slowly. "I was just making a point."

I took a few deep breaths. Suddenly she was just Ariadne again, dark, sparking eyes and tattered jeans. I put my fists down.

"Don't ever do that again," I commented.

"I promise," she nodded solemnly, easing down to the floor. I finally got a good look at her face, which was slightly bruised, like her knuckles.

"So," I said, covering my shaking hands by walking into the bathroom to retrieve a dermal patch. The kittens came flying out of the bathroom the minute I opened the iris, some bounding for the cockpit, some heading toward the ship's innards. None of them seemed to have a plan of what to do once they reached their destinations, however. "What's with the new face art?"

"I found a way to make extra credits. You might not like it, though," she answered when I came back. She was thumbing a whole roll of credits, trying to keep them away from the speckled runt of a kitten on her lap who batted at the metallic fabric playfully.

"You found an illegal fighting ring," I commented, applying the patch to her face.

"Yup," she said. "A good one too, lots of nice rules and regulations but not so many that it gets n the way of the fight."

"How did you even find it?" I asked, sitting across from her. The spotted kitten turned its affection to me.

"Remember that guy whose iguana got stuck in his neighbor's floor next to the house's main artery?" the princess-turned-fighter asked.

"Iguanas love heat." I nodded.

"The iguana guy had a hidden punching bag in his garage and a few cases of the ointment fighters use to calm tired muscles, plus a whole pile of dermal regenerative patches. Myrkheim doesn't have a professional fighting league so I assumed he knew where the good fights would be," she said. All our time making contacts at animal control seems to have paid off a bit.

"He just walked you to the next illegal fight?" I asked.

"Well I kind of threatened to have his iguana deported." Ariadne bit her lip.

"That's cold. And a threat we definitely couldn't have backed up," I said.

"Actually, I checked the manual. Iguanas are new to the ecosystem and certain breedlines aren't allowed," she said.

"Like you know the different breedlines," I huffed, actually feeling a little better.

"Hey, you should see the other guy," Ariacne said, gesturing to her lip.

"Is he still in one piece?" I asked.

"That's why I like the martial arts. You get to beat the crap out of people without as much gore," the princess crinkled her nose at me annoyingly.

"Fine." I rolled my eyes, mocking, before looking back at the credits in her hand. "I was thinking, you can leave me here to deal with Ottoman, while you go start your parcel business."

Ariadne looked at me thoughtfully.

"Nah," she said, shaking her head.. "I was feeling useless, but, not so useless I'm going to up and abandon you the first chance I get."

I nodded.

"So what are we going to do?"

"I can keep fighting," Ariadne said seriously. I winced a little. It was a terrific opportunity to speed up our cashflow, but the fights were not just illegal, they were *incredibly* illegal. If the Myrkheim authorities caught us, we'd be the ones deported. Plus, what happened if Ariadne lost a fight and we ended up with no cash whatsoever?

"Actually, let me put it to you another way," Ariadne said, interrupting my thoughts. "I *am* going to keep fighting. It won't take many more rounds to earn us enough to restock the ship and get back to skiptracing."

"I don't really like the idea, as appealing as it is," I said. The princess leaned a little closer to my face with an expression that was very much not accepting of anything less that my compliance.

I think my brother used it on me once when I refused to eat my ham and algae.

"To be honest, your only choice in this matter is whether or not you want to come cheer me on in the next fight." Ariadne shrugged and disappeared into the bathroom. At least two of the kittens followed her.

I smiled at the runt kitten making a big show of sleeping in my lap.

Of course I was going to come, ninny.

Even if she wasn't as cute as Ignacio Sonata.

• • •

The fighting arena wasn't exactly what I expected, although I didn't have many expectations. I'd only ever been to one live fight in my entire life and even though it was semi-pro, it had felt kind of scummy. This felt even worse. Firstly, it took place in a gooey, slimy part of Myrkheim where ages of factory work with leaking corrosive substances turned the organic components of the floors and nearest wall to a festering mush. Falsebone in little better condition stuck out, corroded almost down to the marrow. The only mercy seemed to be that Myrkheim had far fewer nerve endings in this region, meaning it couldn't feel any of this decay. Not that the colony had any great deal of sensory input or reaction to said input; it had just enough nerves to locate major problems like ruptured veins and broken bones.

Ariadne and I, hoods up to make some sort of overly dramatic entrance, wove our way through the surprisingly thick crowd toward the arena proper, which was little more than a rusted old grain silo. The tall, tubular metallic structure made a great place for an illegal fight, with a clearly delineated fighting area being the inside of the silo and plenty of rust-hole windows to allow everyone and their brother a good look. Of course, it also looked like it could topple over at any minute, but I tried not to think about that.

Ariadne led us straight toward the mustached guy whose iguana she'd threatened earlier. He didn't precisely greet her with a smile or anything close to civility, but he assured her that all the proper arrangements had been made.

"You're fighting Trish Abercrombie at 0300," he said, fidgeting with his nice, expensive suit. It was much different than the stained tank top I'd seen him in while rescuing his iguana, but I didn't judge. I hadn't had a change of clothes in a day or two. At least I'd put on a pair of plain earrings and some eyeliner Ariadne had insisted on. "She's not a strong fighter, but she'll give you a good bout."

"Sounds good, Aether," Ariadne said in a flat tone. "But next time give me somewhat a little more challenging. What's the betting at?"

"You made an impression yesterday, but Trish is a fan favorite. So far the odds are in her favor," Aether said, running a comb through his well-trimmed mustache.

"All right, I'll figure out the money," I said, moving between Ariadne and Aether. "You go scout around or warm up or whatever."

She flashed me what was almost a mischievous grin before disappearing into the crowd.

"Tell me, does she cheat?" Aether asked flat out. It was a rude question to say the least, so I blinked at him a few times just to watch him sweat into that expensive suit. "She's scary."

"Yeah," I nodded before staring the insulting man down with a snarl. "And she's the happy one."

Aether swallowed and didn't say anything more except to acknowledge the odds I'd placed. It wasn't all of our money, but enough to make a sizable return if Ariadne won.

If 'won' was still my choice word, since I'd never actually seen her fight before. I didn't know what to expect.

I found her watching the current bout through a minute rust-hole.

"Couldn't find any better seats?" I chided. She smirked, but didn't look away.

"Next time I want to fight him." Ariadne pointed for me to look through the small rust hole. In the ring were two heavyweights, putting on a decent, if overly-dramatic, show by slamming one another full-body into the ground. I winced a few times, continuously waiting for the cracking of bones. Of course, these guys might have falsebone reinforce-ment grafts along their spines and major joints. Although technically illegal and guaranteed to shorten your life in a very painful fashion, even I knew of a few doctors who'd perform the surgeries... at a great cost.

Either way, they shook the silo each time one of them hit the floor, causing it to rattle terribly. Nobody but me seemed to be bothered by the fact that the rackety structure seemed ready to topple over at any moment.

"Ugh, why?" I finally asked.

"Because the falsebone graft in his right knee is giving out. A well-timed blow and he goes down like a rock," Ariadne whispered with a snap of her fingers for emphasis.

"I didn't notice that," I said.

"That's okay, you're not going to be in there anyway," the princess patted me on the back and went to watch the fight some more. I sneered at her backside and decided to get a better look at the crowd and fighters, a far more interesting view than whatever was going on inside the silo.

For the most part, the crowd was a genuine mix of people — some oily factory workers just off their shifts, some well-dressed businessmen with elegant masks to hide their identities, some little kids and even whole families cheering on their favorite and booing when said favorite disappointed them. It wasn't too difficult to distinguish the fighters from the spectators. Most fighters simply wore whatever was the most nondescript since, if the police raided the place, boring clothes allowed them to pass as inactive participants of this illegal sport. There was still a culture of showing off, of course, and some fighters were dressed to the nines with fancy costumes, headdresses, tattoos, and anything else that helped them stand out loudly.

Trish Abercrombie turned out to be one of these louder fighters. On top of wearing tight, skimpy clothing, she wore copious amounts of jewelry and made a big display of shouting her own name whenever possible. She and her two handmaids even had the word "TRISH" in rhinestones across the legs of their tight shorts. I wandered over to her, er, throne room, which consisted of a few stray falsebone crates arranged to create a big chair that stretched outwards in a semi-circular fashion, making a cleared space for all Trish's adoring fans, none of which seemed to have shown up on this particular evening, to approach their queen. The crate throne was covered with a thick, velvet blanket that had definitely seen better days. Trish sat in it haughtily, not taking any notice of how shabby the whole thing looked. I spent some time watching her movements, trying to see what Ariadne saw.

The rhinestone queen overall looked like more show than go, but she was tall with three long, strong-ish arms. Yes, three. Technically the third one, coming out of her left shoulder, was an organism all to itself with a unique genetic code and falsebone structure. It merely obeyed the commands of its host body, Trish. It probably shared her pulmonary system. It wasn't a great graft, however, because it looked more like the greenish organic floor than Trish's tanned skin. She waved a bejeweled hand almost elegantly in the air, gesturing back and forth to her handmaids, having them fetch everything from coffee to what I was pretty certain was illegal drugs.

Who was I to judge? Actually, I was exactly there to judge. The drugs could prove useful to Ariadne. I pondered my options. It was likely Trish was on stimulants given the fact that her heart now pumped for an extra, mostly parasitic, limb and she needed the boost in heartrate during a fight. Of course, this was only one of a million other options it could be. The only way I could know for sure was to get up close.

I ducked out of sight for a moment into a pile of tarped debris. I pulled out the pocket mirror I always carried and carefully smudged some of the eyeliner I had on across my lower lids. In the area's relatively low light, I'd look just drug-addict enough. Wiping my fingers, I stumbled back toward Trish and her handmaids.

Well, they were more like bodyguards, only a little less built than their charge.

"I just wanna see Trish," I said in the whiniest voice I could muster as the handmaids/former bodybuilders locked tight hands around my arms.

"She isn't in the mood for company," one of the handmaids hissed. She was very threatening, but not very scary with the glitter lipstick she wore.

"But I—" I whined again. This time the handmaids decided to toss me as far as they could, which ended up being a dozen feet or so as I slid across the decaying and slimy epidermis. I was not about to give up, however.

"Fine! If that's the way you want it," I declared, and picked myself up clumsily, staggering back toward the handmaids. While I could use the shock device to bully my way past these two, I preferred to be invited in by Trish due to my fanaticism for her and the fact I was a druggie willing to put up a fight. I hoped she'd consider me something of a withdrawal-ridden pet, but for the most part she just eyed the situation with an unreadable expression.

I continued stalking toward the handmaids who were braced for whatever I had coming. My purposefully ill-fated punch was easily dodged, one handmaid to one side and one to the other. The one on my right caught hold of my punching arm and tripped up my right leg. I didn't go very far as the one on my left caught hold of my left leg and a handful of hair.

"Owww!" I howled indignantly, trying to scratch at any exposed skin I could find. While I landed a few embarrassing hits on the handmaids, they had me completely secure. "Just let me see herrrr."

"Come now, ladies, let's all play fair," Trish finally said from her throne. It was a relatively bored tone, but a wave of her hand called off the handmaid-bodybuilding-bodyguards and beckoned me forward. I stumbled and stuttered a little, putting on what I'd hoped was a good show. I finally made it to Trish's feet where, with some unwarranted assistance from the handmaids, I fell flat on my face.

"Get up, idiot," Trish said. I stood up slowly, painting my slimy face with awe.

"Trish Abercrombie," I whispered vainly.

"Obviously. Now what do you want from me?" Trish said impatiently.

"Oh, you're my idol," I said in a hushed tone. "I've always admired you but never got the courage to come see you."

"I gathered that when you screamed my name. Now you are here, what do you want?" the extra-armed woman looked an awful lot like a scorpion up close.

"Just to sit next to you," I ducked my head down respectfully. "Before your next fight."

Trish flattened her eyebrows at me, but sighed and waved to an empty, velvet-less crate that made up part of her throne.

I eagerly sat down and for a long while just stared at Trish adoringly. It wasn't too difficult to stay in character. I just sat there and stayed quiet like a good subject in Trish's kingdom. A few other fans came up to wish Trish luck, but most spectators were paying more attention to the good time they were having than the actual fighters. I watched Trish's reaction to this apathy. She covered up her disappointment well, scowling and yelling at her handmaids to obey whatever whim managed to cross her mind. I saw the disappointment behind her eyes, however.

After the seventh or eighth spectator passed by without even glancing in Trish's direction, the rhinestone queen glanced in my direction. Her expression was almost relieved. In that moment, I felt like scum. Here Trish was, hoping for at least one real fan, and I was taking advantage of that to betray her wholeheartedly.

Ariadne needed the information, I reminded myself, I'd just have to suck it up.

"So, how long have you been a fan?" Trish asked.

"Ever since the first time I saw you," I said confidently.

"When was that?" the three-armed woman asked.

"Um…" I said, going a little glassy-eyed and starting off at some patch of floor. "I dor't remember. I'm not very good with the days."

Trish raised an eyebrow almost in pity and left me in silence again. I sat there for what felt like almost an hour, watching and listening to people come and go around Trish. It wasn't until a few minutes before the fight that something actually happened. Trish glanced down at my jittery foot, which I'd been twitching to stave off boredom and make my whole drug-addict cover a bit more believable.

"Nerves?" Trish asked. "When was your last fix?"

"I dunno. Tuesday?" I scratched my head.

"Here," Trish handed me one of the pills she had gotten earlier. "I always take these before a fight. It calms everything down."

I accepted the pill, sticking it in my mouth and pretending to swallow.

"Thank you," I said, having tucked the pill beside my tongue and out of sight.

"Wouldn't want my best fan so twitchy she couldn't see straight," Trish smirked.

I kicked myself inwardly, praying that I'd never have to go undercover and completely ruin someone's day ever again.

"I'll see you around," the three-armed woman said, rising to leave and patting my shoulder. I nodded exaggeratedly. The minute she was out of sight, I spit out the pill, wishing for a tall glass of water to rise my mouth out.

I continued to spit as I made a mad dash toward Ariadne, who I found bouncing up and down at one of the silo's old doorways. It was covered by a tattered sheet, ready to be pulled back at the start of the fight.

"Where've you been?" she demanded as I approached.

"Scouting. Trish has two things: an extra arm and a drug problem," I said quickly.

"What drugs?" the princess asked. As if on cue, the whole world went a little quieter and calmer. This was the exact opposite of what was actually going on, since Ariadne and I were standing smack-dab in the middle of a raucous crowd that was pushing and shoving mercilessly to get at the best rust-holes.

"Downers," I said thickly and blinking a lot. I hadn't swallowed the pill, but some of it had probably been absorbed by my mouth.

"I realize we are already knee-deep in illegal here, but what did you—" Ariadne began to shout.

"Nothing, I didn't even swallow it," I said, feeling inappropriately calm. "Just focus on the three-armed lady you'll have to fight."

"If she's got a third arm, why's she on downers?" Ariadne asked. I shrugged helplessly.

The princess looked at me almost petulantly, but nodded and turned back to the curtain.

The subtle bell finally rang for the 0300 fight. No loud announcers like the semi-professionals had, because even though we were tucked fairly far into the uppermost shelf, the sound could still carry into Myrkheim's center and alert the authorities. The curtains for Ariadne and Trish's doors opened up, allowing the fighters to take their positions. The crowd almost pushed me into the ring, trying to get as close to the door's threshold as possible. I stood my ground. Being associated with one of the fighters, I'd earned my prime seating. Plus I didn't have the wherewithal to actually think about sinking into the crowds.

Of course, I wished I hadn't decided to stay in the doorway as Trish saw me. I could hear her growl from across the silo and throw what were probably a few choice words in my direction. I shrugged harmlessly, which only irritated her more. I'd have feared her handmaids, who were standing at the other doorway, undoubtedly plotting a reprisal against me, but as thick as the crowds were, anyone standing at the doorways was completely boxed in.

The fight began as the bell rang again. Trish immediately crouched down and began to make laps around the silo. I was afraid she might burst out of those bedazzled shorts of hers, but they held together pretty well. Ariadne just followed the circle, looking tense but not overly aggressive. Actually, it was much more *passive* than aggressive. I agreed with this strategy, playing defense was always my preferred role.

Of course, having an older brother that wouldn't let me start any fights probably helped with that.

Unsurprisingly, it was Trish that made the first move, lunging at Ariadne. The princess barely had to move to avoid being caught by the three-armed maniac, who left an opening large enough for an insensate mining mite to find. Ariadne, to her credit, seemed to notice the opening, but didn't react quite as strongly as either I or a bunch of random people in the stands would have liked, as we all shouted, "Get her!"

Ariadne didn't even purse her lips in frustration. If nothing else, she had been well-trained to maintain her calm in the midst of a fight and observe her opponent. I'd learned how to take a beating the hard way, so my calm was less calculating and more waiting for the storm to pass. The princess waited for a good opening in Trish's defenses and then exploited it, landing a punch across Trish's right cheek.

Trish howled, an overreaction given the fact that Ariadne had barely been able to put any force into the hit. The rhinestone queen/scorpion began to hit more erratically, trying desperately to avenge Ariadne's love tap. I frowned as the bespangled woman's actions became more and more chaotic. It was as if she was trying too hard to win the fight, a fact Ariadne seemed to recognize and exploit as she landed more and more powerful punches in rapid succession. The princess even managed to catch hold of Trish's wrist and twist, forcing the rhinestone queen into a flip which ended in her landing hard on her backside. Since the epidermis in this area was mostly rotted away, Trish landed on falsebone with a thin veneer of remaining tissue, which hurt a great deal more than if she'd landed on healthy epidermis. By the end of five minutes, Trish had a swollen eye and busted lip to prove where she'd been that evening while Ariadne only had one small cut after being accidentally scratched by one of Trish's rings.

It was right as I thought this would be an easy fight that I realized the reason for Trish's downers. She was a hyperactive individual during a fight who hadn't learned control properly. She got way too excited and that led to chaos and losing. So instead of taking up an apprenticeship with a real fighter and learning control, she decided to self-medicate, downers being the substance of choice. The minute they kicked in, a switch was flipped in Trish's head, she suddenly became cold, calculating, and far more dangerous.

This made Trish's next attacks far less sloppy than previously.

The princess barely had time to flinch as Trish's downers kicked in. She managed to dodge the scorpion's two human arms, but the parasitic arm caught a handful of Araidne's shirt. The arm was probably not great at fine motor movement or reflexes, but its grip was undoubtedly tight and it didn't let go of Ariadne as Trish caught the princess with her other hands. Trish then put her whole body into flinging Ariadne across the silo. The crowd went wild, cheering or booing depending on who they'd put the most money on.

Most of them were cheering.

Ariadne picked herself back up, wiping some of the organic goo off her face. She seemed mostly undaunted by Trish's sudden personality change. The princess once again took up a defensive position. Trish, however, didn't seem to care what posture Ariadne took as she continued to use the parasitic arm to her advantage. Plus, she was playing to the crowd, soaking in their adulation as she now carefully dodged Ariadne's blows. It was not looking good for Team King.

Of course, even the most praising of crowds can get bored. Apparently just watching Trish toss Ariadne around was boring and more than a few cried foul on the subject.

"C'mon! Let's see a *fight*," a raptor-tattooed fan with garlic-breath called out beside me. I moved a little farther away from him.

Finally, Ariadne was forced close enough to the threshold for me to talk to her as Trish took a minute to pose for the crowd.

"I hate drugs," the princess said, picking herself up off the floor again.

"Join the club," I said, scooting as close to the threshold as I could without actually stepping across it. Violating the threshold meant I'd be counted as one of the fighters, so I worked very hard to stay on the correct side. Not that that did me much good when someone decided to push me into the silo anyway.

"I can take care of this!" Ariadne said angrily as I caught my footing several steps into the arena.

"This wasn't my idea!" I said, scrambling back to the doorframe only to find it packed with a group of sneering punks. I landed a punch at one of them in anger, but all he did was grin at me through bloodied teeth.

"You're part of the fight now, princess," Trish said, looking my way. Of course I was the one who had embarrassed her publicly.

"Actually she's the—" I started, as the scorpion crossed over to where I was standing in a few long strides. I got my hands up in time to avoid most of the slap from her parasitic arm. She didn't seem to care, however, as her knee came up to my stomach. I gasped loudly, trying to catch hold of something I could use as leverage against her. I came up empty as Trish began to pound me with more than one of her arms at a time. I finally tried rolling into her. Height wasn't exactly an advantage in her case. While she was much better at protecting her middle after the downers kicked in, she still left a lot open and vulnerable.

As she seemed to be trying to keep me at arm's length, I ran toward her. I pounded as much as I could into her midsection, which felt like punching granite. Given the parasitic arm, she might've also had illegal falsebone plating grafted to her important areas like a built-in suit of armor. Since I couldn't feel any individual ribs when I punched her, I assumed this was correct. That meant I would have to aim somewhere I knew it would be difficult to implant falsebone grafts, like her face. My fist connected with her jaw solidly which, as I had guessed, was not reinforced with falsebone. The scorpion threw me backwards to blink away the hit. As I skidded up to the metallic wall of the silo, I saw Ariadne run full-speed at the back of Trish.

"Watch that arm!" I started to shout as Trish's parasitic arm, not bound by the same bone structure as normal arms, twisted backward toward the incoming Ariadne even as the scorpion began to turn around.

Fortunately, I was mistaken in the idea that Ariadne hadn't seen the issue. Instead of barreling into Trish at full-speed, the princess dropped into a slide, catching hold of the scorpion's parasitic arm and pulling it downward. Trish's head snapped up and back as the parasitic arm was pulled down and under by Ariadne, whose slide ended as she collided with Trish's legs. There was a loud pop as at least one of the parasitic arm's joints snapped out of place. Movement stopped altogether as Trish's head came down on the organic floor sharply and Ariadne shoved the dazed woman out of the way.

"Oh," the crowd gasped in surprise. Ariadne took half a second to collect herself before planting on the biggest, cockiest grin I had ever seen.

"Is that all you got?" she yelled out, much to the delight of the crowd who began to cheer or boo loudly. The princess literally swaggered up to where I was sitting and helped me up, grin still plastered on her face. She made me face the crowd, throwing our arms in the air in victory.

We strode out of the silo just as the subtle bell signaled our victory and Trish's bodyguards ran over to their wounded fighter. We managed to avo d killing scowls from Trish's bodyguards simply because they were too busy trying to get the wounded fighter out of the arena. She was just beginning to regain consciousness, which meant that things were going to hurt.

Although not a natural part of Trish's human body, there were enough connected nerves to make damage to the parasitic arm painful to the host. There had to be in order to control the arm with any measure of success, a fact that Trish demonstrated as her daze wore off and she howled in pain.

Of course, it's a lot easier to hear someone howl when they're not being drowned out by a loud, unruly audience. It took me a minute to figure out if the commotion was good or bad, but as with the conclusion with any fight, it was pretty much half and half with some people threatening Ariadne and my guts and some patting us on the back, declaring us their new favorites. Even the guy I'd punched seemed pleased we'd beaten Trish. Ariadne and I muscled our way through the crowds toward Aether, who was swamped with winners and losers.

"Pay up," Ariadne demanded. Aether grimaced like he'd just choked down a live squid and it was still wriggling.

"I don't think so; your friend here wasn't part of the original fight. I'm not paying anyone," the suited man said with some measure of disgust.

"Listen here—" Ariadne stepped up to the man, obviously still on an adrenaline high from the fight.

She grasped hold of Aether's suit with gooey, grimy hands and pulled him forward.

"Tsk, tsk," a new, smoother voice cut in. It was as if a snake had crawled into my bed as the man's mere presence immediately made me want to run away screaming.

And I hadn't even turned around to look at him.

The air immediately around him felt like cold, rotting fish even though he smelled like roses and leather. The man rested a sizable hand on my shoulder as more of a gesture to move out of the way, with which I complied quickly. He was tall, chiseled, and handsome, no doubt, with dark, greying hair brushed neatly back and a few tasteful gold ear cuffs to declare his opulence, all of which was almost secondary to his million-or-more credit suit of fine red. He was polished, even aristocratic, although not as royal-looking as Ariadne or her brother; no, he was more of a count, a count slimier than the organic residue stuck in my hair.

"Since you two ladies are new, you must not be acquainted with the golden rules of the fighting culture: pay up your debts, and do not rough up the bookie," the man said in a honeyed voice. Ariadne gave him an odd look, but released Aether. The bookie kept his eyes carefully averted from the newcomer's and I moved closer to Ariadne.

Neither Ariadne nor I actually asked the man his name or to identify himself. In fact, the entire crowd within a ten-foot radius seemed to be carefully ignoring him. Even the everyday chatter expected around the bookie's corner had died to whispers.

"I am Piper," the man said, extending a manicured but gnarled hand toward me and then to Ariadne. His gaze wasn't necessarily pinned on either Ariadne or me, but it seemed to be roving, and judging between the two of us with a few almost angry glances at Aether and the crowd around him. I gulped loudly, feeling as though I was being punished for something by this strange and somehow horrible man.

"You're the boss?" I finally managed to ask. He smiled all too perfectly.

"Only to Aether. He and I manage the betting for all of Myrkheim's illegal fighting," Piper said. I nodded dumbly in mute response. I wanted to drag Ariadne out of the fighting ring and go handle some sort of lost rabbit problem. Piper was making me want to react violently by either killing him or throwing up, neither of which was a good response, given the situation.

"I'll mind the rules, next time," Ariadne finally said. She was avoiding Piper and his gaze as well.

"Good," Piper said, smiling again. This time, however, the air around him was warm and inviting. The rotting fish aura he'd produced was replaced with a sedate, friendly atmosphere that encouraged a smile out of Ariadne and let the rose-and-leather cologne dominate. Even the chatter around us returned to normal. I looked at him mostly in shock as he turned from a punishing monster to a kind father.

Not that I could really believe any father could be kind.

"Now, what is this problem we seem to be having, Mr. Aether?" Piper asked warmly. Aether seemed only a little less uncomfortable with his boss's sudden change than I was, but he complied with the question.

"They wanted to collect their money, but the bet was voided because the fight added another fighter without forewarning," Aether said stiffly. I gave him a good hard stare, wondering if he'd noticed everything that'd just gone on or if it was me. He merely frowned and looked away as his boss handled the issue.

"It was unavoidable," Ariadne spoke up. "Marcie was pushed in toward the end, she didn't mean to get involved."

"Well, I was delayed in arriving, so I did not see the fight," Piper said, reaching over to Aether and pulling a metallic case out of the man's pocket. It was locked, but Piper had the key. He began to take some money out of the case, looking over the bookie's records. "How does your whole bet and half of the winnings sound in the interest of fair play?"

Ariadne nodded, but Piper handed me the money. His eyes were still cold and dead, I noted, accepting the still-sizable chunk of credits.

"I would like to see you two fight after a brief business trip I have off-colony. Do you have any scheduled in the next week?" Piper said easily.

"Do you have any you'd like us to fight at?" Ariadne asked, and I almost punched her in the gut. Wherever this guy might want us, I wanted to be far, far away from.

"How does Tuesday sound? There is a fight across the shelf in an abandoned barn, starting at 12:30. Be there before the starting bell and I will line up a suitable opponent for you." Piper smiled again, oozing with civility, kindness, and an overly fatherly attitude. It was like he wanted us to think he actually cared for our wellbeing. "If you win, we might discuss a mutually beneficial sponsorship."

"We'll be there," Ariadne said with a nod, and I immediately grabbed her hand and towed her through the crowd that had decided to flood poor Aether. I shot one last look back at Piper, but he was busy being an altogether polite and well-mannered person.

Nine

"I'm telling you, Ariadne, he's a whackjob," I declared as the princess and I were cleaning the dung from some lost, mammalian pet-type thing I still couldn't identify off our hands and clothes. With the critter delivered, we'd completed our 15-mission success streak for the animal control office, making enough money to live comfortably and visit *Jones'* whenever Ariadne had a hankering for an eyeful of Leopold.

Okay, that might've been unfair, but he seemed just as eager to see her, and I found the whole situation incredibly adorable.

Even with more challenging pet problems like the generic mammalian we'd just caught and returned to a grateful socialite on the second-to-middle shelf, it would take a sizable portion of our lives to save up enough to restock the ship.

While illegal fighting should have solved that problem, the past few fights had turned out more costly than the first few. In fact, out of three fights, we'd only managed to win one, and that was against a rookie greener than his organic face transplant. Ariadne hadn't even needed to step in for that one, I knocked the boy out with one good hit.

I was on the edge of willing to work with Piper.

The *edge* of. He could at least arrange fights that were within our wheelhouse, rather than just having us show up and picking whoever happened to be available. Making a lot of money very quickly so that we could get on with our skiptracing and track down wherever Ottoman Lee could be hiding sounded like a fantastic idea. But all I could remember of Piper was the rotting fish aura he gave off. Apparently it had escaped Ariadne, who thought my observation was over the top. Perhaps she was right; I could be overreacting, or, at this point, misremembering the event. While I acknowledged the idea, I couldn't get rid of the impression Piper had left on me.

"Why? Because he was mad we roughed up his bookie?" Ariadne said, scowling as she tried to wash out her jacket in a public water spout. It was a new-fangled Centauri spigot that was part of a separate system from Myrkheim's main water processing and storage structure. It was installed a few years ago after the colony suffered a dangerous infection that made the processed water undrinkable. While such an infection is not much of a problem in organic structures on earth, where water is bountiful, Myrkheim was on the brink of dehydration before the antibiotics finally kicked in. So the United-Consortium hired the Centauri to develop a whole new way to manufacture, distribute, and store water across the colony, all connected by a streamlined series of public water spouts that spread clean, fresh liquid life 24/7 to whomever might need it.

"No, because..." I scowled, playing with a claw mark the critter had left in my jeans. I had a bruise but no scratches so I wasn't worried about getting a tetanus shot. "He's insane, evil. I can't explain it, I've just seen people like him before," I said half-heartedly.

Ariadne stopped to look at me carefully. It was more curious than questioning, but I looked away as she asked *that* question.

"Who?"

Why did she always have to be so curious?

"No," I said simply. "Piper is just bad news. We shouldn't get involved with him."

The princess sighed greatly, putting on a damp jacket with pursed lips.

"Well, the only way we are going to make enough money to really pursue Otto-whats-his-face is by fighting. And now that Piper has marked us, we won't be able to just waltz into any fight we want with the intention of taking money from him that he didn't offer," Ariadne said. I nodded solemnly.

"Do you ever wish you hadn't paid for my radiation treatment?" I asked.

"Nah, you're cute." Ariadne crinkled her nose irritatingly. I rolled my eyes carefully, since one was still fairly swollen from last night's fight.

• • •

We made it to the old barn at 12:15, each step causing me more and more regret. At least we made it in plenty of time to scope out the place and visit our new lord and master. My pulse quickened, and not in a good way, as Piper spotted us and moved closer. I held close to Ariadne, but let her do most of the talking and interaction.

Unlike his first entrance into my sphere of influence, Piper was altogether charming, commanding, and every bit a polite and necessary member of society. As he pulled cash by the handfuls from hapless bettors and the unrich, I felt uncomfortable with the contrast between his attitude and his actions. But since I was here, at the fight, I may as well get in on the action.

"My newest fighters," Piper said smoothly, tipping the brim of his hat before gently kissing Ariadne's hand. He scooped up my hand with a great deal of force, pinching my knuckles together painfully and giving me a good, long and loveless glare. He then walked between Ariadne and me and placed a hand around each of our shoulders and lead us from group to group. I mostly scowled, to which nobody protested; it was probably a good image for a fighter to be angry and sullen all the time. Even Ariadne wasn't bouncing around like she had been at last morning's match. After a few minutes of being Piper's new chew toy, I excused myself to scope out the area.

"I'll come with—" Ariadne began, but Piper stopped her.

"Actually, m'lady, I need you to stay here to straighten out some official rules for tonight," Piper said, and smiled grandly at the princess.

"Oh, okay," Ariadne said, more confused than concerned. She turned back to me. "You go on without me."

I thought about that for a second. The less suspicious, more compliant course of action would be for me to go off, by myself, leaving Ariadne at Piper's mercy. The safer, more comfortable course of action was to stay and show Piper that I would be his newest challenger.

I looked at Ariadne.

"Nah," I said, flashing her a casual smile. "It's just a big barn in the middle of nowhere. Plus Piper already has our match lined up. I'm sure he chose well."

"Matches. After you win your first one, I have two more lined up," Piper almost growled the word out. I shrugged and sat down on the nearest chair. I could scout well enough from here.

For the most part, the crowd was unchanged from the other morning. Still rowdy with the usual mix of families and individuals of all walks of life, all of which shared the same annoyance at having to weave their way through the old lichen lumps. The chest-high lumps were essentially that, round and elongated hills of calloused, bark-like epidermis that stretched out about a hundred feet in length. They were laid out in neat rows with narrow spaces between, making it difficult for more than one person to walk between. Their purpose was simply to provide a place for lichen to latch on to and grow.

Although wheats and barleys were just as popular here as they were on Earth, it was easier to grow things like lichens, mosses, and mushrooms on the organic Myrkheim. This was largely due to the fact that no one really wanted to ship hundreds of tons of dirt to the colony, upset the ecosystem, and make Myrkheim self-sustaining. Once you introduce dirt, you have to introduce bacteria for the dirt, and once you do that, you have to introduce all kinds of critters for the management and care of the crops like pollinators. All of which has to learn to cooperate and agree with the fauna and flora already maintained by Myrkheim anyway.

While it was an expensive set up, no doubt, with the slim-but-possible potential of completely killing Myrkheim's main organic structure, in the long run it was much cheaper than shipping the necessary grains across the entire system and through the nebula.

Who was I to argue with overgrown monopolies who weren't making enough money pilfering every nook and cranny of the market to let the biggest shipping port in the system be completely self-sustaining?

The barn for this particular farm was a run-down and greying falsebone structure that was less part of Myrkheim and more tacked together with spare bone. Whether that was the reason the farm was being left unused, the farmers couldn't afford the fines that go with building a structure that was attached to the colony biologically, or if they'd simply gone out of business, it was the perfect place for a fight. Even better than the old metallic silo.

Of course, the barn was a whole lot more rickety.

It creaked with the weight of fighters and spectators crammed into its rooms and structures. A few people, mostly the young and the bulletproof, climbed up onto its roof and were looking down on the rest of the crowds.

I finally looked back toward the slimy excuse for a human being. He was, as usual, being altogether charming and friendly. As if he wasn't the complete—

I sighed. It really didn't matter what name I called him.

"Ready for hell, ma'am?" Aether came out of nowhere and whispered to me.

"Don't think I don't know it," I muttered, casting a glare toward Piper. So it appeared Aether did know who he worked for.

"Actually, you don't know it. Do you really think that you and your friend are truly bad at fighting? Or do you think the matches since the one against Ms. Abercrombie have not been in your favor?" Aether looked at me without lying.

I was an *idiot*.

Ariadne and I were not having a string of bad luck, we were being starved. Starved of success and money, becoming desperate enough to actually consider Piper's offer of servitude.

"Why are you telling me this?" I demanded.

"Because I want your forgiveness," Aether said earnestly.

"It's really not mine that you need," I commented.

"Oh, don't worry, I've already had a long conversation with God," Aether said earnestly. "But, please."

I looked the man in the face. It was nothing but honest, and I realized I had nothing real to hate about him. Sure, he was Piper's lackey, but this meeting was proof enough of Aether's remorse.

"I forgive you," I said.

"Then my suggestion is to get out of here as quickly as possible. If you think Piper is evil, you should meet his wife. She is the only person in this universe that he actually fears," Aether said in a hushed tone before leaving as though nothing had happened.

That's it, I decided, standing in a hurry. There was no way I was going to actually make any sort of deal with Piper or let Ariadne do something of the kind. I could already feel the walls closing in around me as I stalked toward the princess, ready to pull her away from Piper. We'd have to find another avenue of monetary gain, it just might take longer that we'd hoped.

A great, pinching hand grabbed hold of my elbow just before I reached her.

"Where are you going, my dear?" Piper said easily as his grip increased, smashing my skin against my bone.

"I was just going over to my friend. That shouldn't bother you," I said.

"No. It shouldn't, but it does," Piper rubbed his chin thoughtfully. "You don't like me, and I'm afraid that won't do for a mutually beneficial—"

"Cut the crap," I said, tired of this game we were playing. "I don't care what mutually beneficial nonsense you think I'm going to commit to, but I don't plan on being your puppet for any amount of time."

"Don't test me, *child*," Piper leaned in to whisper angrily. It was all I could do not to scratch his eyeballs from their sockets.

"We made no arrangements beyond tonight. We made no commitments. We signed no contracts. You will not have us for your new playthings," I sneered back at the man, refusing to back down.

"You will regret this insult to me and my hospitality for all of eternity," Piper said in an even tone, letting my elbow go with a shove.

I gave the man one last, parting sneer before disappearing into the crowd. I had to arrange Ariadne and my bets for the night, hopefully with some insider help.

The bell finally rang for the fighters to take their positions, a side at each of the barn's massive thresholds. It was a teamed effort, with the pair of us facing off against a pair of highly unusual fighters: a tall, blonde-haired and blue-eyed lady with organic-prosthetic limbs from the elbows and knees down and a shorter maniac with a wild glint in his eyes and a white Mohawk. Together, these two had the collective fighting experience of an uncoordinated five-year-old, or so Aether had told me.

This would probably be the easiest fight we'd had all week.

Ariadne and I waited patiently, calmly staring across the fighting area toward the fidgeting duo. The rookie fighters pranced and tried to put on a good show, taking turns flashing rude or "I will kill you" gestures toward the princess and me. It wasn't particularly threatening, nor did the crowd really respond to it with affirmation. The two vertically disparate rookies just didn't know how to excite a crowd.

The bell rang once again for the start of the fight. The shorter fellow decided to take me on, while the tall blonde decided to fight Ariadne. I would have preferred it the other way simply because the blonde's height would put me at a disadvantage and given the princess' specialized fighting style, she would be more than enthusiastic to use the blonde's height as leverage.

But, I surmised, the white-haired fighter's energy and enthusiasm should make for a good fight.

Dodging the first few of his blows gave me feel for how he fought. The answer was 'crudely and without any sort of strategy.' While his technique was reminiscent of Trish Abercrombie, she actually knew how to fight, she simply let adrenaline take control. This guy was just a flaming idiot. His blows usually went wild as he failed to track or predict my movement and he exposed pretty much every weak point on his body for my attacks. It took a great deal of effort to hold back and not take advantage of his utterly obvious failings.

I dodged a few more of his attacks, landing a few punches simply to make it look like it was going to be an actual fight. I was hoping that toying with this rookie would irritate him into doing something useful, but it didn't seem to bother him. He continued with his ineffectual tactics and it was actually me who got irritated. I finally stepped into and passed his guard, landing a solid punch to his stomach. Sometimes what people need is *pain* to make them fight back.

"Hit me, you ninny," I whispered to the rookie as his eyes bulged in pain. All he did was gasp back at me and stumble a few steps away.

I sighed loudly and glanced toward Ariadne as the crowd cheered loudly. The tall blonde was standing up from what had probably been a nice flip, forcibly assisted by the princess. I *knew* the height would be Ariadne's advantage. The blonde blinked slowly, blood seeping into her right eye from a bad gash on her forehead. She didn't have too much fight left in her and the rules of the match stated that the first team to lose a fighter lost the bout.

It was going to have to be me who pulled us out of this one.

So I continued glancing toward Ariadne's fight instead of keeping all of my attention on mine. My opponent couldn't even take advantage of that as he almost toppled over at least twice trying to perform some sort of overly-complicated kick. Had it been executed by a master, it might even have been effective, but instead this idiot mostly ended up off-balance and tangled up in his own feet.

Besides, I'd said *hit* me, not *kick* me.

At least the punch to the stomach was making him react with a little more effort.

The crowd cheered again, and I looked back toward Ariadne fully for an instant, watching out of the corner of my eye as my opponent spotted his chance and charged toward me. It seemed to take an eternity for him to come within range of a punch, and longer than that for him to actually throw it. To his credit, it had a surprising amount of force. In fact, I wondered if I'd made a horrible, life-ending miscalculation as the blow struck my face and I didn't even feel it when I hit the ground, dazed.

It didn't take long for the referee to declare Ariadne and me the losers, and for the former to run over to me, screaming swearwords I couldn't quite make out in my numb face.

"Are you okay?" she finally asked, and I understood. I didn't nod, knowing how much that could hurt. Feeling was slowly returning to my face, and it sucked.

"Yeah," I said, and the princess helped me up.

"How did you lose to that imbecile?" she exclaimed, gesturing wildly toward our defeaters, who were flexing and showing off to the yelling crowd.

I held up a hand as we made our way out of the fighting area, the crowd continuing the tradition of equal boos and cheers. Once outside the barn, I directed Ariadne toward Aether, who was busy paying out a lot of Piper's money to everyone who'd bet that we'd lose, a logical conclusion given our incredible losing streak. Of course, I wasn't happy about the idea that the crowd had thought we would lose to those two rookies, but that was irrelevant at this point. Ariadne and I would probably never fight again on Myrkheim but, with any luck, we wouldn't have to.

"We'd like to collect our bets," I told Aether thickly. He didn't even wince as he reviewed his record book.

"What are you talking about?" Ariadne demanded. "We probably owe them a fortune—"

"I'm afraid I don't have that kind of money on me; you will have to take this up with Piper. He excused himself temporarily before the fight ended, but he will call on you shortly," Aether said, handing me an official statement of the amount Piper owed to Ariadne and me. I showed it to the princess, who gaped at me in a kind of horror and confusion. I tried not to grin, noting that would hurt my face.

• • •

We made it back to the *Lilstar* carefully and slowly, each step jarring my now-swollen face a bit more. It was a quiet trip, however, as Ariadne elected not to say anything to me. I wasn't under the impression that she actually hated my guts, but she seemed to have more questions than she thought I could handle at the moment.

Once inside the *Lilstar*, I showered and placed a dermal patch over the massive bruise that was forming. The patch would infuse my damaged tissue with pluripotent-type cells based on the same biological technology found in Centauri saliva. A while ago we'd discovered that our closest neighbor had remarkable talent in healing minor scrapes and bruises by literally licking their wounds, depositing these stem cells which took the form of all the other cells around them, including skin, blood vessel walls, and even nerves. With their assistance, our genetic engineers worked to reproduce the effect with cells created from genetic facsimiles, setting up an unlimited and mostly less-gross supply of the pluripotent cells. These new facsimile cells could be used in everything from healing minor wounds of all creatures and humans to fixing cuts and scrapes on organic ships and buildings. Of course, the technology was shared with the Centauri for free; this was long before the U.C. became the world's leading supplier of daylight robbery.

The patch wouldn't work ridiculously fast, but with any luck I wouldn't be completely purple by morning. I sat in the bathroom for a while simply resting. It smelled like cat pee but I didn't mind as the mother cat and the kittens had decided to trust me enough to crawl up to me. The little speckled runt of a kitten even crawled into my lap.

For a long while I sat there, petting the kitten and feeling the swelling and bruising go down on my face. Of course, I had just conned an extremely well-powered and angry individual during an illegal fight and cost him a substantial amount of money while embarrassing him publicly. This was my debut fight as one of his champions and I, impossibly he probably thought, blew it completely. Now all that was left was to wait and see if he was going to be honorable and pay up his debt or if he was going to murder us slowly.

After a while, there was a knock on the door. I triggered the mechanism to open the iris and let

Ariadne in. She didn't say anything as she sat down opposite of me and checked my dermal patch.

"How's it look?" I asked. She shrugged, plucking the kitten that was in my lap and putting it in her lap. It even started to purr. I gave the princess and her small, furry traitor a sour expression.

"You totally lost that fight on purpose," she finally said, leaning back. I sighed.

"And won us a lot of money. Enough to restock the ship," I reasoned. Ariane gave me a flat-browed stare.

"That's not the point," she clenched her jaw. For a moment, I waited for her to continue. I certainly wasn't going to say anything that might wiggle my face without a good reason, including asking her what the point was.

I could live without knowing.

"You didn't even tell me what you were doing," she finally said, looking a little hurt.

"You didn't tell me your original plan to make us money was to dive face-first into illegal fighting," I huffed. One of the other kittens mewed in frustration as the paper wad I'd given them earlier was trapped on top of the water spout. I reached up, grabbed it, and returned it to the small one. She didn't even thank me.

"If we're going to make any sort of partnership work, we need to work on telling each other our plans," Ariadne said without accusation. I nodded gently in agreement.

"We never actually declared any sort of partnership beyond sharing the skiptrace license," I pointed out as I shrugged. After a minute, I stuck my hand out in offering. I was more than willing to have a partner for a while. Ariadne put her hand out, but hesitated before shaking mine.

"Are we going to make a pact to tell each other all plans that involve either the skiptracing or, at some future point, a parcel business?" she asked.

"But what if it's a surprise?" I asked in a petty tone.

"What sort of surprise is going to come out of chasing down a bunch of criminals and shipping packages across the solar system?" Ariadne said, wrinkling her nose.

"Maybe I'm hunting some ruffian down for… your birthday and don't want you to know?" I said, grasping at straws.

"That is the lamest thing I have ever heard," Ariadne said blankly. I nodded in acceptance.

"If it involves skiptracing or parceling, I will inform you of all my plans," I finally said.

"So will I," the princess said, satisfied. So we shook hands, to the protestation of the runt kitten, which Ariadne's movement upset.

"We should go get grilled cheese at *Jones'* to celebrate," Ariadne said without shame.

"Oh really?" I asked. She nodded serenely.

I honestly hoped she and Leopold would get married.

And then I would be the weird sort-of aunt who takes all their freaking adorable kids for ride-a-longs to catch debtors and other minor ilk and lets them stay up way past their bedtimes reading cheap comics.

Before we could even get off the bathroom floor to head to *Jones'*, however, there was a loud and unforgiving knock at the *Lilstar's* main hatch. I sighed warily, knowing who that probably was. It was time to figured out if we died here and now as failed fighters, or if we continued living as rich but still failed fighters.

The knocking continued as we made our way to the front of the ship. Ariadne opened the door with caution while I stood back near the pilot's seat, shock device hidden out of the way and ready for use. The iris opened, revealing Piper who stood there front and center, flanked by two thugs and with Aether lurking in the background.

"I've come here to settle my debt," Piper said stiffly. All of his charm seemed to have worn off and what was left was his rotting fish aura. It made me almost physically sick again.

"Is that what you are going to do?" I asked outright, imagining all the horrible ways he could kill us without leaving a trace. Botulism would probably be the most obvious way. He could hide some in an infection on the *Lilstar's* door mechanism, leaving us trapped inside with the disease to die slowly and without any sort of concrete evidence to trace back to him. He could also use some sort of Centauri-made chemical agent not easily detected by the chem-sniffers on either the *Lilstar* or Myrkheim. Some of the new stuff was not only toxic but required specialized Centauri equipment to find and analyze.

I removed all of these thoughts from my head and focused on the problem at hand.

Piper leaned forward to enter the *Lilstar*, I made a gentle move for the shock device. He looked toward Ariadne almost kindly, the roses-and-leather smell returning.

"Your associate and I, m'lady, do not see eye to eye, which is a shame, really," he said smoothly.

"To be quite frank, I don't know why she hates you. But she is my business partner and if she feels that strongly, I don't see a reason to associate with scum such as yourself," Ariadne said easily and with equal charm. I almost blinked at her in surprise. It's not that I didn't assume Ariadne couldn't be charming, it's just that I had never witnessed it before. Flirty, yes; charming, no.

"I think you have insulted me long enough." Piper said, leaning closer. Ariadne stopped him by placing a gentle hand on his chest.

"No, I think you have insulted us, and our intelligence, long enough," she said coyly, gently playing with his suit. "We beat you at your own game and embarrassed you publicly. It'll take a while for your reputation in the fighting community to restore itself after we lost so badly."

"I will recover," Piper growled.

"Yeah, but then there is this thing about telling your *wife* how you lost all that money to a couple of sprites like us..." Ariadne let the end of the sentence hang unfinished while I watched the whole scene bemused and impressed.

Piper gave Ariadne a long and angry look. He almost seemed to be stuck between his evil nature and the elegant charm he'd learned to affect.

He eventually smiled and made it look easy.

"I will give you your money," he said as he gestured toward Aether, who produced a small satchel of credits. He handed them to me with an almost satisfied expression. "In the good faith that I will never, ever see you two ever again."

"Well, I can't promise we won't run into you at a U.C. UberMarket, but I can promise we won't be fighting here anymore," Ariadne said with a shrug. Piper briefly touched the brim of his hat and walked out of the *Lilstar* with all the dignity he had left. The *Lilstar's* hatch closed silently.

"Holy crap, that worked," Ariadne sighed loudly, turning to look at me with an anxious smile of relief.

"How did you know about his wife?" I asked in amazement. The only way I knew about her was from Aether, but Ariadne hadn't been around for that conversation.

"He has her picture in his wallet. I happened to see it when he was going over the rules of the fight earlier," she said, plopping down in the copilot's seat heavily.

"Yeah, but how did you know she scares him?" I asked.

"The picture has a few knife marks in it," Ariadne shrugged. I broke out into a wide, wide grin.

Ten

In the end we did make it to *Jones'* for celebratory grilled cheese when it opened the next day. Of course, we couldn't really discuss with either Leopold or Ylva exactly *what* we were celebrating, given the fact that it involved coming out under the thumb of a ruthless tyrant of the underground illegal fighting community, so we kept our outward cheering down to a minimum and our glasses filled with just water.

"You ladies look cheerful tonight." Leopold said after working his way across the somewhat packed dance floor to visit us, the only two people at the bar.

"We have officially restocked the ship and can now continue with our skiptracing." Ariadne said, raising her glass in a mock toast.

"Ah, well, that calls for a celebration! Have you ladies ever been up to Johanna's Park at this time of night? They usually have live bands. I would be happy to take you, if you have a few hours to spare," Leopold said smoothly and with a toothy grin. I felt honored to be included, but definitely not about to spoil this perfectly lovely idea for a first date of the most perfect couple this modern era had ever seen.

"Oh, I think I'll stay here for now," I said politely, nudging Ariadne gently. "But you two should definitely go enjoy yourselves."

For a second, Ariadne and Leopold just looked at each other, blushing, as if they'd just realized their buffer was gone. Suddenly it was just the two of them, actually going somewhere together without either me or Ylva lurking in the background. For a second I was afraid that I'd made my exit too quickly and neither of them was actually ready to communicate one-on-one. But Leopold finally grinned and ducked his head a little and shrugged. Ariadne mirrored him, batting her big eyelashes.

They were so stinking cute.

"Sure," Ariadne finally managed to croak out.

"Do you have everything under control here, Miss Ylva?" Leopold asked, turning to the barkeep, who nodded vigorously and with a smile.

"Then let us depart," Leopold said, offering his hand to Ariadne. The princess flashed me one quick look before taking the offered hand and following Leopold out of *Jones'*.

Ylva and I waited a full minute after they'd left before bursting out into good-natured laughter.

• • •

I lurked around *Jones'* without anything to do for a few hours, chatting with Ylva and eating a healthy portion of the massive lavender ice cream sundae I'd ordered. After a while, however, I decided that Leopold and Ariadne would still be out for a long time and I could get a head start on tracking down Ottoman Lee. My advertisement hadn't produced any noticeable results, although a few people came with tips that he'd been seen around some very poor parts of the colony under a different name. Overall, though, I took the reports with a grain of salt as they tended to argue over what tattoo the man actually had. Some said he had a 'lover' tattoo and some said it was 'loser,' although they did all agree that it was on the face.

I finally made my way out of the bar and began to make plans to check some of the areas the reports agreed on. That didn't mean he was still in that area, however. In fact, after seeing his face on the advertisement, he might've even skipped town altogether, which would make things extremely difficult. I'd have to basically start all over again, although I hadn't actually made it that far anyway. It was like starting back at square one from square one and a half.

Of course, all that planning lasted until he broke my nose.

Me, glancing down at the somewhat-sizable sum of credits in my hand while plotting out my plan of attack, failed to recognize my quarry, who just so happened to be walking by in the opposite direction. Apparently, he somehow knew who I was, namely the skiptrace that had been trying to hunt him down for the past few weeks, because his elbow came up and smashed the cartilage of my foremost facial feature to almost flush with the rest of my face. To make matters worse, I fell backwards onto the colony's falsebone floor, landing first on my keister and second on my head, sending out bright shards of pain from my bottom to my top.

"Ahhhhhahhhh," I moaned, cradling my nose. My eyes were watering beyond measure and I couldn't quite make out the two people who were standing over me, although I could just see some vague and gaudy face tattoos. The guy with the right-side face tattoo lifted me up just enough to drag into the nearest alley. It was a mucky place, from what I could see, covered in tattoos, some of which were showing signs of infection. My captor then hoisted me up without gentleness and set me down in a chest-high trash bin filled with garbage from the neighboring buildings so he could look me in the face.

"Owww..." I whined, still holding my nose.

"You listen to me, you—" the right-side-face-tattoo guy got up close to my blurred eyes and called me something very insulting. "I want to know who sent you after me."

My eyes were beginning to clear, although I could have sworn I was seeing double. Of course, the fact that they had sacrificed opposite halves of their faces in some extremely questionable fashion statements kept that theory at bay. I was basically looking at the same man, but with two different tattoos and two different facial expressions. The guy who was doing all the yelling had a right-side tattoo that read "LOVER" and the guy who looked a little green and shaky had the left-side tattoo reading "LOSER."

Crappity crap.

"I'll ask you one more time," LOVER said. "Who sent you after me? The cops? The U.C.?"

"Neither, morel brain," I said, sounding a bit hollow through my shattered nose. "I'm a skiptrace."

"Oh really, like I would believe *that*," LOVER yelled into my face. I didn't flinch.

"I'm not certain I really care, Mr. Lee. It's not like you're the first one to not believe me," I said plainly, sniffling somewhat.

LOVER laughed loudly. There was something about him that began to give me the creeps. I began to doubt the validity of Aristotle's file on this guy. Even the most violent debtor was usually not quite so...unhinged. That added "mental instability" to their files and put them in a whole other class of ruffian. I glanced at the shaky Mr. LOSER and realized that, somehow, either the picture or the name in Aristotle's file had gotten mixed up. LOSER was probably the debtor, LOVER was something a little less human.

"So which of you is Ottoman?" I asked, making no obvious move to stand.

"That would be me, you pig," LOVER said, now waving around a very big knife as he paced back and forth, obviously trying to think.

"So who are you?" I asked LOSER, who had yet to speak anything. He was far from LOVER in demeanor, being mostly a deer-eyed fright who was shaking so much he could have been one of those little, neurotic dogs all the celebrities liked to own.

I wondered what drug he was addicted to.

"Oh me? I'm just Set or Setesh, if you are feeling fancy. Otto's twin. Or clone. I'm really not sure anymore," LOSER said, and, in a moment of stupidity, decided to introduce himself properly and shake my hand. I took it right as LOVER/Ottoman protested the action.

"Stop, you idiot!" Ottoman cried, right as I activated the shock device. Set seized up and fell to the ground. While LOVER had been busy yelling at me, I carefully removed one of the shock device's pads, tucking it out of sight in my hand. Of course, I hadn't expected LOSER to make it as easy as shaking my hand, but I wasn't going to complain too loudly.

Of course, that meant I still had to deal with the obviously more violent twin/clone, but he also decided to make my job easy.

"What did you do to him?!" Ottoman screamed, looking at his unconscious twin/clone.

Now, the smart thing in this situation would be to throw a knife at me, from a distance. Instead, Ottoman charged, and I merely leaned to one side and let him stab the trash behind me while I slapped the second shock pad onto Ottoman's neck. Unfortunately, I was still touching him when I activated the device. Electricity shot through my arm all the way to my shoulder and eked toward my core, bringing two or three times the amount of zing as when Sasha had demonstrated the device on just my arm. Thankfully, I didn't lose consciousness like Ottoman did.

"Owww…" I moaned again.

The good news was that I didn't have to carry both unconscious ruffians back to the *Lilstar* myself. After relieving them of all weapons — Ottoman had somewhere close to six knives shoved in various places on his person — I secured the two Lees to the walls of the alley with slats of epidermis I had scraped off other portions of the colony earlier and had been carrying around for such an occasion. The Lees wouldn't be going anywhere without a really sharp knife. I then limped my way back to *Jones'*. Of course, Leopold and Ariadne were still out on their, well, *date*, but Ylva was there and, thankfully, not very busy as the late-night crowd began to thin.

"My goodness, what happened to ye?" Ylva asked, hurriedly gathering a wet cloth for my nose. Having a completely sober patron stumble in with a bloody nose and a few odd muscle spasms from an electric shock was not something seen every day.

"I found my quarry," I said with blood dripping down my entire hand. I tried not to get any on the nightclub's floor, but that was impossible. Ylva rounded the bar, handing me a cloth to cover my nose and ushering me to one of the bar stools.

"Want me to straighten that a bit?" she asked, gesturing to the nose. I couldn't see how crooked it was over how swollen it was. "It'll hurt."

I nodded anyway, and she leaned over the bar to give me a lemon slice to bite down on. She was a more than capable nurse, so I wondered why she was tending bar, but I didn't want to ask and make my procedure even worse. So I just explained exactly how my nose got broken and the predicament I was now in.

While Ylva did a good job straightening my nose, it might've just been quicker and less painful to rip my entire face off, or so I believed. In no time, however, it was neatly bandaged with a layer of pluripotent cell patches underneath some medical tape.

"Ye may need a bit o' plastic surgery to get this looking right again, but I did the best I could," the barkeep warned me. I shrugged. It's not like I hadn't had my nose broken before, although never to this extent. I wondered how long I would have to save on a skiptrace's bounties to afford surgery.

Eh, ponderings for another time.

The next step for me was to figure out what to do about transporting the Lees from the alley to the *Lilstar*. I looked toward the massive bouncers who were busy cleaning up and stacking tables and chairs.

"Think I could borrow your hunks to move my bounties?" I asked Ylva. "I'll compensate them."

"I dunno, let me ask them. Dara, Nakajima, feel like making a few extra credits?" Ylva called out to them. The two brawny men shrugged and ambled over.

"I need some help moving a couple of unconscious quarries for my skiptracing," I said, pulling some credits out of my pocket. It was more than enough to pay both men to help. I waved it a bit in the air.

"Sure," Dara, as his nametag identified, said. He and the other guy, who I presumed was Nakajima, looked like they could bench press small Boots, so I was secure with the idea that they could heft the twins/clones.

I led the two bouncers back to the alley and cut my two still-unconscious quarries free from the wall. I went ahead and switched out their Myrkheim bindings to epidermis from the *Lilstar*. Ariadne hadn't been excited about the idea of me shaving off thin layers of the ship's epidermis in different areas until I had enough to secure a person to the wall, but after I promised to take it from insensate areas like the floor, she acquiesced. There was just barely enough to bind both of their hands together. Since I presumed we were after one person, I didn't think to get enough epidermis for two.

Dara and Nakajima carried the two Lees over their shoulders with ease, and in no time we'd made it back to the ship.

The *Lilstar* was going to be very cramped with five cats, two bounties, and two mostly lucky skiptraces who could barely afford to restock the ship enough for three people. I sighed as I handed Dara and Nakajima their credits.

"Tell Ylva to send Ariadne back this way when she gets back from her date," I said.

"Uh, for no extra cost, would you like one of us to stay here to make it a fair fight in case those two decide to wake up?" Dara's baritone voice suggested. I looked at the two Lees, bound on either side of the threshold that divided the cockpit of the ship from the living space. I imagined the positions they were in, seated on the ground with arms stretched up over their heads, secured at the wrists to the ship's walls, was going to be uncomfortable for long periods of time. I hadn't decided if I felt like putting them in the bunks or not. The bouncer was right, however, numbers were not on my side, at least until Ariadne got here.

"Nah, I'll pay whichever of you wants to stay," I said. Dara nodded.

"Nakajima will be out here if you need him," the bouncer said as he left. Nakajima took a seat in the airlock outside the *Lilstar*.

I waited patiently for Ariadne to return, which didn't happen for another few hours. I tried talking to Nakajima, but the man only grunted or replied in yeses and nos. So I re-checked the ship's supplies, calculated how much we needed with an extra passenger, and fed the cats. Of course, thinking about the cats made me have to go visit the cats. I opened up the bathroom's iris carefully, but not carefully enough, as one of the kittens decided to make a break for it and dashed out of the bathroom before I could catch him.

"No!" I yelled, chasing after the little furball as he bounded through the living space and over to the unconscious Set. I feared what would happen if the poor thing became lost on the station. One cat wasn't necessarily going to upset the whole ecosystem but he would still have a bounty on his wee head. I rounded the corner and made it into the cockpit to see Nakajima in the ship's threshold, gently cradling the small kitten, who protested loudly at being caught.

"Sorry, he escaped," I muttered. The bouncer nodded, stroking the little feline's head.

Nakajima looked into my ship with big, brown — but scrutinizing — eyes.

"That is a *Birdsong*-class ship, yes?" he said.

"I dunno," I shrugged. I'm sure Ariadne had mentioned it.

"Yes," he said, nodding, keeping his attention largely on the kitten who was gnawing his finger with all the power it could muster. The bouncer didn't even wince; in fact, he made little, amused faces at the kitten. At one point he literally cooed at it. "It's made for two people and you have four and...cats?"

"Five cats..." I muttered again.

"Are you trying to find a home for the cats?" he asked, looking up at me. I felt a smile creeping up on my face.

"They can't live on the colony," I said.

"I live on a ship docked not far from here. Technically I am not on the colony," he said, tone laden with hinting.

"Do I have any guarantee you will give these guys a proper life?" I challenged, but was in reality definitely willing to entertain the idea of letting him have them. He seemed to be gentle and caring toward the kitten in his hand and had even managed to calm it from its near-rage mentality to a content, almost sleepy demeanor. I suppose, if the kitten was that comfortable with him, he must be good with cats.

"I already have four. They're the reason I didn't sell my ship in the first place," Nakajima said.

"Well, come back tomorrow. I need to make sure Ariadne isn't attached to any of them," I said, although I also had to make sure *I* wasn't attached. The little runt that was still in the bathroom seemed to hold a piece of my heart.

Nakajima nodded and, reluctantly, gave me back the kitten, who mewed in protest.

I returned the kitten back to a grateful mother as I heard Ariadne's voice come into the airlock.

"Hi, I'm back—holy crap, Marcie, what did you do?" Ariadne's tone went from singsong to demanding in almost no time as she entered the ship and got a good look at my face. I tried not to scream when she touched the puffy skin around my nose curiously.

"I ran into somebody's elbow," I said plainly, fighting back the reflex tears that had started after the princess' prodding.

"Your nose is all—" Ariadne started, twisting back to look at our quarry. Of course, Dara had probably alerted her to their existence and capture like I'd told him to do. "Which one of these idiots did that to you?"

"Why?" I asked suspiciously.

"I dunno I kinda wanted to kiss him," Ariadne crinkled her nose sarcastically.

I made a gagging motion.

"Are we really going to transport *both* of these?" the princess asked, gesturing generically to the Lees.

"That was what I was thinking. Technically I have no idea which one is the debtor." I shrugged helplessly. "Plus I found an adopter for the cats."

"Oh," Ariadne said a little sadly.

"I mean, they would be much happier with this guy. He already has four cats of his own," I reasoned. Ariadne nodded.

"Of course. It's not like we could keep all of them on the ship," the princess said. There was a moment of silence. She finally looked at me with an almost conniving expression.

"The little speckled runt?" she asked.

"I've already named him Albert," I confessed. She gave me a wry sort of grin.

"It's settled. We'll keep Albert. But the ship is still overstuffed," Ariadne said.

"Nakajima?" I moved to stick my head out the airlock.

"Yes?" the bouncer asked.

"How would you like to have four more cats and babysit a fifth?" I asked. "We'll pay you for upkeep until we can take him back."

"That sounds good," Nakajima said with a ghost of a smile.

• • •

With Nakajima sticking around a bit longer waiting for us to relinquish the kittens to him, Ariadne and I were free to begin planning our departure from Myrkheim and the return trip to Earth. While Ariadne began prepping the ship and announcing our departure to the colony's ship control, I went back to buy the extra supplies we would need to support ourselves and our quarries.

While out, I also took the time to send a solar-system-spanning communique to Aristotle, hoping it could allay any fears he might have that we were goofing off with his license. The communique would take about a full day and a half to get from Myrkheim to Dinium, Earth, time which included bouncing around a few communication processing stations before finally being sent to Aristotle's office in the form of a phone call. Of course, I sent the communication with the notion that the somewhat delicate radio-wave based transmissions would avoid being scattered in all directions by any odd pocket of gas that happened to stray into its path. The fact that long-distance communication existed through the nebulous pea soup that engulfed the system was an amazing feat of engineering, but there was always a high chance of something failing. I just hoped this particular message made it through.

It was always good to assure your new employers that you were not slacking off.

This message also explained that we had *caught* Ottoman within the required month, although we would be bringing him back about a week late. I prided myself on the legal loophole I'd discovered and hoped it would convince Aristotle not to fire us the instant we stepped foot inside his office again. I also mentioned the addition of Set, hoping that would convince Aristotle of Ariadne and my abilities to capture the human realm's most wanted.

Of course, I could always fall back on becoming Myrkheim's foremost animal control officer.

I returned with the supplies shortly to hear a great deal of noise as the mother cat and four of her kittens mewed from a box seated next to Nakajima. The bouncer did get up long enough to help me move the new supplies into the *Lilstar*, but promptly went back to the cats, leaving me to sort and organize while Ariadne ducked into the ship's bowels to check for any infections or irritations that might have occurred while we were docked.

After I stuffed the closet as full as it could get, I began to unload the rest of the supplies onto one of the bunks — Ariadne's of course. We'd just have to take shifts, unless one of us felt like sleeping on the floor eerily close to the Lees. It would be better to have at least one of us awake at all times, anyway.

I shoved any doubts I might've had about the safety of having four people all in the same, small, two-person spacecraft for the two weeks it would take to get back to Earth.

"All set!" Ariadne finally called. I turned to the still-open hatch.

"Thank Mr. Jones for us," I said, slapping the promised extra credit into Nakajima's hand. Included in it was an invitation for Leopold Jones to send letters to Miss Ariadne King whenever she and her partner, Marcie, made it back to Earth with their quarry. It included the *Lilstar*'s radio callsign, although it was very difficult to contact a ship in flight, and the information for the transmission station nearest to Aristotle's office. The cat-owning bouncer nodded understandingly after reading the note. I gave him a wink goodbye and stepped through to the *Lilstar*, closing the hatch behind me.

"Strapped in?" I asked, moving toward the bunk area. Set was still unconscious, but Ottoman was glaring from around his mouth gag, still a little loopy, if I was reading his unsteady expression right. I nudged Set slightly with my shoe and he moaned just a little. Still alive, thankfully.

I muttered at nothing in particular before moving to the copilot's seat. Ariadne was just getting clearance to undock as I buckled my seatbelt.

I cast an irritating glance toward our captives. Ottoman's scowl never changed in pitch, so I assumed he was comfortable.

Ariadne made a low growl in frustration.

"What was that for?" I asked, giving her a strange look.

"I forgot to give Leopold my number," Ariadne said as the *Lilstar* let go of Myrkheim. I hid a sly smile.

"Maybe you should call *him*," I said easily.

"I don't know, he is awfully busy being a proprietor," the princess said, looking downcast.

"He took you on a freaking *date*! I don't care how busy his business is," I said, pulling out a pen and notebook. If we were going to cram four people — two of which were immobile and potentially murderous ruffians — into a two-person craft, there would need to be rules and a set schedule. It was a more or less long trip back to Earth and our captives would need food, water, and to use the facilities more than once throughout the two weeks of travel.

While I considered making a stopover at a station or Meropis-C, I didn't think it was worth the risk. Ariadne and I would undoubtedly want to take time outside the ship during those stopovers, leaving only one of us to handle the predictable escape attempts made by our two captives.

"Technically, you were invited too," Ariadne muttered.

"Yeah, but he didn't exactly fight for me to stay when I refused," I countered.

"You're right," Ariadne sighed. I shook my head with a wry grin.

It took me a little while to come up with an acceptable plan, which included everything from bathroom breaks, showers, naps, and feeding times. The Lees would just have to be content with washing fully clothed and handcuffed. Actually it would be more of a rinse-down and face wash simply to keep the smell at bay. Between the two, I didn't figure Set would give me quite as much trouble as Ottoman, who seemed to be some kind of addict—

Ah. Addict.

I looked at the still-unconscious twin/clone with some horror and surprise. I hadn't thought through this far enough. I never was a great strategizer. If Set was an addict, I doubted his poison of choice would remain in his system from the time he last took it until we made it to Earth. I certainly wasn't going to stop and get him more of it; my illegal activities stopped at acquiring and giving illicit drugs to my bounties. I rubbed my forehead, setting the new schedule aside and began writing out a battle plan for any signs of withdrawal. While it would all depend largely on what Set preferred, the *Lilstar*'s medical kit might have some non-addictive substitutes to keep his symptoms at bay, but it was duct tape on a space suit, a temporary fix to a long-term problem.

Ottoman let out a sniveling laugh behind me through his taped mouth. I glared through his LOVER tattoo and judgement of me, realizing he knew I had just realized what my predicament was.

Great, not only was he a sociopath, he was also perceptive.

"What's up?" Ariadne said, looking in concern from me to Ottoman.

"We're in it up to here," I gestured to my neck.

Eleven

T he first few days of the trip went along
smoothly. Everyone was fed properly, allowed to
use the facilities, and rinsed down at least once.
Ottoman was actually behaving himself, something
that surprised me, but every so often I would catch a
weird glare from the corner of his eye. He was still
someone I wouldn't trifle with. So that was why I
quickly adopted the policy of attaching a shock plate
to our captives' necks whenever they weren't
strapped to the ship. I kept it on the lowest setting,
figuring that was just enough to startle them into
submission. I never even had to use it, except once
on Ottoman who decided to half-heartedly attempt a
takeover. That time, however, I made sure I wasn't in
direct contact with him when I turned it on.

Set remained lethargic almost to the point of
unconsciousness. Since he was so apathetic to his
surroundings, I went so far as to removing the tape
from his mouth most of the time. Besides, if he went
through withdrawal, it would be better keep his
mouth unobstructed.

It wasn't until the fourth day, about halfway to
Earth, that things began to go badly — even setting
aside the fact Ariadne and I had passed our month-

long probation from Aristotle. That, fortunately, was something to be dealt with once we had reached home. No, the more immediate and dire situation we faced came from one simple sentence:

"Where are the unicorns?"

It came from a soft voice situated behind Ariadne's chair. She was napping, of course, and I was left awake to keep an eye on everything.

"What unicorns?" I asked with genuine fear, wondering if all of my anti-withdrawal plans would be enough to keep Set and everyone comfortable for the mere five days we had left until Earth.

"The... unicorns. Like fairies, but with less... misogyny," Set said, eyes narrow, skin damp, muscles spasming, and fingernails the palest of blues. Even his LOSER tattoo seemed to be ashy.

"Misogyny...?" I let the word roll out of my mouth as I wracked my brain to both diagnose his withdrawal symptoms and plan what to do next. The good news was, I'd shown an aptitude for biology as a kid. After I'd graduated from the Basics, the rest of my education through high school was centered heavily on human and organic structure, anatomy, diagnosis, and a lot of basic first-aid. There had been some more advanced topics, of course, of which I had only scratched the surface, but between my education and stories of my brother's work, I was reasonably confident that I could handle a withdrawal-ridden addict. Unfortunately, everyone reacts to either drugs, or a sudden lack of them, a little differently, although each poison had its own calling card, so to speak. Even with that spectrum of symptom variance and signatures, Set seemed to be reacting very generically.

Great.

I glanced at Ottoman for any kind of help he might offer. Surprisingly, he was looking at his clone/twin with an amount of empathy or pity I wouldn't have assumed possible. I suppose if I shared a face with someone, I would feel connected to them through any sort of narcosis that might be affecting me congruently.

"What's his fix?" I asked Ottoman, fishing for just how deep his empathy toward Set might exist before I removed the tape.

He looked at me with wild, yet not wholly un-pleading eyes that I took as a sign he wanted to help. I leaped out of the chair and freed his mouth.

"He likes crystals of any kind, but the last he took were a few adams," the sociopath told me, still glancing warily at his deeply-suffering counterpart. Set seemed to be caught between crying, laughing, and thrashing around violently. I nodded, retaped Ottoman's mouth, and went for the medical kit.

Adams, *adamas*, or simply "diamonds" started out like many other illegal drugs: as a prescription medicine. During the U.C.'s rise to control the creation and sale of pharmaceuticals, private companies fought to be competitive by creating and marketing so-called wonder drugs on a daily basis. Most of the drugs did more harm than good, such as diamonds. Originally meant to cure all insanity, adams quickly caught on in the underworld as the best way to empty your mind. Sure, it cured mental ailments, but that was because it was slowly eating away every aspect of your brain, leaving you a drooling, empty shell with no muscle control.

I dashed toward the cabinet with the medical kit, waking up Ariadne in the process.

"What's the problem?" she asked, just after sitting up too quickly and banging her head on the ceiling above her bunk.

"Just keep an eye on those two!" I shouted in return. The moment I reached the cabinet I began pulling out all the non-medical provisions that had the misfortune of standing between me and my prize. I finally found it shoved in the farthest corner of the highest shelf and made a mental note never to put it back there again. I ripped it open almost violently, spilling half the contents all over the floor. I finally found the medicines I was looking for. From what I remembered of close adams encounters, someone going through withdrawal needed two things: a sedative to calm their spastic brain and nervous system and something to relax their stomach.

Of course, they could still *die* from the withdrawal, but these medicines could keep the more dramatic of the symptoms at bay.

I found an all-night dermal sedative for Set along with an anti-nausea pill. The patch would be easy enough to administer, and I would probably put it directly on his neck for a quicker effect, but getting him to swallow the pill was another matter entirely. I seriously considered crushing it into a glass of water, but getting him to swallow a whole glass of water seemed even messier. In the end, I started with the patch.

"Marcie!" Ariadne demanded once I returned with the medicines. She said it quietly, however, while kneeling cautiously beside Set. She didn't seem panicked or frightened by the addict's inane babbling or thrashing, just concerned.

"I've got stuff, hold this," I said simply, handing her the bottle of anti-nausea pills while I unwrapped the sedative patch. At this point, Set was shrieking, sweaty, and somehow pale and flushed at the same time. He pulled so much on the epidermis slats that bound him to the ship that I was afraid he might break his wrists.

Without being asked, Ariadne helped me apply the sedative patch by holding down the addict's kicking legs. Of course, that brought more and louder screams from the brainless man, but I was wholly focused on the task at hand. Just get the patch to his neck, I told myself, then wait a few minutes for it to kick in. In the sweet spot between him being hyperactive and being sedated, I could force-feed him the anti-nausea pill. With any luck, we'd be good for a few hours until the patch wore off.

He fought like a pinned and mostly rabid opossum, trying to bite at my hand as I attempted to place the patch on his neck. I placed my hand just behind his ear and pushed his head firmly to the side, exposing his neck enough for me to put the patch just over his carotid artery. The location meant that it would be able to enter the bloodstream much faster than if I'd put it on muscle or fat. Although, even if I missed the artery a little, it was still fast-acting. I didn't miss, however, and by the time I had collected myself, he was just dazed enough to force feed the anti-nausea pill without causing him to choke. For a moment, he was so green I figured it wouldn't stay down. But within ten minutes he was resting peacefully.

"Aaaahhhh..." I moaned softly.

"I'll see if there is a faster course we can take," Ariadne said as she slid into the pilot's seat.

"And one without a lot of turbulence," I suggested, watching Set's face lose its green hue temporarily.

I continued to sit on the floor between our two captives, resting my head against my palm. Ottoman nudged me with his foot and I gave him a pretty nasty side-eye. He remained undaunted by my glare and lifted his chin in a motion that suggested I take the tape off.

I did so grudgingly and with a demanding, "What?"

"How long do you think you can keep that up?" he asked accusingly. "Set is bad off and won't get much better without medical attention. *Real* medical attention."

"Ah, shut your mouth," I said and taped him back up off-handedly.

Ottoman yelled formless words at me from underneath his tape, gesturing to his twin/clone repeatedly. I didn't have much room to judge him on the matter; I'd be concerned if my brother was in that same position. However, I was tired, and it was Ariadne's turn to be awake, so I tumbled into the open bunk and fell promptly asleep, taking the opportunity to pretend that the Lees were already in police custody and that Aristotle hadn't banished us from his employment.

• • •

The next two days consisted of the same routine: give Set a new sedative patch and anti-nausea pill. For the most part, these two substitutions seemed to keep his withdrawal symptoms down, but even Ariadne recognized that the addict was not coming even close to being stabilized. We needed to get to Earth fast or find some kind of clinic that could handle him. I spent many an hour simply chewing my lip out of frustration. On the one hand, we had a sick twin/clone who was close to dying and few options to help him. On the other hand, we had a vicious twin/clone who would undoubtedly take any and all opportunities to escape when possible.

But someone was technically *dying*.

"Could we be brought up on charges?" Ariadne asked on cue, glancing toward the sleeping addict.

"How far are we from a station or colony?" I finally asked.

"We're not far from Baltia, Mars. Plus, we're on something of an intercept course with Edonite," the princess said, gesturing to something on the control panel I couldn't make sense of.

Actually, I wasn't paying attention to what she was pointing at, having swiveled my head around to watch out of the corner of my eye. I watched Ottoman's face to make sure he didn't have any preference in the matter. The last thing I wanted to do was take him directly to one of his favorite hideouts or a station he was familiar with. His LOVER-tattooed face revealed an irritating amount of nothing.

"Baltia has a great clinic," the princess offered.

"Edonite has fewer laws and traffic," I countered. Ariadne looked at me briefly, then nodded and then input the proper coordinates.

I turned to look at Ottoman full-on. His gaze was now fully fixed on Set. He seemed to actually care for his twin/clone. I wondered exactly what made him the way he was, insane and likely far more dangerous than had originally been reported. While there was still a chance he was just a debtor, I somehow doubted that covered the subject. He probably was a debtor, but it was also likely that my over-exaggerated advert on Myrkheim was less exaggerated than I'd originally believed.

There was always a chance I could have become like that. Some skiptrace might have had me tied to their ship, dragging me home to an arrest and trial. I'd had plenty of opportunities to do so even as far back as my childhood. The situation involving my brother could have been a catalyst for a downward spiral, but it wasn't. Against all that had happened to me, I'd managed to stay afloat in terms of sanity. Of course, I always had days where I doubted my mental stability, but looking at real crazy put those concerns to rest.

I must have shown some sort of pity toward the sociopath because suddenly he looked at me, got angry, and strained against his bonds as if to fight me. Of course, the copilot's seat was far out of his reach, but he managed to kick it once or twice.

Without a sound I placed the final sedative patch I was holding on his exposed ankle.

• • •

We arrived at Edonite within a few hours and contacted their medical facilities to warn them of our situation, just as Set's most recent dermal patch was beginning to wear off. Ottoman was still sleeping like a murderous baby, however, so I moved him farther into the ship. As I told the princess, the station was light on laws, but I figured it would be best not to advertise having four people in a two-person craft, although the *Lilstar* was beginning to smell like it was overpopulated.

Besides, I wasn't quite certain Ottoman was a small fish. Having him snatched out from under me by another skiptrace or overeager station security would probably evaporate any chance I might have with impressing Aristotle.

And I really needed to impress the carrot-top lawyer.

After moving Ottoman, I turned to the rousing Set and began to prepare him for the medical officer that was waiting for us at Edonite. He was starting to mutter and spasm weakly, like he was having a nightmare. Right now, of course, his life pretty much *was* a nightmare, most of which was my doing. Not that I truly pitied anyone who decided to ruin their lives with drugs or other destructive vices. I only felt sorry for the waste of human potential they exhibited.

Like now, Set refused to give Ariadne and me any cooperation in moving him toward the airlock and the awaiting nurse. His thrashing increased and his inane muttering became a full-on scream even through the tape I put on his mouth.

"Cut him free!" I yelled tersely at Ariadne as I tried to hold down the addict. She produced a folding knife from her pocket and proceeded to cut the organic slats holding Set immobile. Well, *somewhat* immobile. Ariadne was attempted to be careful enough not to nick one of the *Lilstar*'s nerves, which translated into her taking forever to cut the slats free from the ship.

I had to switch tactics from simply holding down Set's free legs to sitting on top of them. Each agonizing moment brought a new wish from me that usually involved speeding up the princess's cutting efforts or ensuring my meager frame was enough to keep this addle-brain from hurting himself or anyone else.

"Hurry!" I let myself cry out once as Ariadne continued to move slowly.

"Yes, I know!" the princess yelled back at me. She was only about halfway through. Just another half to go.

Of course, things are never as easy as '*just* halfway more to go,' especially when it's imperative that they *do* go smoothly. In this case, Set broke one of his wrists trying to thrash about. The break let him wiggle a hand free and before I could stop him, he hit Ariadne across the face, sending her flying backward, crashing into the back of the pilot's seat.

To her credit, the princess was back up without any kind of hesitation. Of course, she caused me a great deal of panic when she completely ignored her original task and instead stepped over Set and moved deeper into the ship.

"What the—" "I bit off a choice word as I sat on the addict's struggling legs, trying to pin his free arm at the same time. His wrist didn't seem to be causing any more pain than the rest of his symptoms, but even so, I tried to grab his arm instead of the wrist itself. Even if he wasn't feeling any pain in the break, it wouldn't do for me to make things even worse.

Ariadne returned a second later, placing a semi-used dermal patch from Ottoman on Set's free shoulder. I could see she was resisting the urge to smirk at me as we waited for the addict to calm down. This lasted until Set's breathing became more or less regular and she turned to give me a knowing side-eye.

"Yeah, yeah. Your name is I. Genius; I get it," I waved her off. "How's that cheek?"

"Ow," Ariadne said as she reached up and touched her fresh wound, which comprised of what would be an excellent black eye and scar, if the surprisingly massive pressure cut wasn't treated properly.

"You'll accompany Set to the clinic, I'll stay here with Ottoman," I nodded toward Ariadne, who seemed to agree with that plan.

"Are you sure you can handle *him*?" the princess asked in a low tone. I glanced toward Ottoman, who was looking around somewhat bleary-eyed.

"Yeah, I should be all right. The tough part is you making sure someone doesn't try to snatch Set from us." I contemplated giving Ariadne the shock device, but decided against it. It wouldn't do to have her caught zapping a hospital patient even if he legally was one of our prisoners.

"I think I can handle a druggy," she said and smiled, turning to pick up the addict's front half. I grabbed his legs and helped Ariadne weave the unconscious and miserable man to the airlock.

"Fresh air, hallelujah," I gasped as I stepped over the threshold into Edonite, realizing just how ripe the inside of the *Lilstar* had become. The nurse with the stretcher gave me one odd look before strapping Set down to the wheeled bed and giving him a brief inspection.

Without any real word toward me or the princess, the nurse whisked the withdrawal-riddled addict toward the clinic with Ariadne in tow.

I stood in the airlock for a moment breathing in the fresh-ish station air.

We were so close to Earth. In just a few days we'd be free of these troublesome twins/clones and their hideous tattoo choices and, hopefully, be gainfully employed by a company known as Aristotle & Sons. Of course, this could all go to the dogs if Set managed to die while technically in our custody.

Why couldn't I have just become a nurse like my brother? Revenge was having a longer-lasting impact on my life than I figured it would.

Plus, I had to deal with this guy.

The *Lilstar* let out a shrill, bright tone which was her way of warning me that the prisoner had escaped. I spun around and landed a good punch across Ottoman's nose before elbowing him in the throat. He stumbled backwards and tripped over the *Lilstar*'s hatchway, landing soundly on his keister, gasping for breath.

"I thought I made it clear to you to sit in the ship like a good boy. How'd you even get loose?" I huffed loudly before dragging him by his still-bound hands back into the ship. His wrists were a little bloodied and the epidermis slats that bound his hands were covered in jagged cuts. Somehow he'd managed to get hold of a sharp edge. The sociopath moaned quietly. "Oh, suck it up."

• • •

It was a few hours before I heard anything from Ariadne. Although Set had gone into cardiac arrest more than once, the addict was now in stable condition. In a few days, the doctor had assured her, he might even be stable enough to travel. The important thing was, however, that Ariadne and I would not be brought up on involuntary manslaughter charges.

Negligence charges could prove worrisome, but skiptraces were given a lot more leeway in such matters than regular citizens. This was not precisely a fair deal toward ordinary citizens, due to the fact that there was no real reason for it. Skiptracing was a booming business and a lot of governments actively encouraged it as a way to take pressure off of their underpaid and overworked police forces. It essentially saved them from having to hire so many detectives.

The downside to this was the fact that, with encouragement from powerful people, came the abuse of said praise. The governments couldn't very well risk angering the skiptrace community, nor could they risk looking like idiots who hired indiscriminate thugs to track down simple debtors. So skiptraces were allowed the luxury of bent laws. It saved the governments from admitting that their hires were actually acting very illegally.

This policy was more than repulsive, but it would allow Ariadne and me some breathing room in this situation with Set.

I twisted around in the copilot's seat and rested my chin on its headrest to keep an eye on Ottoman, who was trying futilely to escape for the second time in only a few hours. I had discovered the small scalpel the sociopath had used to cut himself free of the ship. It must have fallen out of the medical kit when I was scrambling to find sedatives and anti-nausea medicine for Set and rolled into some sort of crevice that I missed when I was cleaning everything back up. I treated and bandaged the small cuts he had on his wrists. It wouldn't do for him to suddenly catch an infection, especially not when we were this close to dragging his sorry behind back to Earth.

I was thankful the *Lilstar* had warned me when Ottoman was free. It might have been a little more helpful had the warning come when Ottoman was cutting his bonds, an act I'm more than positive the ship should have felt, but like human beings, each ship had a different level of sensitivity toward pain. Even if the ship's genetic facsimile had been engineered down to the last nucleotide, there were always variables, usually caused by environmental stimuli.

Even more basic than that, genetic facsimiles were simply not as precise an art as real genetics. They paled in comparison to the genes found in every other, non-man-made living organism. Organic ships and structures were a complete anomaly in the natural world. Real genetics, with all of their information and nuances, were almost impossible to replicate without major issues cropping up later. This was part of the reason why genetic manipulation on all non-plant creatures was outlawed and even manipulating plant genes was a highly regulated process.

Cloning was still legal and even cloning humans was not as controversial as it probably should be, but that's a whole other bag of worms.

To put a long story short, the *Lilstar* could have an extremely high pain tolerance to withstand Ottoman slicing through the epidermis, and that could have caused the warning's delay. In any event, it was good information to have for later situations

Ottoman continued to strain at his bonds. Freedom was just beyond the *Lilstar*'s airlock. His situation could be considered cruel, but, aside from releasing him to terrorize Edonite, there was little I could do about it.

"You're going to break something," I finally said. He glared at me from over his taped mouth. He seemed to process something, however, and then thrashed even harder. The nice bandages I'd put on his wrists began to rub off but, thankfully, he wasn't bleeding noticeably.

"No, don't do that. I'm not taking you to the clinic," I said and frowned, an expression the sociopath returned. He sat glumly for a few minutes before deciding to work the tape off of his mouth.

I suppose with the blood from his nose, it was a lot easier for the captive to lick the tape's glue off and dislodge it from his lips. Getting up and replacing it seemed like an awful lot of effort and I was very bored, so I let him alone with tape hanging uselessly off the side of his face for the time being.

"What are you after?" Ottoman asked. I blinked at his words apathetically. "I mean it. What are you after at this moment?"

"Atonement for my sins," I finally said.

The sociopath actually laughed in my face. It was a raucous, grating sound and I felt a bit of his spit all the way from the copilot's seat. Even after I rubbed it off with contempt and disgust, I could still almost feel all of his germs crawling around on my skin.

"Cute. Very cute. Like your sins are more important than mine," he said.

"Are you trying to imply that you are on some mission to atone for your own?" I asked, and he nodded.

"That's what I was doing when you went after me," Ottoman said. He was actually doing a fair job of trying to manipulate me. Unfortunately, I'd spent most of my early life being manipulated, so that just wasn't something I would fall for. Especially not from him. "I just want to make right what I've done wrong. Can't you empathize with that?"

"What do you want me to do about that?" I asked, more curious than anything else.

"Nothing," the sociopath said dramatically, not looking me in the eye. It was a nice game he played. "I just wanted you to understand my situation a little better."

Smooth, I complimented him internally, but it was ultimately futile. Even as he tried to pretend to be a victim, there was a tangible evil around him.

"No," I said, standing up and getting two fresh pieces of tape. I placed them carefully across his mouth in an 'x' pattern. "I'm just trying to get a job done. Sins aren't something you can simply atone for, anyway, they're something you have to be forgiven for."

Within a split second, the sociopath went from empathy-greedy to insane as he screamed and lunged at me, still captive by his bonds and tape.

Catching his chin in my hand, I forced him to look up at me. His eyes were cold and empty. Devoid of everything that could have made him human.

"I saw the way you looked at your brother," I whispered. "But don't think you will ever know what empathy is."

I tried to enforce my point as I held his face immobile. It was unlikely anything could really break through, but for the moment I was in complete control; and it was he who blinked first.

Releasing him with a slight shove, I went back to my seat, waiting impatiently for Ariadne to make contact again.

TWELVE

At about the station's supper time, Ariadne arrived back at the *Lilstar* with a few fresh boxed meals and some extra supplies; the latter included new dermal sleep aids. I promptly placed one on Ottoman's forehead and went back to eat the first warm-ish meal I'd had since that grilled cheese at *Jones'*. The pasta wasn't exactly world-class, but I was secure in the knowledge that I'd eaten far worse in my lifetime.

"Now what?" Ariadne asked in the middle of a mouthful.

"Now we wait around until Set is good enough to travel, and head back to Earth," I shrugged. The plan didn't need to be complicated, just efficient if we wanted to make sure Aristotle would be happy, or at least impressed.

"We should be at one of the orbital ReHy stations within three days, which should take about six hours to process the *Lilstar* through," the princess said.

"Agh, that'll seem like forever," I said, mentally counting all of the unread books I had left. I sighed inwardly; I'd probably have to reread one or two of them. "I wish the ship could bypass that whole process."

"They are trying to make ships with epidermis that can handle atmospheric entry without rehydration, but that's still a few years off," Ariadne sighed greatly, as if she were mourning the out-of-reach technology.

"Could the *Lilstar* be refitted with that epidermis when it comes out?" I asked.

"Maybe; I'm sure it'd take a complete genetic overhaul to do it, though. To be honest, it would probably just be easier to buy a new ship," the princess said.

"I suppose it would." I chewed my lip thoughtfully, wondering just how expensive an overhaul like that would be. Of course, who was I kidding, I could barely afford surgery to correct my own broken nose, much less a genetic facsimile rewrite for an entire runabout. In a few years, however, it could make a good present for a certain, up-to-her-eyeballs-in-debt-with-me pilot I know.

"What happened to his nose?" Ariadne suddenly asked, looking back at our sleeping captive.

"Vengeance," I said. I told Ariadne about Ottoman's whole and futile escape and the scalpel I had found.

"Didn't the warning bells go off?" she asked, looking curiously at Ottoman.

"Yeah, but not until he was literally right behind me," I said, scooping up the last bite of pasta in a perfect pasta-to-cheese sauce ratio. I paused for a second to mentally prepare myself for the best part of the meal, even if the noodles were mediocre.

"Hm," the princess seemed uncertain.

"What?" I countered, swallowing the last of the pasta.

"Did you search him?" she asked pointedly.

"Yes," I said, giving her a strange look.

"Like, really search him?" Ariadne said.

"Down to his underwear. Why?" I said.

"You didn't find any... I dunno, vials of any kind?"

"No, I definitely would have noticed something like that. He was clean." I watched the princess's face, hoping to see something that would tell me where she was going with this. All I could figure out was that she was worrying about something.

Something I should probably be worrying about too.

"Never mind," she decided to frustrate me. I let it go for the time being. She reached up and touched her newly-bandaged cheek. "Now we look like a matching bar fight set."

"Nah," I grinned a little as I stood up. "You'd need a split lip for that."

"Owie." The princess crinkled her nose. "I think I'll pass."

"Wise choice," I said, yawning greatly.

It was a day or two, as promised, before Set was determined 'fit for travel.' The doctors gave Ariadne not only the medicine required to keep the addict calm for the next few days, but also taught her how to administer it properly using a syringe. She explained the whole procedure to me but, of course, I already knew how to use a syringe on everything from mice to a superliner, although the latter was not something I had any practical experience in.

No more need to force-feed Set pills, thank goodness.

• • •

Within three days of our arrival, we were back on course for Earth. I inwardly groaned at the delay, but knowing that Set wouldn't just up and die on us was a relief.

Ottoman remained uncharacteristically quiet, which I didn't take as a good sign. He was probably plotting something or biding his time for some kind of opening, which I was not obliged to give him. He had already tried talking his way out of this, which had failed, as had his escape attempt, so his next effort was bound to be impressive.

Of course, I figured Ariadne had an idea of what was going on, she just declined to tell me.

I wondered if her brother could be just as irritating, or if the princess was the exception to the King family trait pool. She didn't seem to be doing it intentionally, so I didn't let it bother me too much. Or at least, not as much as it should have bothered me.

We didn't notice anything unusual until we bounced off an asteroid. That in itself was nothing too unusual; ships often collided with rogue rocks and space debris, because, although equipped with optical sensors that mimicked eyes, it was extremely difficult to *see* inside a nebula. That's why they had pilots with Orbit-Time books and kept up with any news flashes about rogue asteroids. Of course, things always slip through the cracks.

It wasn't as though Ariadne and I actually knew what we were doing, anyway.

Usually these run-ins were barely dangerous even to a small ship like the *Lilstar*, resulting in only a few bruises and some broken falsebone, with a tear in the epidermis only on occasion and often with sick or old ships. The good news was that a tear didn't happen; the bad news was that the *Lilstar* was not as healthy as usual.

"What happened?" Ariadne said, rubbing her head where she'd hit it on the control console during the ship-to-asteroid collision.

"I think we hit a big rock," I said unhelpfully, closing my book quickly and attempting to look over the *Lilstar*'s controls. Even after almost a collective month aboard, I still had no idea what any of it meant.

"No, we didn't," the princess's impeccably smooth brow furrowed. "The ship's not in pain."

"I heard something crack, so she's got to be aching at least a little," I countered. Breaking falsebone sounded slightly lower in pitch than a breaking human bone, but it was still highly distinctive. I shivered imperceptibly, involuntarily imagining my own little bones breaking. I shook the thoughts out of my head.

Ariadne growled a little as she searched for some tangible evidence that I wasn't lying. She got up out of her chair, stepping carefully around the tied-up Lees, and in two quick strides was in the ship's innards. She came back quickly with a scowl on her face.

"You're right," she had finally found the evidence. "The *Lilstar*'s cracked a few ribs. It's not bad, it's just... um..."

"Um...?" I looked at Ariadne strangely. She blinked at me slowly and carefully.

"I dunno, Marcie..." the princess's eyes seemed to get really heavy. Her voice was thick and uncertain. For a brief second, her eyes opened wide and she looked down at her ankle. Sitting neatly on it was a dermal sleep patch. By the time she'd registered it, Ottoman reached out a grimy hand and clamped it tightly around Ariadne's ankle, keeping the patch in place until the princess toppled over, asleep.

The whole tableau had taken as long as it took me to yell "Crap!"

I reached down to grab the shock device, which I had stowed underneath my seat, hoping to get up out and ready before Ottoman could stop me.

I failed, miserably. Ottoman reached over the seat, grabbing a handful of my hair and pulling my head back against the headrest. He reached around the seat and pulled his forearm across my neck with immense pressure, effectively choking me. I coughed and sputtered as I tried to fight him off, reaching for any part of his person I could scratch, slap, or injure in some way. Unfortunately, I was getting weaker and more panicky by the minute, meaning my efforts were less than par.

He definitely won this particular battle.

"I suppose this makes us even for injury, Marcie," the sociopath whispered into my ear as he forced my entire head backward against the seat. His breath was hot as it raked across my jawline. I craned my eyes to look toward him, wildly trying to figure out how he had escaped.

"Don't worry," the insane man almost cooed. "I won't harm you or King until we've landed. I might need you to trick the communications."

In one of the most disgusting moments I'd ever faced in just over twenty years of existence, Ottoman kissed the side of my cheek slowly.

Fortunately, I didn't remain conscious long enough to vomit.

Thirteen

I woke up sputtering and coughing horribly. My throat felt like it was seriously bruised, I had a headache, and to top it all off, the bandage that had been protecting my still-healing nose was crooked and pinching one of my nostrils.

"Ngghh," I moaned underneath a swatch of tape that held my mouth shut. Fair is fair, I surmised unhappily.

"Mmph." Ariadne kicked my toe. She was situated in the same place Set had been, behind the pilot's seat, arms stretched up to connect her epidermis bonds with the ship's wall. I realized I was in the same position Ottoman had been, behind the copilot's seat.

"Humph," I huffed wordlessly. The princess rolled her eyes dramatically. I looked around for our should-be captives.

One of the twins/clones seemed to be sleeping in the copilot's seat just in front of me. Judging from what I knew of the two, it was probably the drugged-out Set. That left Ottoman hiding somewhere around the rest of the ship. It wasn't until he started snoring that I could pinpoint his location as sleeping on the ship's only open bunk. I growled a little.

I jerked my head toward Ottoman, trying to ask Ariadne how long he'd been like that. I have no idea if that was how she interpreted it or not, because her answer was a whole lot of odd winks and nods I couldn't decipher.

Instead of trying to establish communication with the princess again, I decided to try and work my way out of these bonds. Of course, I'd learned the epidermis trick at a skiptrace seminar and the people who developed said trick were extremely good at keeping wanted criminals under control. This was a tried-and-true method of villain incarceration and wasn't about to be subdued by an underprepared sprite.

Ariadne eventually cocked her head to one side, staring intently at the spot where Ottoman's arms had been secured over my head. She jutted out her chin as if to suggest I look at it. I craned my head as much as I could with my arms bound to the wall above my head. After a minute, I found what she was looking at.

The wall tissue where Ottoman's arms had been bound up looked almost necrotic, like it had been hit with some kind of acid or venom. This would definitely explain how he had escaped the second time. The epidermis was so bad, I had no doubt that the slats holding his wrists in place decayed to the point that they fell completely off. All he had to do was wait for the right moment to jump Ariadne and me. Since the ship's alarms didn't go off while the acid/venom ate through the epidermis in what would have been a painful process, I had to assume that the compound had some sort of anesthetic property. That would also explain why the ship bounced off an asteroid without so much as an *ouch*.

Venom and acids were tricky because the ReHy station orbiting Earth wouldn't care. Unlike viral, bacterial, or even fungal infections, venom-like compounds were not threatening to other organic ships or Earth's ecosystem. In fact, many old warships still had their weapons either because no one had bothered to rewrite their genetic facsimiles, or because they made for a useful defense against pirate attacks. The managers of the ReHy station might give the *Lilstar* a small dose of antivenom if they happened to detect the problem, but by the time the ship reached the ReHy station, the venom would have probably been processed by the *Lilstar's* natural defenses. Even if anyone detected and complained about the venom, it would be more than easy to spin up some story about some kind of huge pet snake getting loose.

I hate reptiles.

I moaned again, more loudly this time, as if the noise could stir up some kind of result or advantage I could use.

The evil twins/clones remained content to nap peacefully until my stomach started to growl loudly. I tried to scrunch up my legs as close as possible to keep it from doing that again. Though I was trying to get a reaction out of them earlier, I decided I needed more time to think my way out of this mess. Unfortunately, I was too late and Ottoman began to wake.

"Oh, is it feeding time?" Ottoman yawned grandly, taking time to stretch his arms and ease out of the bunk, the entire process taking about ten agonizing minutes. He face actually seemed a little swollen and red, like he'd had some kind of bad allergic reaction.

"Not to worry," he said, patting the princess's and my heads as he walked by, bringing a pair of low growls from each of us. "I'll feed you in a moment."

The sociopath stretched a little more before plopping down into the pilot's seat and humming a contemporary tune. At least someone was enjoying themselves.

"Oh, by the way, your ship is fine now. Aside from the broken ribs, of course, but those shouldn't affect our reentry," Ottoman said.

"What did you do to my ship?" Ariadne demanded, surprising me with how fast she'd licked the tape off. Of course, I wasn't certain how long she'd been awake before me.

"Oh, now that is a treat," Ottoman looked over his shoulder to grin at her. He pointed at the wound on the *Lilstar's* wall. "I suppose you saw that."

"What did you do to my ship?" Ariadne spit out the words one-by-one.

"I think Marcie will like this better," he got up from his seat and knelt down beside me. Watching me intently, he opened up his mouth widely, using his finger pull back his cheek.

I looked at him in horror. Sitting in the middle of his massively swollen cheek was an organic component. It didn't take me too long to realize that it was probably the source of the venom that had damaged the ship. The freaking sociopath had a *venom sac*. Venom that, given the condition of his cheeks and the almost acidic decay of his back molars, wasn't harmlessly absorbed by the more human-like parts of his body. I couldn't imagine that was in any way painless, and if his skin was reacting this badly, his bloodstream and nervous system were probably no better off. No wonder he was insane. I wondered briefly if Set had the same implants.

"Like it?" Ottoman showed the venom sac to Ariadne, who winced painfully. "That's what I get for being a son of Mill Hew."

"What is that stuff, *exactly*?" the princess asked. Ottoman stood up and walked into the ship's living area.

"Oh nothing, just your typical cytotoxic compound. Lots of pretty little proteins and polypeptides," Ottoman said, pulling a box of oat-and-wheat space rations from the pantry and pouring half of it into two bowls. He snapped his fingers for emphasis. "All non-resistant cell walls, poof, just like that. It's pretty brutal against ships and, in high doses, people. Of course, like real venom, it has its other advantages."

Anesthetic, totally called it, I muttered with my mouth still taped. I didn't bother actually licking the tape off my mouth, because I didn't have anything useful to say for the moment. Ottoman walked between us with a bowl of the space rations.

"You could have killed us all! If the compound reached the ship's heart, or eaten through its outer epidermis, we'd all be dead!" Ariadne yelled.

Ottoman shoveled a spoonful of the rations into her gaping mouth, which she proceeded to spit out on the floor in defiance. The sociopath growled and slapped her across the face. I felt the slap as if it had been my own face.

"Fine. I don't have to feed you," he cursed at Ariadne, getting up almost calmly.

"You—" Ariadne began an expletive, only to have Ottoman roughly cover her mouth with his palm. The other hand held a knife to her temple. Ariadne looked at him in genuine surprise, as neither she nor I had actually seen him take the knife out, despite the fact that it involved spilling the space rations all over the floor. I was considering his proximity for a chance to strike, but that knife looked very sharp.

"Shhh... I'd really hate to kill you and be forced to bribe my way through the ReHy station," Ottoman whispered to her. The princess seemed to get the message, although she looked much more angry than obedient.

The princess made a silent spitting motion to the sociopath's back as he moved to sit in her rightful seat, leaving the oat-and-wheat mess on the floor.

I'll get your ship back, I promised Ariadne.

• • •

Ariadne and I spent the better part of the morning scowling at one another. While it had started as a scowl of blame, anger, and accusation, it eventually morphed into a we're-so-screwed-and-out-of-ideas-what-should-we-do-next kind of expression. It was amazing what we could communicate through just the upper half of our faces. But even that didn't last long, and the princess eventually zoned out, flexing her arms and wrists a little.

I figured the exercise was hopeless, but if it made her feel better.

I must have been behaving to the sociopath's standards, because come supper time I was spoon-fed warmed rations. Ottoman made a point of feeding the princess last, although her stomach was growling loudly, which I didn't appreciate.

We sat there for what felt like an eternity before anything interesting happened. Well, more interesting than Ottoman busting out into a full-on jam session to music only he could hear. Not even Set joined him in his third rendition of a song by the band Bubblegum Goose. I'll admit, I was expecting his tastes to run more toward heavy metal, not sickeningly sweet pop. It's best not to try and understand insanity.

Things were going as okay as they could until the *Lilstar* started crying.

It was more of a whistle-like whimper, but it grew steadily louder as the painkilling compound in Ottoman's venom wore off and the ship began to feel the broken rib and what was probably massive bruising. While the crying didn't reach its maximum capacity, which was reserved for internal damage or serious infections, the whimpering was almost impossible to ignore.

Ottoman responded to it by trying to fix the issue. I watched him walk in and out of the ship's innards, where the rib had been broken, getting more and more frustrated by the minute. As far as I could tell, he was attempting to fix a sub-dermal problem with a pluripotent patch. Sure, that could fix some of the damage on this side of the epidermis, but it wouldn't do anything for the broken rib.

The best way to fix broken falsebone on a ship was by making an incision in the epidermis, cutting through the tough outer layers, and then snapping the bone back into place, wrapping a mesh sleeve around the break. It wasn't a super-complicated procedure, but for someone who didn't specialize in organic nursing, like I did, it was both gross and undoable without causing further injury.

Fixing the *Lilstar*'s broken rib would be child's play, but at a cost.

I could leave things as they were and the *Lilstar's* broken rib would definitely catch some attention from the ReHy station. They probably wouldn't let the ship land without fixing the issue and performing a final inspection to make sure the ship was worthy of a safe landing, which would mean a boarding party that could easily solve our predicament. The problem with this plan was that it left the *Lilstar* in pain for the duration of the trip to the ReHy station. That was beyond unfair. In fact, it bordered on cruel.

I didn't look at Ariadne as I tried to figure out my next step. While I knew the injury to the ship wasn't fatal, at least, that wasn't how the *Lilstar* was acting. Her cry hadn't reached that certain holy-crap-I'm-dying-somebody-help pitch just yet. If I fixed the injury, that could allow Ottoman and Set the chance to land on Earth and escape, and if I had judged them correctly, they were not harmless debtors. Having them loose on the streets was not a great thought.

So I could let the ship suffer, giving Ariadne and me a chance to escape, or I could fix the problem and essentially give the twins/clones a free pass through the ReHy station.

I finally glanced at Ariadne. She seemed to be on the edge of crying, flicking her eyes between Ottoman and her ship in concern. The princess caught me looking at her intently. I was glad she couldn't see me chewing my lip nervously.

"Aaahhhh!" Ottoman yelled from the ship's innards. It was followed by a corresponding *thump* and the *Lilstar's* crying jumped a few frequencies to more high-pitched than before.

That pig just smacked the *Lilstar*.

Ariadne screamed in anger, lunging at Ottoman's form as he entered the living area.

"Stop it!" I yelled, letting the tape I'd spent hours licking off fall from my mouth. "I can fix this!"

Ottoman stalked toward the cockpit with murder in his eyes.

"What?" he yelled, ripping what was left of the tape from my face. I didn't wince.

"I can fix the ship," I said, and stared the socio-path down. He looked my face up and down for a moment.

"How?" he asked.

"There is a bone repair kit in the back. It has an anesthetic, a sharp knife, and a mesh sleeve. I have to make an incision, put the bone back in place, and stabilize it," I outlined the procedure. Ottoman backed off slightly, thinking.

"I'm not giving you a knife," he said plainly.

"Then when we reach the ReHy station, the *Lilstar* will not be cleared for atmospheric entry, meaning that they'll send an inspection team and maybe even do the surgery themselves," I said in a measured tone. He seemed unconvinced. "You have my word I will not try to escape."

"I won't need your word, pet," Ottoman said with a sneer that meant he knew something I didn't. He took the shock device out of his pocket and stuck one of the pads on to Ariadne's forehead. "Setesh!"

The sleeping drug-addict stirred slightly and mumbled many incoherent words before turning around in his chair. At least he was looking better than he had a few days ago.

"I need you to hold on to this for me and, if Marcie here attempts to escape, you press this button and Ariadne here is dead," Ottoman said, looking at me for effect, as he gave his twin/clone the instructions. Set nodded sleepily and Ottoman repeated the instructions a second time, but more slowly.

Ottoman took a knife from his pocket and cut the slats holding me to the ship. Part of the epidermis slats were still in place, keeping my hands still bound together.

"I'll cut your hands free once we get to the innards," Ottoman said, hefting me roughly to my feet and shoving me down the hallway. I cast one last look at the cockpit, hoping maybe I'd have the opportunity to escape without forcing Set to fry Ariadne, but the drug addict seemed to be much more clear-headed. He even looked dangerous.

I decided against escaping. For the moment.

I moved to the ship's innards, which was comprised of an empty, hall-like structure running the width of the ship. Right in front was a relatively thin membrane that separated the actual, greenish-brown guts of the ship from the habitable region. Everything looked relatively healthy, by my evaluation. Ottoman's venom didn't seem to have had any real, long-lasting effects aside from the localized necrosis.

The broken rib was located along the ship's port side, or along the right when you first step into the innards, facing aft. The good news was that the falsebone had broken inward, not outward, meaning that it probably had not punctured the ship's outer epidermis layer. The bad news was that it had almost broken through the ship's inner epidermis layer and was in at least three or four separate pieces. It was going to require a lot more surgery than I had originally hoped.

"Can you fix it?" Ottoman asked, lurking in the doorway, keeping his distance from me.

"Yes," I said plainly, sticking my hands out so he could cut the remaining slats. The sociopath grabbed the slats and pulled me forward, closer to him. So close I could feel his breath on my face. He kissed the top of my forehead lightly, a gesture I took with a defiant, angry gaze. He merely laughed, bringing the slats that held my wrists up to his mouth, spitting a giant glob of his venom on them.

It only took seconds for the venom to kill all the cells in the epidermis, causing the slat to melt off my wrists. I winced through the pain as some of the venom that hadn't been busy eating the epidermis burned my own skin. Thankfully, it was much less effective on humans than ships.

It still hurt like the dickens, however.

"Get to work," Ottoman said, shoving me back into the innards. I shot him a glare, which he ignored, and walked left to the small alcove that held all of the ship's emergency medical supplies.

The broken bone kit was right up front, and I quickly had all of its contents organized on a tarp on the floor. It wasn't as sanitary as I would have liked, but beggars can't be choosers and the ReHy station would blast the *Lilstar* with a whole cocktail of antibiotics before it would be allowed to enter the atmosphere. The risk of a widespread infection before we actually made landfall was minimal.

The kit contained a lot of redundancy, which would come in handy if something else went wrong. There were at least three knives of varying sizes since normal scalpels were entirely too small to be useful when cutting into a large organic structure, two full sets of clamps for keeping damaged arteries closed until they could be stitched, biodegradable thread, an over-sized needle, for the stitches themselves, a metallic-like mesh with a hard metal splint that could be wrapped directly around the bone to provide stability, a local anesthetic to numb the area for surgery, a massive bottle of iodine, a few rolls of tape to keep the incision from either healing back on itself or bleeding, multiple pairs of gloves, masks, and two chemical-based headlamp.

The kit was also one roll of tape short - which was being used for keeping whoever happened to be captive at the time quiet. Despite this shortage, there was still plenty left over.

The first step was to don the rubber gloves, face mask, and chemical headlamp. The gloves and mask were fairly straightforward, basic rubber and mesh that created a barrier between myself and the ship. Even though the *Lilstar* had successfully incorporated me and my germs into its own microecosystem, I still had a few nasty bugs that could wreak havoc on a ship's open wound, making the gloves and mask a definite fashion choice for on-the-spot organic ship surgery.

The headlight was a bit more complicated, being comprised of three parts: a small vial of one chemical component, a larger vial of a second component, and a lens-like apparatus. The larger vial was basically a sphere on top of a throat that was about two inches or so in length. Inside the larger vial, sitting right on top of the throat, was the small, much more delicate vial that had an opening closed off by a small ball-bearing. This kept both of the liquids separate before the headlight was needed.

The ball-bearing was attached to a small string that ran down the throat, through a rubber seal, and out with a long enough tail to grasp. Using the light was as easy as pulling on the string, releasing the ball-bearing from the smaller vial and allowing the two chemicals to mix. It produced an almost-white glow that wasn't fantastic, but would be enough to see for surgery.

Once I had activated the headlight and put it on, I picked up the bottle of iodine and painted the entire area around the broken falsebone. The smell was incredibly strong, causing Ottoman to double over in a coughing fit. I thought about taking advantage of it - until I saw him wave back down into the ship, probably to Set who was poised and ready to zap the crap out of Ariadne over an unexpected coughing fit. I decided just to stick with the task at hand.

The next step was to take the local anesthetic and fill the sizable syringe as much as I could, taking care to tap out the extra air that had been trapped inside. I walked up to the site of the broken bone. Being as gentle as I could, I injected the anesthetic at different points around the wound.

I knew it was working because the *Lilstar* finally stopped crying.

After I was sure the ship couldn't feel any pain in the local area, I ran my hand gently across the break, trying to ascertain the exact type of injury it was and what kind of damage it had caused. I could barely make out the falsebone structure through the sem - translucent epidermis. It seemed that the rib was in three salvageable pieces. It was a significant wound, but there was surprisingly minimal tissue or vessel damage from it. Of course, I'd probably cause more damage creating an incision in the epidermis and trying to put the falsebone back together into something that looked like a functional ship's rib.

That, unfortunately, was going to hurt and there was no general anesthetic I could give the *Lilstar* to make it go away. The only places that were allowed to have that kind of anesthetic in stock were shipyards that fixed bones like this on a regular basis.

The other problem was that I was going to need an assistant for this. The four-inch-diameter falsebone was broken inward, making it difficult to push back into place *and* put the mesh splint on it at the same time. Plus, I wasn't certain I was actually strong enough to pop the rib back into place anyway. Falsebone was almost as strong as steel and far less malleable.

I looked at the sociopath, who had a nasty scowl on his face.

"I need help," I said plainly. "Someone has to hold the bone in place while I put the mesh on."

"I'm not releasing Miss King," Ottoman said.

"No, I figured you would help," I said honestly. Ottoman snorted at me.

"I'm not going anywhere near you with those knives nearby, imp," Ottoman grinned wolfishly. I took a step toward him.

"Then you open up the possibility of a ReHy station inspector sending a team of nurses to board the ship and fix the rib themselves, in the process discovering this entire hostage situation. My only concern right now is fixing this ship, which is hurting. I'm not going to try to escape," I spoke the words in a measured, don't-mess-with-me tone. I was not lying, either, which Ottoman seemed to recognize.

"Setesh, come stand here and watch what's going on," the sociopath called his twin/clone. The drug addict stumbled down the narrow hall and took Ottoman's place in the threshold. "If Marcie does something wrong, fry Miss King."

Set nodded slowly, and Ottoman followed me to the injury. He put on the plastic gloves and mask that I gestured to. He almost looked like he could be an actual organic nurse, if I did know he was a cold-blooded killer.

Also the 'LOVER' face tattoo was a little obvious.

I handed the sociopath a roll of tape from the kit and picked up one of the knives.

"I'm going to cut down to the falsebone. You put tape along either side of the incision so that it doesn't try to heal itself before I can do anything else. Got it?" I asked, feeling very much like I was a teacher's assistant for the younger organic biology classes.

"How about I make the cut, you tape it up?" Ottoman reached for the knife I held.

"Don't get grabby," I chastised him. "You'll only cause more damage than you fix."

The sociopath sighed loudly in resignation.

Satisfied he wouldn't try to take the knife again, I went to the injury and began the incision, trying to cut as straight as possible while avoiding any of the arteries and veins that ran along the ship's ribcage. The thousands of small capillaries I had to cut through began to ooze nutrient-rich...ooze. Organic structures didn't have blood by any stretch of the imagination, but they did utilize a fluidic system that acted similarly to the circulatory system found in more natural beings, like humans. It helped mostly with transporting nutrients and for space-side injuries, would clot very quickly. Inside, however, it just oozed, making the tape invaluable.

It took quite a while to cut the incision, despite the fact that the epidermis layer wasn't all that thick and the knife I had was really sharp. Ship epidermis was designed quite a bit tougher than its building counterparts for the simple reason that, in atmosphere, a hole in the wall was a lot less dangerous than in the vastness of space. At least there was very little muscle in this region, so it was just a lot of really tough skin that I had to cut. There was a bit of connective tissue between the falsebone and the skin, but it was already damaged from the break, so I didn't have to cut through it.

When I was finally done with the incision, I gently pulled back the two sides, allowing Ottoman to apply the tape. Once I was satisfied that the incision wasn't going to close in on itself and that most of the bleeding was stopped, I released the two halves a bit, taking a moment to survey the damage more closely.

The falsebone was broken, as I had surmised, into three big pieces with a few smaller shards all around. I made Ottoman hold one side of the incision back so I could take out the shards. They wouldn't heal properly even if I could put them back together, so it was easier just to remove them.

Once I had cleaned up the area, I looked carefully at the massive artery that ran alongside the left of the rib to make sure it hadn't been punctured by any of the broken falsebone. After I had confirmed it was intact, I grasped it gently, running my hand up and down, feeling for any hidden weaknesses along the walls. The gloves made that somewhat difficult, but with a visual inspection it appeared to be a relatively strong artery. I could even feel the *Lilstar*'s heart pumping through it.

The next task was setting the rib to rights. I decided the best way to fix this would be to straighten out the two relatively intact pieces of falsebone and then try to work the third piece into place. It was a reasonable plan, of course, and it wasn't even the most complicated fracture I had ever had to deal with.

It might have been one of the biggest, since I never actually finished my education as an organic nurse, but it definitely wasn't the most complicated.

The difficult part was that since the broken section was bent inward, I'd have to push the pieces out as opposed to pulling them in. I tentatively tugged at the falsebone. The *Lilstar* released a single, whistling note as sort of a hey-you-know-that-hurt-a-little. Even with the local anesthetic, it was still going to suck for the ship. I took a deep breath and braced myself, then I shoved up against the broken falsebone with as much force as I could muster.

The *Lilstar* let out a few more notes that I tried very hard to ignore.

After a few tries to make sure I wasn't strong enough, I motioned for Ottoman to push the rib back together. He shoved against it as hard as he could, succeeding on the first try. Unfortunately, he also screwed up big time. As the falsebone snapped into place, his left hand slipped and hit the artery dead on, tearing a big hole into the side of it and causing it to spew nutrient-rich ooze everywhere. The *Lilstar* began to shriek horribly.

"You idiot!" I screamed, "Get out of my way!" I reached for Ottoman's right hand and pulling it across me, exposing his front. As he was bewildered at what was going on and blinded by a spray of nutrient ooze, I kneed him where it hurt. Honestly it was just to get him out of the way as quickly as possible, but I couldn't say I hadn't been waiting for the opportunity.

I wrapped both my hands around the broken artery to stop the bleeding and looked back over my shoulder at Ottoman. He didn't seem to be too retaliatory over my attacking him and Set was nowhere to be found.

"Get up, you big baby! Before the ship bleeds out!" I yelled at Ottoman. He stood up slowly, with murder lurking in his eyes.

I ignored it.

"I need two of those clamps. Now!" I gestured to the metallic clamps on the tarp. Ottoman, probably despite himself, reached down and grabbed the clamps. "Put one above and one below my hands."

The sociopath complied, successfully clamping off the artery. I slowly released my hands to make sure it wasn't still bleeding. While it was leaking a little nutrient ooze, it wasn't as bad as it had been. I dabbed my forehead on my sleeve. Of course, Ottoman couldn't just leave me alone. He grabbed a handful of my hair and yanked my head back so I'd have to look at his face. He also pressed one of the knives from the bone mending kit up against my neck. I could feel the metal biting into my skin.

"Don't ever do that again," he whispered harshly. Although I had a million comebacks of varying degrees of crass, I decided just to keep my mouth shut. Thankfully he got distracted.

"Where have you been?" he spat at Set as the drug addict reappeared.

"Restroom. These meds are kicker," Set said. Internally, I had a lot of thanks to give that the drug addict wasn't there to see me attack his twin/clone. If he had been, Ariadne would definitely be toast by now.

Despite this interruption, the rest of the surgery was relatively easy. I stitched up the artery with the biodegradable thread, meaning I wouldn't have to come back and remove the stitches after the artery had healed. The good news was that it was much less delicate work than if it were on a human being, meaning I could go at a relatively fast pace and get back to the broken falsebone quickly.

Ottoman held the three falsebone fragments in place while I wrapped the mesh sleeve around the whole thing. It was designed to fit any of the *Lilstar's* fifty-plus ribs that served as the main structure for the ship's interior. In some ways, the ship was one big ribcage with plenty of room and protection to house the small, livable interior and the innards needed for the organic components to function.

I tugged the sleeve on tight with the split on the inside of the rib, shoring up the break. Once I had fitted the sleeve and cut off the excess mesh, the final step was to take the tape off and let the incision seal once again, providing the bone with even more stability. It was immensely satisfying to watch the epidermis seal without a crack or scar. There would be some scar tissue underneath, of course, and nerve damage was inevitable, meaning the *Lilstar* would always be a little numb in that spot, but everything looked much healthier than it had been. Plus, the ship wasn't crying anymore.

The mesh was now a permanent part of the ship's rib, unless some strange incident forced surgeons at a shipyard to cut it out. That was not necessarily unheard of, especially if the mesh was causing any sort of major discomfort to the ship. This was a good mesh sleeve, however, and I doubted it would ever need to be removed.

After being assured that all of the bone kit's knives were accounted for, Ottoman marched me back to my seat next to Ariadne. I felt exhausted, even though the surgery had only taken an hour at the most. I had forgotten what it felt like to be an organic nurse. In some ways, I was glad that wasn't my current path, but it would definitely come in handy if I stuck around with Ariadne and the *Lilstar*.

I'm sure Ariadne had more than her fair share of knowledge regarding ship first-aid and even basic surgery skills. All pilots had to pass the rudimentary organic biology exams. Having studied to be an organic nurse, however, made me feel much more useful when we were bouncing between destinations and there wasn't any skiptracing to be done.

I sighed heavily, trying to settle comfortably in a very uncomfortable position. At least Ottoman had let me wash most of the nutrient ooze from my hands and face. Although it didn't have any sort of smell, it got sticky after a while.

"Thank you," Ariadne whispered, tape hanging off her face.

I gave her a genuine smile.

"Yeah, I almost got you killed," I confessed. She nodded her head understandingly.

FOURTEEN

I bided my time and strength in hopes of retaking the ship before the next meal. And the next. And the meal after that. We finally made it to the ReHy station and I hadn't come up with any great ideas. The *Lilstar* seemed to be doing perfectly well with the mended rib. There was an almost undetectable sort of *shudder* whenever we passed through a pocket of ionized helium and the drastic change in temperature caused some discomfort to the ship's injury. There was no crying, however, which I took to be a good sign.

I was glad the ship seemed to be feeling better, even if it meant we'd have to figure out Plan B for escaping. Unless someone from the ReHy really thought that my patch-up job on the *Lilstar's* injury was a threat to itself and its crew, it was highly unlikely an inspector would board the ship. To add to my stress, my shoulders were cramping up something fierce; Ottoman let us loose far less often than we let him loose.

"Alright" Ottoman called the princess and me something very rude as the *Lilstar* pulled into the ReHy station's queue. Apparently, our displays of mental and physical defiance soured his impressions of us. He hadn't used the terms 'pet' or 'imp' since the *Lilstar*'s surgery. "Miss King, you'll stay with me and ensure that everything is in order for the station master, and Miss Dunn, you'll accompany my friend to the lavatory. Of course, with these attached."

Under muffled protests, Ottoman placed one shock disc to my forehead and the other to Ariadne's. He handed the device to the semi-lucid Set, once again explaining the rules of the shock device to the drug addict.

"It's just like before. Activate this whenever they seem to be getting uppity, do you understand me, Setesh?" The addict nodded a weary reply and Ottoman moved to slash the epidermis that held me to the ship. I was tempted to try and escape then and there with Ottoman within easy range of kicking, punching, or biting if I tried really hard, but thought better of it. Although Set seemed placid, I didn't know which setting the shock device was on.

And, either way, the disc was stuck to my *head*. Ariadne was probably familiar with the sensation of a small, rubber-like disc fully capable of frying one's entire brain by now, but it made me quite uncomfortable.

Ottoman hefted me up roughly and pushed me down the corridor to the ship's bathroom, shoving me into the narrow shower and reattaching the epidermis that bound me to the shower's floor. My knees came up to my chin with my arms wrapped around them. I glared at the sociopath until he vanished back down the corridor, returning a moment later with Set.

"Go sit with Marcie, okay?" he cooed to his twin/clone. The addict nodded and started toward the shower. Ottoman followed, ensuring Set's comfort before placing the second of the shock pads to my chest just above my heart. "This is set to the maximum level. Only a few meager layers of bone and skin are between your brain and heart and the discs. I've suggested to Miss King that she obey me to the letter or I may activate the device."

I jerked my head toward Set, who was literally toe-to-toe with me and dozing.

"I really can't have him wandering around in his fugue state; this is a two-person craft, if you remember, and Earth has always been so picky about that. I suppose, if you get zapped and die, he does, but I'm hopeful your friend will see everything my way," Ottoman said, with what could have been a reassuring smile if it had been on pretty much anyone else's face.

The sociopath turned to leave, sliding the shower's translucent falsebone door closed. I heard the bathroom's iris door open and close slowly, and then it was just me and Set.

I yelled internally with all of the helpless anger I'd built up over the past day and a half, while making some feeble attempt to yank my bonds free from the shower floor. It mostly just bruised my wrists and made me angrier. Set moaned slightly in reply, but didn't stir.

After venting what little I could, I tried to look at the situation rationally. What could I do that would get Ariadne and me out of here without making

Ottoman fry my entire nervous system? I stared up at a few patches of beneficial and bioluminescent fungi that covered the shower's ceiling like they made up some kind of all-answers-oracle, which of course they didn't.

The ReHy station itself wouldn't provide much of an opportunity for escape, given that it required very little contact between stationmasters and pilots. The short-range radio was more than enough to confirm the ship's identification, Ariadne's pilot's license, and a list of vaccines and injuries the *Lilstar* had in the past few months, including the broken rib I'd repaired. While it was entirely possible a nervous stationmaster might order the ship to be inspected because of the injury, that was unlikely. Not only was I a great surgeon, but the ReHy station would undoubtedly be able to see that the rib was not that serious and had been treated properly.

There wasn't much to the ReHy stations. They had a fleet of smaller inspection ships, and ships that functioned a lot like tug boats, guiding bigger, clunkier superliners and such into the station itself. ReHy stations themselves have been described a number of ways in varying degrees of accuracy, but I always saw them as giant, legless frogs with next to no discernible body and one, big, gaping maw that had to be miles across. Unlike most organic ships, ReHy stations were not matured in a shipyard and *then* slung into space. Since their internal structure more closely resembled the simplicity of a single-cell organism, it didn't require the constant monitoring of scientists, surgeons, and genetic facsimile experts that normal ships did to make sure everything was growing properly. This meant that ReHy stations could be grown partially on Earth and then sent into orbit to mature to full-size.

The station's big mouth would open up every six to twelve hours, essentially swallowing dozens of ships at a time. Once inside the station, the ships were subjected to a humid environment and to a special treatment applied via a fleet of small lamprey-like ships that oozed a lotion from their mouths, rehydrating the ships in preparation for the considerably moister atmosphere on Earth. This kept the outer epidermis, which had hardened and formed a shell in space, from cracking and splitting upon reentry, spilling the ship's entire complement halfway to the surface.

I needn't discuss the horror stories involved with that.

ReHy stations also subject ships to standard antibiotics and other treatments to ensure no new space pathogen would be introduced to Earth's ecosystem. While humanity had been traveling both its own system and the Centauri for thousands of years now and had developed innate immunities to most interstellar pathogens, there was still a chance a plague could be introduced that could wipe out most life on Earth, organic structure and human alike. It was always better to be safe than sorry.

I listened carefully, trying to make out any of the words Ariadne and Ottoman were exchanging with the station master. The interview seemed to go one slightly longer than usual, which was not a surprise.

Ariadne was talking very calmly to the station master, probably convincing him that the broken rib was not in any danger of becoming worse. The station master finally signed off, and after many minutes of radio silence and no sudden course changes from the *Lilstar* to pull her out of the queue for an inspection, I presumed that the ship was given the all-clear to descend to Earth once the ReHy station had done its job.

Entering the ReHy station felt like nothing, which was always surprising. It looks like a big mouth inhaling ships, but since there isn't any significant atmosphere in space, nebulous gases being too light to be considered a real atmosphere, there isn't any pull from the station as there would be if it was actually taking a big, deep breath. Of course, given the bathroom was windowless, I couldn't even see how dark it got once the mouth closed and the *Lilstar*, with probably a dozen or so other ships of varying sizes, sat patiently inside the station's mouth, waiting for what was basically a spa treatment.

It was an incredibly long set of hours sitting in one place as the sauna did its job. I spent most of those hours licking the tape off my mouth.

"Phoo," I said, finally free to speak. Of course, my companion was a strung-out druggy who mostly just moaned incoherently and twitched on occasion.

"Hey," I said, tapping Set's foot with my toe.

"Hush," he said, almost coherently.

"No. I will not hush. I will never hush so long as your evil doppelgänger is holding me, my friend, and my friend's ship hostage!" I stated in an angry whisper. Set rolled a baggy, blood-shot eye toward me.

"You look like a unicorn," he said unhelpfully.

"Would you stop it with the unicorns? What does that have to do with *anything*?!" I asked him incredulously.

"Your thingie," Set continued, pointing slightly to my forehead. "It looks like a horn kind of thing."

"You mean, the thingie that has the potential to kill all of us?" I asked, a little incredulous.

Set actually smiled as he nodded in reply. He had the expression of a five-year-old who had just stepped on his younger sibling's paper crane.

I stared at the man for a good long minute, trying to figure out exactly what to say next. How does one hold a conversation with a person who wasn't all there by choice?

"You're missing more than a few bones upstairs, aren't you?" I said.

"It's better that way," Set said in a tone that sounded very honest but a little sing-song. "I was worse than him, before."

"Adams rot your brain out," I commented.

"That's the idea. That's why I take them. At least now I'm not quite so...violent," Set said. "Actually, it was Ottoman's idea. They were going to kick me out until the adams calmed me down. Mill Hew doesn't handle failures. Not even ones with brothers."

The drug addict's eyes began to well up as he brought his knees up to his chest. I internally removed myself from the situation completely, like I had a million times before when someone violent decided to cry in front of me. Whether or not Set was trying to manipulate me or was genuinely crying about the situation was irrelevant.

"Don't make me pity you," I said quietly.

"Did I ask for pity?" Set sighed. "I don't need pity. I don't even care about it."

Unfortunately, I did pity him, as much as neither of us wanted that. It wasn't for the addiction, however, but more for whatever events had led to it. I glared at the addict for a long time as he sat there, weeping silently. I tried to think of a way I could steer the conversation to my favor. The addict had a lot going on and maybe just enough of a conscience, evidenced by his crying fit, to make something work.

Of course, at this point I also realized that Set was just lucid enough to make tricking him difficult. He was less of the bumbling idiot he had been when we first met, probably an effect of being off the adams for at least a week.

"At least you seem remorseful about the whole deal," I commented.

"Ottoman regrets things, but he won't give himself up for emptiness," the addict said. "He's always been afraid of it, of being empty. I was always afraid of spiders."

"I've always been afraid of not being able to protect people," I said truthfully. My brother, for example; he went away without even the slightest chance of me saving him. I didn't need to be a hero, I just needed to be a guardian. "Like right now."

Set shrugged.

"I 'spose it's not *really* my problem," he said.

"Of course, if Ariadne messes something up and I get my brains fried, you'll undoubtedly come with me," I reasoned.

"Imagine how empty that'd leave me," the addict said wistfully. This conversation was going in the wrong direction.

"Don't make me kick you in the face." I gave up trying to reason or persuade the addict into sense.

"I saw you trip over the deck for no reason the other day. I doubt you have that much coordination," Set said, after eying my wrists-bound-to-the-floor position.

I growled.

Given the fact that I *hadn't* yet been fried by my hostage keeper, I could reasonably assume that everything was going according to the sociopath's wishes. And since there hadn't yet been an inspection, it was also reasonable to assume that they'd deemed the *Lilstar* safe for descent, meaning the next best thing for Ariadne and me to do was wait until we finally landed.

"Do you know where we are going?" I asked the addict. Set gave another annoying non-answer in the form of a shrug.

"Ottoman doesn't tell me anything. Some things, but not something like that," he said.

"Where do you usually go on Earth?" I pressed.

"Somewhere in the Olds. Ottoman has a…" Set's voice trailed off as he eyed me. "I don't care if you escape. I don't care if you die. I just want Ottoman to keep breathing."

"I can probably make that kind of deal," I said, trying not to feel too hopeful about making a deal with a strung-out addict who, purportedly, was even more dangerous than my ex-captive/now-captor. "If you'll help me and Ariadne escape."

"I dunno if I want to make *that* kind of deal." Set laughed weakly.

"Will Ottoman kill us when we land?"

"Probably."

"Then I'll have to kill him first."

"I don't think you can do that," Set said, although he looked me over warily.

"Of course I can," I said, building up confidence it the idea. Believing what you are bluffing about is incredibly important. Although I *would* kill Ottoman if he threatened either Ariadne or myself in any serious way, I wasn't as bent on the idea as I pretended to be. "But I don't have to if you help me."

"I'm just kidding, I don't care if Ottoman dies," Set said the words easily. Unfortunately, he was a bad liar.

"I doubt that. You care about Ottoman, and you don't want me to kill him," I said. Set swallowed loudly enough for me to hear it as he looked at me. "He's the only person in this world that might understand you."

Set silently watched me until the *Lilstar* was finally underway for descent. His face was dull but worried, the kind of worry that I knew was gnawing his brain even more than any adams ever could. He really did have an affection for Ottoman, just like the sociopath seemed to care for him. It was the twins/clones' only really obvious weakness. That and maybe spiders.

It wasn't until the *Lilstar* entered the rocky upper atmosphere that he decided to say anything.

"Fine. But Ottoman lives through this."

Fifteen

"**H**ow are we doing, Set and, well, you?" Ottoman said, the 'you' rolling out of his mouth with a great deal of disgust. At least it was better than an expletive. The *Lilstar* had landed a few minutes ago and, from what I could tell, it was raining heavily outside. It had been a rough descent with the ship's tender rib, and on more than one occasion, I could hear Ottoman and Ariadne yelling at each other about whatever technical problems arose. Still, it was a better landing than that one time I was on a 97-year-old cruiser which had a pulmonary blockage halfway down to the planet's surface. The poor ship managed to hold on until about ten feet above ground, after which it bounced painfully for about a hundred feet. Always wear your safety belts, kids.

"Mhmmph," Set said, pretending to doze better than I could have. I merely glared at the sociopath.

"Wake up, Setesh, we need to get moving." Ottoman's coo was a little more urgent than usual, although it still took a great deal of prying to get the addict out of the shower. When Ottoman finally succeeded in that task, Set was upright, but remained bleary-eyed and a little wobbly on his feet.

253

No doubt about it, the addict was an excellent actor.

I growled low in my throat for show.

"Tsk, tsk; so unhappy," Ottoman said, producing the shock device controller for me to see. "No worries; we've landed and will be disembarking in just a moment. You and Miss King will, unfortunately, not be coming with us."

He almost grinned at me as he pressed the shock device's button, frying my entire nervous system and leaving me a smoldering corpse on an abandoned ship, a testament to my complete and utter failure as a skiptrace and the greater failure of the skiptracing community to train and prepare their newest skiptraces for the villainous ruffians they might encounter. It was an entirely philosophical situation that could cause lasting repercussions across the whole of the system and even into Centauri space, but would be traced back to one solitary moment where a barely-trained skiptrace got her brains scrambled by her overzealous, venom-packing quarry. It could, for certain, eventually lead to the downfall of the skiptracing community as a whole, leading to rampant lawlessness across the whole of humanity.

Except none of that happened. The shock device didn't fry me to a crisp and the greater skiptracing community was not held liable for my failure. I gave Ottoman my evilest grin, which of course he couldn't see because my mouth was still taped.

As with most people, his first reaction was to press the shock device button again, and then hit it a few times in his hand in frustration. Just before he gave up on the Centauri device and slashed my throat with one of the many knives I knew he had, Set came up behind his twin/clone and with a surprising amount of skill, wrapped his arm around Ottoman's neck in a sleeper hold.

Ottoman was, of course, irate and attempted to plead and fight off his compatriot, but Set refused to yield until the sociopath was unconscious. Actually, he held on a little longer than that. So long, in fact, I thought he'd actually kill Ottoman. Although Ottoman's bounty was probably closer to alive-or-dead than just plain old alive, I really didn't want to open that particular can of worms at the moment. Besides, Set was scaring me. At least Ottoman had been blunt about his murderous side, Set was letting his get away with him.

"Stop!" I shouted under the tape. It proved to be just enough to break whatever bloodthirsty trance had come over Set, and he dropped his slightly-purple but still breathing twin/clone.

Set removed his twin/clone's knife from its scabbard and cut me free of the ship. I ripped the tape off my mouth quickly, getting out of the shower and going to the medicine cabinet.

"I thought you wanted him alive," I said, turning back to Set. The addict's eyes were hollow.

"Me too," he said. I swallowed painfully and offered my hand to shake. He took it, falling asleep almost immediately as the dermal patch went to work. I breathed a little easier as he slumped to the floor.

"You're never going to learn that trick, are you?" I muttered, taking the epidermis slats that had been holding me to the ship and securing both the Lees to the bathroom floor. I could move them later.

I walked into the cockpit, finding Ariadne slumped over in the pilot's seat, at least eight dermal patches covering her arms and face. I ripped them off as quickly as I could, thankful she was still breathing and her pulse was strong and steady. One patch was guaranteed for a full night's sleep; eight were guaranteed to stop your heart in about half an hour.

"Wake up, princess!" I said harshly as I removed the last patch. Ariadne blinked many times, trying to speak repeatedly but failing. Finally, after becoming very frustrated, she tried again.

"They've got—"

"Shh!" I clamped a hand over her mouth for a minute, hearing voices outside. It was difficult to pick up because it was obviously in the middle of a fairly impressive downpour, but these guys were being loud about whatever their discussion was.

Finally Ariadne pried my hand off her mouth.

"Friends! Marcie, Ottoman has friends! *Those* friends!" she said, panicked.

"How many?" I whispered quietly, wishing the *Lilstar*'s opaque eyelid was open.

"I dunno. Probably more than we can take. Especially if they are like the Lees," Ariadne said, trying to look through the eyelid too. The voices were getting closer.

My thoughts ran around loudly inside my head as I tried to figure out the next best move. I collected the shock device, flipping the toggles on the pads back to the ON position. The Centauri were definitely creatures of safety, designing the shock pads with independent ON/OFF switches to prevent any accidental use of the device. Given that, I surmised the device wasn't really a weapon, but that was ponderings for another time. I handed Ottoman's knife to Ariadne and we crouched by the door, prepared to run out like our lives depended on it.

"Ready?" Ariadne asked in a whisper. The voices seemed to be coming from directly in front of the ship, which was both good and bad. Good, because that meant the princess and I could exit the ship's only hatch without being directly confronted. The bad was that whoever was outside would be able to see the ship's door opening, and probably see which direction we were traveling.

"Wait," I said, walking back into the ship's living quarters. I plucked my favorite pair of jeans off the bunk and tied them around my waist.

"Is now really the time for these kinds of fashion choices?" Ariadne asked in an almost rude and very impatient voice.

"These jeans just might save our lives someday," I whispered harshly. The princess didn't counter. She counted down on her fingers, pressing the mechanism for the door's iris promptly once she'd reached three. I barely waited for the iris to open fully before I leapt out, landing a little roughly on the shipyard's concrete pad. I scrambled back to my feet and set out in a dead run as far from the *Lilstar* as I could get. I heard some shouting, but I ignored it.

It was almost impossible to see anything through the fact that it was nighttime and raining. Not even the Centauri-grade floodlight that seemed to beckon me forward could fully pierce the deluge. I panicked slightly when I heard footsteps behind me, which in turn made me miss a whole, nasty pothole in front of me. My foot went out from under me and I landed solidly on the ground.

"Ow," I muttered a curse as the footsteps got even closer. By this time, however, I recognized it as the princess.

"Get up, you ninny!" Ariadne cried, as she helped pull me to my feet.

"This way!" she shouted, and veered off to the right.

It was about a minute of blind jogging before we made it to the enormous organic building. Light could be seen from a few glass-implant windows and, thankfully, the door was open.

I couldn't even begin to imagine what we looked like, two damp and bruised sprites suddenly entering a warm, clean, and semi-bustling terminal. It wasn't as packed as I would have liked for escaping, but it was better than tromping around the airfield all day.

"Ladies room is this way; we can dry off and take a breather," the princess said without really stopping inside the door. I continued to follow.

We wound our way past the main public area and toward the innards of the building that I wasn't so sure we should actually be in. I didn't argue with

Ariadne, however, who seemed to know exactly where we needed to be. Besides, there were very few people around, and those who were didn't seem to care about the two of us, lost children though we might look.

The building itself went on for a lot longer than I thought it should have, but the biggest kicker was the fact that it was made like a bunker. It was a clearly-visible fusion of Earth and Centauri technologies that made it little less than a cyborg. Electronic touch screens decorated the walls, and metal shunts, designed to be flexible and manipulative to a degree, stuck out from the layers of epidermis like a bad piercing. I doubted this building had any true nerve endings left, just as much as I figured it would have armor plating, both metallic and super-dense falsebone, covering the outside.

After we passed the sixth uniformed officer, a deer-eyed junior lieutenant if I knew the insignia on her shoulders, I began to get a sneaking suspicion about this place. I held my tongue until we'd arrived at a ladies' locker room, a hormone-sniffer locked room complete with showers and a sauna. The sniffer lock was just impressive enough to keep any male, including our ex-captives/ex-captors out, meaning Ariadne and I could take all the breather we needed.

"Where are we?" I asked the princess point-blank as she went to go pillage a stack of new towels.

"Carlion's Foremost Pilot's Academy, Olds III," she said, not really looking me in the face.

"A *military* base?" I asked, voice squeaking in disbelief. That would explain all of the uniforms and the fact that the building was an incredible abomination to organic craft.

"Shhh!" Ariadne whispered fiercely. "Technically, it was an academy, not a base, and now it's not even either, you ninny. It's strictly a pilot's school, completely open to the public."

"That's what they say to the public, but what sort of pilot's school has ranks?" I demanded, forgetting to dry my hair.

"Look," Ariadne said, getting up in my face. "I don't care what your opinion is of the military. I don't care what the public thinks of the military. They protected us and I was more than honored to go to school here. I'm a better pilot than any commercially-taught U.C. lackey could ever think to be because *I* was trained for combat. They also taught me how to fight that fancy martial arts stuff that saved our butts on Myrkheim, so take that!"

I blinked in surprise.

"I have no problem with the military. My brother was a corporal before the media forced him and his whole division out. The military gave him a safe place to be, as ironic as that sounds, and I would have followed him if I could," I said quietly. "I just have a problem that we *broke into* a military base. Won't that be, I dunno, treason or something?"

The princess' eyebrows went up in a motion that was a little surprised, a little confused, and just a touch embarrassed.

"Oh," she said, still processing what I'd said. "OH. No, it's not treason. Firstly, this place calls itself a civilian pilot's school, so they can't make a big deal of it with the media watchdogs on their case and secondly, if anyone shows up, I know the commandant. He'd let us stay and rest even if he knew we were here."

"Whew," I sighed in relief, laughing just a little.

Ariadne grinned.

"You're all right, Marcie Dunn."

"I could say the same to you, Ariadne King," I said, grinning.

A thought suddenly struck me.

"If you were trained for combat piloting, how'd you nearly hit an entire space station after we left Earth?" I put my hands on my hips to demand an answer.

The princess blinked at me.

"I'm going to take a shower," she said, and dashed off.

I was a little too unsettled to enjoy a comfortable shower, despite the fact that I was covered nearly head-to-toe in mud. After drying off and partaking in a quick snack from a nearby vending machine, I tried to figure out what our next move would be. At the moment, we were lacking everything. Our ship, our quarry, our chance for actually getting out of debt, and any respect we might have had in the skiptracing community. My dried algae flakes tasted like overly salted sadness.

Of course, we had two options: admit defeat, turn in our skiptrace license as failures, and go find jobs that normal human beings would take like managers, repairmen, and organic nurses. The second option was to re-capture the Lees and try to salvage our current career paths. I tried to figure out how we could accomplish that as I set my favorite jeans out to dry.

I swore loudly as I realized the shock device was no longer safely tucked into my pocket, surmising it must have fallen when I slipped outside. There was no real way I was going back outside to get it in the pouring rain with a whole bunch of blackguards chasing us. Just another setback to add to the list.

I stretched out across a bench that ran in front of the metallic lockers, musing how things had gone so completely wrong so quickly. I wouldn't necessarily mind a normal job. Actually, it would probably suck. Yes, I could pass myself off as an organic nurse, but tending houses with the sniffles all day seemed anticlimactic. To be honest, I kind of enjoyed the skiptrace life. It was a familiar challenge I'd been baptized into after my brother's death and it didn't just use one of my skills, like organic nursing would, it used most if not all of them. My head for strategy, my problem-solving skills, my ability to give as good as I get, and even my mediocre acting ability were useful to skiptracing.

Plus I was still technically in Ariadne's debt and would forever be in said debt if I became an entry-level organic nurse. I could always work for the princess in her parcel delivery job, as long as Ottoman and Set hadn't completely wrecked the

Lilstar. How many years would it take to pay off radiation therapy on that salary?

I sighed defeatedly and sat up, and Ariadne took that as an impetus to slap the back of my head soundly.

"C'mon now," I said miserably, crossing my arms defensively.

"While I can technically start up my parcel business at any time, given the fact that I can now access my bank accounts, you're still broke," Ariadne said, sitting across from me, producing a medical kit. She took off the old, tattered, and rain-soaked bandage that held my nose together and replaced it. I muttered a thank you, feeling somewhat sorry for myself.

"Quit acting like a child," the princess rolled her eyes at me. "It's not like you haven't already captured the two twerps anyway. All we need to do is do that again."

"You make it sound like it's easy." I said. "I feel completely stuck like the floor is nothing but organic waste from the *Lilstar*. Anywhere I turn I'm getting nowhere."

"Don't make me slap the front of your head, especially with that nose," Ariadne said. She seemed to be far more confident and comfortable than I was, something I attributed to the familiar surroundings. This was the beginning for her, where she learned the most. My beginning, my learning place was somewhere I swore I'd never return to.

"Fine," I almost whined. "But we are going to need a lot more information on the Lees."

"Okay, where do we get it?" Ariadne asked. I rubbed my fingers together thoughtfully. We needed power, which most cheaply could be described as hiring thugs. Skiptraces did that kind of thing all the time, there was even a Thugs' Guild designed to help manage all of the legal and ethical lines associated with muscle-for-hire. A few good, well-trained thugs wouldn't run too much for a few days' work, but finding reliable ones was more important. The question then was where the best place in the Olds was to find reliable thugs.

I looked at my favorite jeans, still dripping with water.

"How far are we from Ascalon?" I demanded.

"What the heck is Ascalon?" she asked.

"Right, you wouldn't know that one..." I corrected myself. "Where's Olds V?"

"Well, we're on the extreme north-ish edge of Olds III, so I guess about sixty or seventy miles. Why?" the princess asked.

"I know how we can get back the Lees." I tried not to grin too wide at my own genius. I had been laughed out of Aristotle's office entirely too many times in my life and I would show the pudgy lawyer and Mr. Carver that I could be a good skiptrace, at least this once. "We have access to the greatest skiptrace library of bad guys in the whole system."

Sixteen

A cab took us to the train station, wherein we boarded a positively rickety train and made our way to Olds V. I kept pretty mum about my plan for a few reasons, none of which kept Ariadne from demanding answers the entire train ride.

"What is Ascalon?" she demanded.

"Why is it a good place to go?"

"Stop grinning like an idiot if you're not going to tell me."

Of course, it wasn't until we got into another cab at Olds V that I finally decided to give her some answers.

"Take us to Ascalon," I told the cabbie. The scruffy-looking man with wild hair shot me an incredulous expression.

"I'm not sure that place is for the likes of you two..." he trailed off.

"Stop fretting, I know Silene personally," I told the cabbie. He still didn't seem quite as confident about the whole deal as I was, but I ignored that. I was paying him to take me wherever I darn well pleased.

"Who is this Selene person?" Ariadne demanded as soon as we were underway. Metal and store buildings began to speed by as the cab zipped toward its destination. The Olds were not like Dinium or Theopa, where growing organic buildings was both cost-effective and reasonable. Most of the Olds' territory rested on highly polluted ground, in many cases too toxic for organic buildings to inhabit for very long. It was just easier to build houses and community buildings with inorganic materials. There were other advantages to inorganic structures — some of these buildings were thousands of years old, patched up and fixed as best they could. While organic buildings were being made with a longer lifespan in each new genetic generation, they couldn't last much longer than a few hundred at best.

This, of course, meant the whole place felt a little empty or impersonal. There was no rhythmic thrumming from a hundred synchronized pulmonary systems, but neither was there the often-overpowering, warmed-over wheat smell that came with the standard brand of genetic facsimile. There was also an increased risk for human infections in non-organic cities, as the rocks and mortar had no self-regulating immune system or pluripotent cells to speed up the healing process for both the building and its occupants. In fact, they probably had to use disinfectants like chlorine and alcohol to keep down the dangerous viruses and bacteria, making it all the more likely that said viruses and bacteria would eventually mutate into superbugs.

"It's *Silene*, pronounced SI-lean; practice pronouncing it like that," I said, pulling out some of the stitches in my favorite jeans' left pocket.

"Marcie!" the princess said, finally placing her hands on my shoulders and forcing me to look up at her. "Focus!"

"Relax," I told her. "We are going to meet an old acquaintance of mine who is going to help us find Ottoman and Set, recapture them, and drag their sorry butts back to Aristotle."

"That sounds very expensive," Ariadne commented.

"Nope, it's a favor," I said, working to wiggle out the piece of treated paper I'd had sewn into the pocket.

"Who owes you that big of a favor?" the princess asked.

"Someone who may or may not realize it yet," I admitted, unfolding the paper. It had just two words printed on it, "Silene" on the front and "Ascalon" on the back in metallic ink, but the important part was what was scribbled and signed in the corner: "I.O.U. if alive."

I was still alive, so it was a valid favor-in-print.

I glanced over at Ariadne, who had decided to pout even as I waved around the piece of paper triumphantly.

"Are you two sure this is where you need to be?" the cabbie asked, stopping the cab in front of a dilapidated-looking stone building. I knew that it was probably sturdier than most organic buildings and that the inside would be very well-cared-for, but it still *looked* dilapidated. A scruffy outside hid the nice, neat inside.

Silene was not a person to let things get soft, although she recognized the usefulness of not looking *too* pristine and painting a big target on yourself.

I paid the cabbie and led Ariadne through the building's front yard, which went for more of a wild, unkempt look with tall grass, lots of vines, and two surprisingly beautiful trees. The ground might be too toxic for artificially made organics, but the natural flora seemed to do just fine. Plus, they always seemed to make the air even fresher than any city's shared pulmonary system could.

I strode up to the structure's big, wooden door, not even bothering to knock at the princess' almost irate protest.

Given this building was the epicenter of a skip-trace nest, the front room and main hall were surprisingly devoid of people. The few that were there glared at the pair of us like we were plague victims. which I ignored completely. The princess seemed to be deciding on whether or not she was actually going to grab hold of my hand in fear.

"Treat them like the media," I said, casting a scowl back at a particularly cruel-looking woman in a corner. She actually looked like a ghoul, I surmised, with pale, almost greyish skin, long dark hair, and layers of flowing black robes.

"What?" the princess said, still slinking directly behind me.

"They're the media, you're a pilot at Carlion, and you want to beat the crap out of them," I said, taking an immediate right and striding up to a pair of really big, really heavy doors.

"How the h—" Ariadne bit off a choice word as a man even bigger than the doors moved to intercept us.

"What do you two want?" he demanded, plain green eyes attempting to pierce my soul and scare me.

I looked up at him without wavering. He may have been a mountain of a man, dressed mostly in black with piercings, tattoos, and a few wicked-sweet scars, but he also didn't scare me. I had a card personally signed by his boss. Besides, I also knew he was bluffing.

"I'm Marcie Dunn. Do you remember me now, Kohinoor?" I asked. It took the giant a moment.

"Oh, yeah! Little Marcie from SkipCon in Baltia," the speaking mountain said with a sniffle, taking his sightless eyes off me in recognition. He shook my hand gently in remembrance and smiled. "How have you been keeping yourself?"

"So-so," I said honestly. "I was hoping to talk to Silene; I fulfilled our agreement." I of course didn't wave the signed I.O.U. card in his face.

"That should be no problem. I don't know your friend, however," Kohinoor shifted his face toward Ariadne, looking somewhere just over her shoulder.

"She's new," I said, looking back at Ariadne. "Say something, he can't see you."

"I'm Ariadne King," the princess said, casting wary glances from me to the speaking mountain and back again.

"She's new," Kohinoor said with a cautious sniffle.

"She's my pilot," I said, ignoring the fact he had just repeated what I said. "Is Silene in?"

"Should be. But she's in a meeting. I'll let you in once she's done," Kohinoor said, and in the most graceful of gestures he could manage, swept a giant arm toward a few empty chairs. I gave the man the last credit I had in my pocket.

"For your sister's medical fund," I said.

"Thank you much, Marcie, she will appreciate it greatly," the mountain of a man beamed brightly, rubbing the credit in his hands.

I moved to flop satisfactorily into the empty chair near Ariadne.

Ariadne sat almost on the edge of her seat, uncertain as to what to do or say next, though she opened her mouth on more or one occasion.

"His sister?" she finally asked.

"Zvonimir. If I remember correctly, she crashed into a flyer and broke her leg chasing down Cassia Lodger, the fourteenth most wanted exotic animal smuggler in the system," I said matter-of-factly.

"You need a hobby. Like, a real hobby," Ariadne said, with a concerned look on her face.

I nodded ruefully. For a moment, we sat there in the eerily quiet hallway. For a house of skiptraces and thugs — whose outward appearance and mannerisms differed only very slightly from the criminals they caught — Ascalon was a surprisingly rigid and orderly company. I always figured it was because it was built just as much on secrets and information as it was on actually hunting down ruffians and dragging their sorry keisters to the proper authorities.

"Marcie..." the princess finally said. A glance toward the creepy, most-likely-a-real-ghoul lady sitting across from us shut her up.

"This is Silene's operation. She runs a whole skiptrace network that is mostly the best of the best. It's not as big as something like Trynod, but it's the place to go if you want to hire experts," I commented, looking around the room, trying to identify the other occupants. I hadn't seen any of them aside from Kohinoor before.

"And how do you know these people?' Ariadne said, not really taking her eyes off the creepy lady.

"I met Silene at a skiptrace seminar not long ago when I was doing...research for a personal matter," I said. "She and Kohinoor dragged me around for the whole two days, letting me in on a few trade secrets."

"Why?" the princess asked, looking at me with a sort of disgusted, mostly surprised expression.

"Because I swore to take down one of her biggest rivals," I said, *almost* nonchalantly.

"The guy you took the license from?" the princess said.

"Yep," I said.

"He was a rival to all this?" Ariadne said incredulous.

"Well, I suppose rival is a strong word. He was more of a nuisance skiptrace who caused problems for everybody. Only Silene really hated his guts like I do." I shrugged off the information, thumbing the I.O.U.

"This is an entire world I know nothing about," the princess finally sighed.

"If it's any consolation, I feel the same way about pilots," I said with a wry expression.

Ariadne just stared at me.

I mostly ignored her until Kohinoor called us over.

"Silene'll let you in," the speaking mountain said, opening the large doors to the heart of Ascalon.

I strode through it with what I'd hoped was a measure of confidence. Silene was a person I actually looked up to, and I wanted to put on a good face to meet her. Although she'd only mentored me for two days, she'd given me a card, signed with an I.O.U., and she was *Silene of Ascalon*, and I was going to impress her all over again.

And then grovel a little for help.

It was a little more difficult than I had imagined. Sure, I'd been in stone structures, but this was opulent to a fault. Dark wooden walls were decorated with tapestries and paintings. A massive fireplace sat to one side, heating the whole room in a warm glow, contrasted by the deep bluish lights coming from the only stained-glass window I'd ever seen, real or in pictures. It sat directly across from the door, fully prepared to intimidate any business rival or impress any potential client that might make it all the way to Ascalon. It had Silene's crest, a roguish soldier standing over a speared dragon in triumph. Good has conquered evil.

I stared with my mouth falling open as I looked at the glass. It was such a simple thing, the gruff, logical part of my brain chided me, is it really worth getting so doe-eyed over?

Given the fact that Ariadne poked my side, it probably wasn't worth any amount of slobbering, but I was too far entrenched. The blues were holding me captive in a moment of pure strength and beauty. How did they refuse to let the greenish, almost sickly nebula-filtered sunlight that penetrated them wash out their colors? How could shards of glass present such a grand moment like slaying a dragon so easily? I didn't know and almost didn't want to. I was far too entranced in the intoxicating idea of it; a shining bright good versus a dark, potent evil. Someday, I might even be that soldier, proud and regal, all enemies I encountered laying at my feet.

I remained lost to the glass until an enthusiastic peal of laughter broke toward my right. I forcibly shook myself back into reality and there she was, laughing at me from behind her desk.

The princess and I didn't say anything while the master skiptrace continued her laughter. She wasn't a wholly intimidating person, being just a touch taller than either myself or Ariadne. While she wore a well-decorated suit and business-woman-like bun to the seminar, now she sported black leather and her dark-purple-almost-black hair was pulled back in a severe braid. The barest hint of her soldier-and-speared-dragon tattoo could be seen on the left side of her neck.

She sat behind a huge, real-wood desk that seemed to take up much of the room. It, like everything else about Ascalon, was sturdy and powerful. It didn't quite dwarf the master skiptrace that sat in its seat, but I knew if I sat behind it, I'd look like a toddler.

At the moment, I very much *felt* like a toddler.

"I'd forgotten how much I've missed your sparkling innocence, Marcie," Silene grinned once she'd finished laughing. My cheeks got hot and probably very red, but I accepted her hug when she walked over to me. "I'm glad you're here, sprite! What happened to your nose?"

"I ran into somebody's elbow," I said, finally matching Silene's grin. "This is Ariadne King, my pilot."

"Pleasure, Miss King," the master skiptrace greeted Ariadne with a handshake. The princess remained quiet. "What brings you this way, dear ladies?"

"I'm actually here to cash this in," I said, holding up the I.O.U. Silene nodded in understanding and took the card. She rounded to the other side of her table and gestured to two empty chairs for Ariadne and me.

"That's very quick. I'd only heard about that..." she broke off and glanced from the princess to myself, "...charming fellow's de-licensing a few weeks ago. I suppose you two need help with your first official case?"

Silene pointed directly to my still-broken nose and Ariadne's bruised cheek. I pursed my lips in a measure of irritation. Of course, I was dealing with one of the *best* skiptraces. Silene could connect random pieces of information into a whole far faster than anyone else, correctly guessing where even the most well-hidden and unpredictable criminals might be hiding.

"Yes," I confessed, still trying to determine just how much of the story I was ready to admit. "We need help tracking down a couple of criminals and dragging them back to Dinium."

"What kind of help are you looking for?" Silene asked, beginning to take notes.

"Information, mostly," I said. "The information we got from our lawyer was incomplete, to say the least."

"We can definitely do that," Silene scribbled a few notes and then looked both of us over carefully. "Are you sure you want to use the favor card up so soon?"

"We're kind of out of options," Ariadne finally piped up. "The job turned out to be a lot bigger than we originally thought and Marcie and I are kind of bumbling idiots when it comes to skiptracing."

I punched the princess in the arm with a great measure of force.

"Who gave you the assignment?" the master skiptrace asked.

"Aristotle Simon of *Aristotle & Sons*," I said. "It wasn't his fault, he thought he was just sending us after a debtor but—"

"There turned out to be two of them and they're both major creeps," the princess cut in, shooting me an I-dare-you-to-hit-me-again glance. Silene just nodded at the information.

"I've heard Aristotle's a fair enough lawyer, for all the contradictions that implies," the master skiptrace said, rubbing her fingers together in thought. "If that's what you want to use the card for, I do owe you one for taking that menace off the skiptrace market. Kohinoor!"

The speaking mountain stuck his head inside the door with little hesitation.

"Yes ma'am?" Kohinoor asked.

"Talk to the Librarian, we need information on…" Silene looked toward me.

"Ottoman and Setesh Lee, they're twins or clones or something," I said, and the master skiptrace's eyebrows shot up a little as she wrote down the names.

"Any information on Ottoman and Setesh Lee," Silene said. The speaking mountain nodded solemnly and ducked back into the hallway.

"Thank you," I said sincerely, standing up as if to leave.

"What else do you need, Marcie?" the master skiptrace/mind reader asked me pointedly. I swallowed. Watching Setesh almost murder his own twin/clone offhandedly had been giving me the willies ever since. I wasn't at all convinced that

Ariadne and I could capture the Lees by ourselves a second time, let alone capture them now that they had friends.

"Ahh...I might need a few thugs," I said, tapping my fingers uncertainly on her desk, suddenly feeling like I was on the spot.

Which I was, according to Silene's face.

"You demand a lot, Marcie," the master skip-trace said, with a smile covering some expression I couldn't read, but hoped was amusement.

I didn't say anything, trying to reinforce my statement through silence and bravery. It didn't seem to be making a difference, but it was the best option I had - other than running out the door and fleeing Ascalon altogether, I suppose.

"All right, give me until tomorrow. I'll get you what I can," she said, handing me one of her business cards. "That's for your employer. Tell him I can help keep his criminal information pool more complete for a meager fee."

I thanked the master of Ascalon and started toward the door.

"Marcie," Silene said in a serious tone once my hand hit the doorknob. "Always let the thugs in the door first. That's what they signed up for."

I nodded.

That should be no problem at all.

• • •

The princess and I bid Kohinoor goodbye as we headed back to the Olds V city center. All of our clothing had been on the *Lilstar*, which was hopefully still at Carlion unless our two captives-turned-captors had decided to keep it. Given the way they had treated Ariadne, I doubted either had the expertise to actually pilot the ship. Besides, Set indicated they'd had a hideout in the Olds. Which Old and what city, I didn't know. Hopefully Silene's information would point us in at least a general direction.

I mulled all of these things over as Ariadne and I got a cheap meal of grits and lichen chips. Then we headed to the nearest and cheapest hotel. I had suggested that we go find one of those sleeping pod companies that rent out bed-sized chambers for overnight travelers who didn't really need an entire room, but Ariadne made a good case for having our own bathroom.

We arrived at Ascalon the next day to an even more sickly Kohinoor and an appreciable pile of information regarding Ottoman and Setesh Lee. While Silene couldn't help us sift through all of it, she did lend us one of the miniature castle's many conference rooms to plan our attack and brief our new crew of thugs.

"I'll have your thugs together in a minute, Marcie," Kohinoor sniffled as he led Ariadne and me to the conference room.

"Thank you, Kohinoor," I said, trying to be polite but also anxious to get into the four sizable file folders that sat on the conference room's huge desk. Ariadne wasted no time cracking open one of the files. Kohinoor was overcome with a sneezing fit and disappeared from the doorway.

I closed the door behind him and turned to Ariadne.

Judging from her face, we were a little more than screwed.

"Ohhh..." she moaned, looking sick as she read one of the files. In fact, I almost reached for a bucket to hand her. "Oh—"

"Yeah, yeah I got it," I said, picking up what looked like Ottoman's file. I barely made it through the entire thing without muttering the serious cuss word that was floating around my mind. If this was only Ottoman's rap sheet, I would have hated to see Set's. These guys made homicide look like a hobby.

I hoped and prayed Silene let us borrow a *lot* of thugs.

"*Marcie*." Ariadne emphasized her words with hand gestures. "These guys take psycho to a complete and entire new level. I'm not certain they can be measured in normal psychological, um, measuring things!"

"Breathe," I told the princess. She complied after a moment. "We will have several professional thugs who will be going through the doors before us. We should be able to handle these sick idiots."

Ariadne said nothing, but seemed to tap out the phrase "this is a bad idea" on the table with her very judgmental albeit nervous fingers.

"Even if we catch them, why should we work for someone who can't even get their information straight?" the princess said, looking me in the eye for a direct answer.

"Silene said she'd keep Aristotle's records up-to-date," I answered almost too easily, gathering fistfuls of paper as if to show her proof this would work. "She has the good stuff, too. I've found a whole list of hotels and motels the Lees have stayed at, including one just before they left for Myrkheim. We can start there."

"And if the good lawyer doesn't or can't take her up on the offer?" Ariadne challenged.

"Then I'll find a skiptracing job somewhere else. Maybe Silene will hire me," I sort of muttered the last part, glancing warily at the door. I didn't want to seem desperate in having a job on top of being desperate for my first real mission as a skiptrace to succeed.

"What if I just hire you for my parcel business? You should be able to pay me off in a couple of years," the princess said.

"There is no way your parcel business will make enough for me to pay you off before retiring age. If we really want to be debt-free in any sort of reasonable timeframe, we'll need both the skiptracing and the parcel business," I said without challenging Ariadne. She chewed her lip thoughtfully.

"Fine," she finally relented.

I gave the shuffled papers on the solid table a quick scan, hoping I hadn't missed anything important. If the motel didn't pan out, the other options included a diner they'd been at recently and a couple of other hotels and apartments of varying degrees of reputability. A few stores and one shady doctor's office were added to the mix as well. I wrote down the most important addresses and a few more for good measure. It seemed that, when the twins/clones were in town, they hopped from place to place, never settling down. Of course, they spent more of their time off-world. I didn't want to think about how easily they could be halfway to Proxima by now.

"Where do we go from here?" Ariadne asked, looking over the papers.

"This says the Lees like to hang out at a motel in Olds II, Criley's Motel and Spa. I think we should start there first," I said, plucking a sheet of paper out of its pile and waving it in the air.

"I'd rather we head back to Carlion and pick up the *Lilstar*," Ariadne said, moving to rest her head in her hands. I couldn't see her face for all her curls, but I surmised it had shifted from worried to stressed.

I chewed the inside of my lip thoughtfully. At the moment, retaking the *Lilstar* was less of a priority. I doubted the Lees trashed the ship out of spite. More than likely, they would have fled Carlion with their friends to Olds II where they could better hide from the authorities. The priority was still tracking down the Lees, and I knew Ariadne wouldn't like that.

"I'm sure she is fine," I said, trying to be somewhat comforting. "You have contacts at Carlion, yes? Why don't you give them a call?"

Ariadne looked at me for a long minute before sighing in a resigned manner.

"I suppose that would work," she agreed. I patted her shoulder.

Just as I was starting to get comfortable into my mind, the door to the conference room burst open and in came five very punctual thugs.

SEVENTEEN

"**H**ey, *younglings*, when do we head out?" A stocky, red-headed thug stormed into the conference room and nearly yelled in my face. He stood, arms crossed, in defiance of me.

I slammed my hands into the table as hard as I could before meeting his gaze.

"You will address me as 'boss' or 'Miss Dunn.' This is my operation," I growled, not letting go of the big man's stare. He seemed to want to snarl at me, maybe even take a swing. The rest of the thugs filed in behind him, watching with interest.

The red-head started to open his mouth before he was slapped unceremoniously upside his head. I looked at the slapper in surprise to see it was the ghoul-lady from earlier. She looked at the red-head with what could only be described as contempt.

"Shhh, you ape," the ghoul-lady said in a hushed tone as the red-head attempted to glare her into submission. Of course it didn't work. How could one scare a ghost, anyway?

"Need introductions, Marcie?" Kohinoor said, sticking his head into the conference room.

"No, I think we will do just fine," I said, looking over each of the thugs carefully and pointedly.

"Now that you all know *my* name, how about you give me yours?"

The ghoul-lady actually smirked slightly.

"I am Alyx," she said, presenting a long, pale, and well-manicured hand. "The flame-haired idiot here is Addie; that is Skirm, Griffin, and Cabochon."

The ghoul-lady proceeded to point toward a tall, malnourished-looking man with a big hat, a well-dressed man that would have looked better in a board room than as a thug in a skiptrace's office, and a man with ebony eyes who bore Silene's dragon-slayer-and-slayed crest on his neck. I gave each of them the slightest nod and gestured for them all to sit down. I continued to stand, however.

"What's the plan, boss?" the hatted guy called Skirm asked, letting the last word roll easily off his tongue. I gave him a mental nod of gratitude and turned back to the rest of the thugs, trying to look at each of them with what I'd hoped was confidence.

"Here are the targets," I said, passing around the Lees' files for the thugs to look at. None of them reacted as strongly as Silene or Fredericks at the Lees' name, which wasn't surprising; these were hired thugs, their purpose was to not be surprised by the bad guys.

"The plan is to travel directly to Olds II by train where we will investigate a number of locations that the Lees have been known to frequent over the past two or three years. Here are the list of addresses we will be investigating, in order of frequency that the Lees visited, and the route we will take once we enter Olds II," I said, passing around papers with the information on it. All of the thugs looked over the papers carefully except Addie, who was seated far away from Alyx.

"Question," Skirm said once the paper with the addresses reached him, "are we going to split up into teams to save time searching the addresses?"

"No," I said, "These guys are way too dangerous for that. I need everybody together to take them down."

The ebony-eyed guy called Cabochon jumped in.

"We are trained to take down the toughest quarries. We can handle these guys," he said, getting a nod from Addie. The red-head hadn't been looking at me the entire meeting.

"The files on Ottoman and Set leave out three important things Miss King and I learned while tracking them down," I said. "Firstly, Ottoman has venom sacs implanted in his mouth that can eat through organic structures and, in high enough doses, can probably eat through human skin. Second, they have an unknown number of friends. And third, they're both complete psychopaths and druggies. All of this means I'm not going to split up the group into teams until I absolutely have to. Any more questions?"

There was a great deal of silence in the room, which I preferred over protests or taunts.

"Alright, I'll ask one: what resources does anyone have for transportation?" I asked.

"I get discounts at the Nor'easter Country Train Station," Griffin offered after an uncertain silence.

"Okay, you get the tickets, we'll refund you. Is everything clear? Good, we will meet at the Nor'easter Country Train Station tomorrow morning at 0800 sharp. Dismissed." I said finally.

With little hesitation, all of the thugs got up and meandered out the door.

"Ow..." I moaned, holding my palms that were still stinging from my display of power. I could even see a few minute bruises starting to form from the table's rough surface.

"Well, I'm impressed," Ariadne said, leaning on the table to face me. I glanced at her to see if that was a sarcastic remark or an honest one. I decided both was an acceptable answer.

Ariadne and I snaked our way outside Ascalon to head back to the hotel a few hours later. I, of course, couldn't take Silene's information out of the building, but I made copies of all the relevant data. Actually, I even made copies of my copies, as if to overcompensate for my lack of real skiptracing experience by organizing. It was an okay strategy, but it didn't actually make me more qualified.

At least the meeting seemed to go okay.

"Eh, not bad," a thin voice startled me as I reached the end of the main hall. Skirm suddenly materialized in front of me, opening the door and, with a flourish, gestured Ariadne and me out into the afternoon light.

"What wasn't bad?" I demanded as the thug caught up.

"You and your backbone," Skirm said, looking toward the mostly empty road. "I don't think I'll have any trouble following your lead."

"I didn't say anything especially leadership-like," I challenged.

"You could have been as silent as the grave, Miss Dunn, and that's all I would have needed." Skirm waved down a cab before winking at me. "Taking Addie head-on. Plus the great skiptrace Silene of Ascalon likes you."

"You're easily impressed," I commented, noting that Ariadne was staying very far out of the conversation.

"If any of the other thugs give you trouble, let me know. I'll set them straight," Skirm said.

"Are there any of the thugs I should be worried about?" I asked.

Skirm smiled. It was a wolfish kind of expression, but it intimidated me even less than Kohinoor.

"Alyx is scary, but not evil. Griffin is a master of disguises, Cabochon is a professional liar but neither are things to worry about. I can't speak for Addie, since I just met him in the hallway," Skirm said, sidling up to the stopped cab to once again open the door for the princess and me.

"What about you? Can I trust you?" I asked, before stepping into the cab. The thin-voiced man merely grinned wider.

"I'm a hurricane, Miss Dunn." I wanted to scowl at him for being so vague and demand a more specific description, but I couldn't get past his eyes. A strange sort of washed-out hazel that bordered on yellow. Like the rest of him, hardly attractive, but even then, they held a taut sort of power. Like the string on a bow, something I really didn't want to be on the receiving end of. I realized I didn't need him to elaborate any further.

I bid the disquieting man a farewell and settled into my seat of the cab. Ariadne didn't look at me as I ordered the cabbie to the cheapest hotel.

"What?" I finally asked the princess.

"Is it really a good idea to work with a whole bunch of completely strange thugs we don't even know?" Ariadne said, a concerned look on her face.

"I'm sure they're not *dangerous*. Kohinoor wouldn't have picked them for us if they were," I commented, wishing I had a needle to sew the card for Aristotle into the pocket where I had kept the I.O.U.

"Would he have? I don't even know the man! And who gives their child who was undoubtedly a very large baby boy a girly name like Kohinoor?!" Ariadne threw her hands into the air dramatically. I sat by, letting her stew for a moment.

"Are you done yet?" I asked neutrally. The princess sighed and nodded. "Do you have any spare credits?"

"Why?" She gave me a suspicious side-eye.

"I figured you'd want a new pair of jeans. Those are getting ripe."

• • •

It was exactly midday when Ariadne and I strode into the train station. It wasn't difficult to spot the gaggle of thugs that were waiting on us, even as crowded as the place was. Alyx, Skirm, Cabochon, and Griffin were all accounted for.

"Where's Addie?" I asked. Skirm shrugged twig-like shoulders.

"Late. Some sort of family business. He said he'd be back within an hour, hoping we'd be inclined to wait," Cabochon snorted with some measure of disapproval.

"Alright," I said, trying not to scratch my freshly-bandaged nose. "We'll wait here for a bit, but if he doesn't catch up within an hour I'm just going to leave him a ticket with the station master."

We waited nearly two whole hours, me deciding to be all too generous with the thug. By the time we were well into the afternoon, I finally called waiting quits and left a nice ticket with the thug's name on it with the station master. I chided myself the entire trip to Olds II for taking so long to wait for Addie, but I was still confident that the thugs we had with us would be enough to help the princess and me take down Set and Ottoman.

We arrived at Olds II just as dark was setting in. I considered going straight to the hotel we were staying at, but the first of the Lees' favorite motels, called Criley's Motel and Spa, was only a short cab ride away. This could be easy, I'd almost begun to convince myself, perhaps the twins/clones were at the motel and we'd be heading back toward Dinium within two days.

Of course, as with most of the things I assume or dream up, this easy way out never came to fruition.

Ariadne swore as we stepped into the main office at Criley's. The place was an absolute disaster with deep gouges in the wood walls, upset pictures, smashed tile floors, and two beaten proprietors picking up shards of glass.

"I swear we have no idea where they are!" the woman with a severe black eye held up her hands. "Please don't finish the job like your friends said you would."

"Who is they? What friends?" I asked, feeling a little panicked but determined not to make this couple's day even worse.

"The red-headed fellow from the Manners," the man with missing teeth and a swollen tongue said thickly. "He said you'd be by to ask us where those Lee fellows are and if we still didn't know, you'd burn our motel down."

"Red-head?" I demanded. "What was his name? Did he give you his name?"

"I-I-" the man stuttered. He began whimpering just a little.

"It's okay," Ariadne said calmly, stepping toward the couple just a little. Her voice was magnificently soothing. I wondered if she could teach me to do that. "We're not part of whoever it was that beat you up. We're skiptraces simply looking for the Lees."

The woman glanced from one of us to the other with terrified paranoia. I supposed it was difficult to have a civil conversation when outnumbered. I made a gesture to the thugs to wait outside, and they complied without protest.

"Now," Ariadne said, righting a few chairs. Her voice was still soothing. "We need to know everything that happened."

The woman, sitting down in one of the chairs, nodded slightly. She still seemed suspicious, but that seemed to be giving way to tiredness. She almost aged two decades just sitting in a chair.

"The red-haired man came in a few hours ago and demanded we tell him if a pair of our regulars had shown up," the man said, his voice steadying.

"Did the red-haired man give you his name?" I asked, and both proprietors shook their heads.

"No. Just that the Manners would come and get us if we refused to give him the information," the woman held my gaze intently.

"What are the Manners?" Ariadne asked.

"A massive up-and-coming gang," I said. I'd never actually met a member of the Manners in person, but they already had a reputation of being merciless and fully prepared to ruin anyone's day.

I could hear the princess swallowing.

Yeah, if the Lees weren't enough, we now had the opportunity to tangle with a particularly malicious gang.

"We don't know where they are," the toothless man asserted. "They used to come here regularly, but they haven't been around in years."

I nodded. It was reasonable that the twins/clones wouldn't return to places they had once been. With their supposed line of work, they would need to bounce from place to place to keep the police and skiptraces off their tails. But, of course, it was human nature to stick to a pattern. Unlike those lovely Centauri-built number machines, humans weren't random no matter how hard they tried. So, if I could track their movements, I might be able to figure out where they'd be next.

Of course, if the Manners were after these guys too, that'd be a bigger problem. Thankfully it looked like Addie had already shown his stripes as a member and hopefully my in-depth knowledge of Ottoman and Set would give us the advantage.

"We need to be going," I finally said, standing. "Do you need anything?"

"No, thank you," the woman said, and I led Ariadne out the door.

My neutral expression turned to a great and dark scowl the moment my feet hit the sidewalk.

"Marcie—" Ariadne started. I held up a hand as the thugs joined us.

"Do you guys care if we do a little night work?" I asked, barely waiting for the thugs to catch up before I hailed a cab.

"You're the boss," Alyx said. I nodded, pulling out the piece of paper that I had with all the places the Lees had been to on it. The next place was a hotel called Maribel, about a fifteen-minute cab ride away from here.

We set out to Maribel Hotel, where the Lees had been spotted six months ago, only to face the same story. The Manners had beat us to it a few hours before, beating up the proprietors and trashing the place, claiming the next wave of gang members was on the way. These particular owners were less forgiving than the first ones and chased us off the property with a nasty-looking crossbow. So we made it to the Lees' favorite diner, once again trashed. Thankfully the Manners didn't seem intent on actually killing anyone, though they'd sent more than one person to the hospital.

I resisted the urge to yell out in frustration as we entered a small grocer with a bloodied owner.

"They just came out of nowhere, demanding we tell them the location of some ruffians I'd never seen before!" the bespectacled man held his slashed arm.

"Was there a red-head leading the group?" I asked wearily. The man nodded enthusiastically.

"I think one of them called him Addie or some-thing," the owner said, finally confirming what I had begun to suspect each time we encountered another known location of Set and Ottoman ransacked by a red-headed gang leader long before we reached there.

"Alright, that's all we need to know," I said, turning to leave.

"Uh, wait!" the owner said. "I've seen those two, er, whoever they are."

"The Lees?" I filled in the gap.

"Yes! Them! I saw them enter that store over there," the man said. I eyed the store at which the grocer was pointing with suspicion. It was a pristine store with a pudgy proprietor standing out front, scoffing so loudly and with such amusement at this grocer's misfortune I could almost hear him. It only took me a minute to figure out what was actually going on. I reached out calmly and grabbed a handful of the owner's shirt, upsetting his glasses slightly. Thankfully, he was short, so I could pull him nose-to-nose without craning my neck.

"Tell me something," I whispered harshly. "And be honest, I'm having a bad day. How can you have not seen the Lees in your own store but have seen them in your biggest competitor's store?"

The wide-eyed man gulped great swallows of air.

"I-I just wanted you and your friends to beat him up too. It's unfair," the unscrupulous shop owner gasped. I released his shirt after a moment and stormed out.

After that failure, I had us head back to the hotel we had reservations at. We made it in well past three in the morning, but I still spent the rest of the night pacing. I'd need to have a talk with Kohinoor about Addie when this was all over. Having a Manners spy in Ascalon was not an ideal situation for the company's reputation. It also showed off just how capable they really were to get a guy through Ascalon's hefty thug vetting system. The Lees must have been terribly important to the Manners if they were willing to sacrifice such a position inside one of the biggest and most well-informed skiptracing companies in the system.

Why did the Manners want Set and Ottoman in the first place? Given the Lees' almost flippant relationship with killing, it was possible that the whole situation was a vendetta. Yes, the Manners could be out to hire the Lees for their services, but

Addie's crew was *hunting* the twins/clones. They were making a lot of noise, trying to scare us off their trail, and intimidating anyone who may have come in contact with the Lees. That wasn't exactly a great recruitment tactic, especially if they knew just how undaunted the Lees really were. This had to be something more, like a vendetta.

Well, at least revenge was a language I spoke.

The bigger problem was the Manners themselves. I couldn't have them just swipe my very important bounty right out from under me, but if I attacked them directly, or beat them to the Lees, things would get ugly quickly. Not even the Trynod would have enough thugs to take on the Manners. So that left me with scaring them. Or calling the whole thing off and demanding that Aristotle give me another bounty to work because the one he gave me turned out to be a catastrophe of massive, system-spanning proportions.

Of course, that would have meant I wasted Silene's I.O.U., a more terrible thought than going head-to-head with the Manners.

I could always try bargaining with the Manners, but that seemed even less likely to succeed than attacking them. The only way to do this would be to scare them off. I needed something big and intimidating to get the Manners to back off. Ascalon wouldn't be enough; they had at least one spy already embedded in the organization, so it was likely that they knew more about Silene's operation than I did. No, the Manners needed something scarier. Something with far bigger teeth than they sported. Something that was intimidating enough to force them into a change of plans.

Something like—

"Marcie," Ariadne appeared in the doorway, dressed in new pajamas. "How about I take over the pacing and you get some sleep?"

"Sorry," I said glumly slumping onto the couch. I don't know if she actually meant to fulfill her suggestion, but as soon as I was out of the way, the princess started pacing.

For a while there, it was all quiet, save the wood floor that squeaked every time Ariadne stepped near the table. The noise was high-pitched, regular, and extremely irritating. Falsebone floors rarely made that kind of noise. No wonder I'd stirred the princess.

"My question is how?" Ariadne finally said. She still looked drowsy, even though she'd probably walked the equivalent of a quarter of a mile now.

"How do we get the Manners off our quarry?" I asked.

The princess nodded.

"Also note that we just agreed to take on one of the biggest new mobs in existence," Ariadne pointed out.

"We're idiots," I said, nodding ruefully.

"Well, that's not news to *me*," she said, plopping down on the couch beside me. "I assume it's not news to you either."

"My brother always said I had a skull thicker than a rhinoceros," I said. The princess nodded silently.

I replayed the idea I had in my head repeatedly, debating whether or not to tell Ariadne. Of course, I'd already figured out the answer to that; it wasn't something Ariadne was going to like. It wasn't even really something that I was going to like. Or that I thought I could pull off, but that was beside the point. It was a do-or-die kind of situation.

"You're scowling again," the princess said, without actually looking in my direction.

"So?" I asked.

"You're not exactly subtle. You've got some ideas floating around that head and you are going to tell me about them," she said. I glanced at her with tired eyes.

"I may have an idea or two," I said cryptically. Ariadne pursed her lips with irritation I tried to ignore. "Look, it's a long shot and I'm not sure I really want to go through with it just yet."

"Stubborn goat," the princess muttered.

"Drama llama," I muttered back. Ariadne rolled her eyes dramatically as if to emphasize my point.

"Seriously, go sleep," she finally said. "You're the boss and it won't do to have you slacking off from exhaustion."

"*Fine.*" I took my turn to roll my eyes and shuffled to my bed.

It still took me an hour to finally fall asleep. I tossed and turned, trying to straighten out my brain. Now that I had a plan, what I needed was a meeting with the Manners, which in turn meant I needed some way to actually arrange it. It's not as though I could just call them up on the telephone. They might not even *have* a telephone and, if they did, their number was probably not in the registry.

Skiptracing wasn't as easy as I'd like.

On top of all my inner moping, the bed was also incredibly uncomfortable. Although I didn't miss much about my life after my brother died, the apartment I'd stayed at immediately following his death had the best mattress. Not even the *Lilstar* with all her padding could quite match that old bed.

Of course, I'd had to sell the apartment to pay for expenses tracking down the skiptrace, which just added to the of holes in my life - things most people had. Family, a home, security, a job, even a social life were all things that seemed to exist just outside my grasp. Not that I was completely empty; I had Ariadne and a mission, if nothing else. With any luck, I'd always have a mission. Something to do. Something to drag me forward in time. I didn't really want to settle down anywhere, unless I was well and truly spent. For now, I needed to keep moving.

Even so, part of me still wanted to go home.

An idea shot through me like a shock from my Centauri device. I tried not to bolt out of bed and act too quickly.

I missed *home*. Me, a person who was never really sentimental. If I was missing home, I knew two people who were probably missing home too.

And I had the address to their home.

Eighteen

"You're going to Carlion," I said the next morning, as everybody met in the hotel's lobby. Ariadne's face lit up with more confusion and less joy than I would have liked.

"Are we giving up here?" she asked, the question echoing in the eyes of the entire party of thugs, except Alyx, of course. Her face was as cool and passive as ever.

"Not yet, but I need something from the *Lilstar*. Take everybody but Alyx with you; I might need her here," I said. Apparently, my idea was not as pleasing to the princess as I had thought it would be, as she dragged me by the elbow a few paces away from the thugs.

"What are you planning?" she asked, hands on hips like a disappointed mother. To be honest, she looked more like a disappointed kitten, but that was beside the point.

"I'm not going to do anything too stupid," I said, "I just have to contact somebody. That's it."

Ariadne glared at me for what felt like an eternity.

"Fine, but you have to take Cabochon with you. He's creepy," the princess finally relented. "What do I need to get from the *Lilstar*?"

"It's in the back of the bathroom closet, a little leather case. It has biohazard warnings all over it but don't worry, it's not contagious," I said easily.

"Oh, yeah, let me just go get the unknown biohazard box you smuggled onto my ship," the princess said sarcastically, throwing her arms into the air for emphasis.

I rolled my jaw around in an I'm-so-done-with-this-conversation expression. The princess wasn't impressed.

"It's fake tattoos," I finally confessed, speaking even more slowly than before. "They're engineered on clone grafts of my own skin, that's why they have biohazard on them, they don't want people sharing. It's a liability thing. Happy now?"

"Clone-graft tattoos? No wonder you're broke," Ariadne said with a sigh. "All right, I'll go pick them up, but you are not allowed to do anything stupid while I'm gone. I want to be there to witness it."

"Thanks," I said flatly as Ariadne headed out with Skirm and Griffin. Alyx and Cabochon turned toward me. "You guys ready to poke the tiger?"

Alyx actually smiled.

• • •

My plan was relatively simple: get ahead of the Manners and force them to talk to me. Of course, that meant I had to predict their next move. Since Addie's gang was following my original game plan, I safely assumed that he would continue to do so until he reached the end of my list. If I simply skipped ahead, I could theoretically beat them to one of the locations on the list. I picked one of the abandoned locations, an old townhouse about twenty miles from the hotel. It was the only location on the list that was visited by the Lees repeatedly over the course of about thirty years, meaning that it was more than likely their childhood home or some other place that was significant to them. Since they hadn't actually been seen at the location in over five years, it was at the bottom of my list. That may have been a rookie mistake on my part, given the fact that five years was more than enough time for the Lees to feel safe returning to their old home, but for getting ahead of the Manners, it worked out perfectly.

The next step was to figure out the best way to communicate with said Manners.

Bringing my best handwriting to the table, I wrote out a carefully-worded note to Addie and his gang, requesting a meeting with his boss to discuss a mutually troubling development. I signed it as someone I knew the Manners would never turn down or resist, and tied it with an appropriate green ribbon. The final step was to drop the note off at the abandoned townhouse, a maneuver that went off without a hitch and, given the level of undisturbed dust covering everything in the house, it was a safe bet Addie hadn't yet reached the end of my list. The only thing left to do was wait until Ariadne and company made it back with my fake tattoos.

"Marcie!" Ariadne shouted the second she entered the hotel room.

"What's up?" I asked.

301

"The Lees, those… *pigs*," Ariadne spat out, "took all of my clothes just to spite me."

I tried not to sigh loudly.

"We bought you new ones, didn't we?" I asked, taking the leather case she offered me and opening it up. Thankfully the evil twins/clones hadn't bothered to steal it from the ship. Not that it would do any good for anyone who wasn't me; clone grafts were finicky, acting almost like the epidermis of organic structures that always clung to its host creature. The clone grafts didn't act exactly like that, but they would adhere to my skin until I decided to peel them off with a special solution that destroyed the graft's cells that were holding onto my skin. Theoretically, I could put on and take off a clone graft about two times before it was too thin to use. The graft I needed for this particular situation, however, was one I hadn't needed to use before.

"I also found this," Ariadne said, presenting the shock device. It was in about five or six pieces.

"Can you do anything with it?" I asked, sifting through the vials of clone grafts until I found the one I was looking for.

"Uhhh…" she started, looking at the jumbled pieces. "I'm a pilot, not a mechanic."

"It doesn't look too broken," I offered, making a beeline for the bathroom. "Maybe it just needs some glue?"

"Brilliant, Marcie. You—"

I lost the other half of her sentence as I closed the door.

• • •

I waited until about two hours before midnight to try and sneak out of the hotel room. No, I hadn't invited Ariadne to my little party. Although I did agree with the idea that I would need some backup, namely Alyx and Cabochon who were *already* in on my plan, I didn't feel the need to unnecessarily involve the princess in what could very easily get everyone killed if I wasn't as great an actress as I needed to be.

My mind was well and fully made up about the situation; Ariadne was not coming with me. I even let her have the real bed while I pretended to nap on the couch, which was a grand total of twelve steps from the door. At the correct time, I eased up on the springy piece of furniture, grabbed the small bag of make-up that I had already prepared, and stepped between the squeaky spots in the flooring to the door.

Unfortunately, it proved very difficult to sneak out of a hotel room when your roommate was sitting in front of the door, looking altogether shameless and elegantly put-out.

"Hi," Ariadne blinked at me innocently. I tried not to scream in surprise. How did she get in front of the door without me noticing?

"Why?" I asked, getting to the point.

The princess merely patted the ground beside her.

"You might want to sit, unless you are going to tell me what your plan is."

I scowled at her impish face for a moment.

"I'm going to make the Manners back off," I said, reaching for the doorknob. The blasted metallic lock zapped me with enough force to make me swear a little.

"Oh, this?" Ariadne rolled the shock device between her fingers. "All it needed was some glue."

I reached for the knob again, this time placing my hand determinedly on the shock pad, reaching for my favorite indentation in their usually smooth surface.

The cursed thing still shocked me and I growled loudly.

"Yeah, found the ON/OFF switch for the pads too. Guess what, the off switches have an off switch. Don't worry, I'll turn them back on once you stop trying to open the door," Ariadne said, looking up at me with big, round eyes that were entirely too pleased with themselves.

"What? Why?" I demanded, feeling less-than-elegantly put out.

"Because you are a ninny, Marcie Dunn, and I'm beginning to get the hang of this skiptracing thing," the princess said.

"Fine!" I said in a harsh whisper. "You can come with me. But you have to do *everything*, I say without question because these people are more likely to kill you than me."

"Why? Is it because I'm the pretty one?" Ariadne whispered harshly, rising to stand. I punched her in the arm and led the way out the door.

Of course, when attempting to sneak *two* out of a hotel room, it's a good idea to check the floor for legs that you might trip over. I hit the ground first, just managing to turn my head to avoid re-injuring my nose. I had taken the bandage off because it looked out-of-place, but it was still far-ish from healed and a collision with a hotel floor would not do it much better. Ariadne toppled on top of me with a surprisingly quiet yell.

"Tsk, tsk," a narrow, hatted man clucked his tongue at us, retracting his leg.

"Can I not go through a door without someone stopping me this evening?" I whispered angrily.

"It might help if you stop doing stupid things without us, you ninny," Skrim said in an all-to-easy tone.

"You're not coming with us," I said, dusting myself off and walking quickly down the hallway as if to make my point.

"Do you really think you can stop me, Mss Dunn?" the narrow man said.

"I think that I already have many times more people than I was planning on taking on this particular trip," I said in a soft but accusatory tone. "I promised I'd have two people with me, not four."

"Hm?" the tawny-eyed man raised an almost condescending eyebrow.

"Shut up," I said, making my way out of the hotel room.

I practically stomped all the way downstairs with Ariadne and Skirm in tow. Alyx and Cabochon were waiting in the lobby like I had planned.

"All we're missing is Griffin," Skirm said a big off-handedly.

"He's waiting in the rented car. It wouldn't do to arrive in a cab." Alyx smiled a ghoul's smile at me.

"Fine" I sighed in defeat and led the small mob outside.

"Since we've left no one behind, does everyone know the plan?" I asked as soon as we'd all piled into the car. Cabochon sat in the front with Griffin, Ariadne and I sat in the middle seat, with Skirm and Alyx in the back.

"We meet the Manners and scare them into backing offa the Lees, yeah?" Griffin said, twisting around from the front row of streets.

"Follow my cues. I'm the only one with a passably real tattoo," I said, unzipping my jacket to reveal a power-red top that was just barely modest. I was a gang member, I needed to look like one.

"Eyeliner." Ariadne said, forcing my head toward her and expertly decorating my eyelids with the charcoal black makeup, having already put on a healthy amount herself.

"More," Alyx said, reaching from the back to take the eyeliner from the princess. The ghoul-lady made me twist awkwardly in my seat so she could reach my eyelids.

"Stop before I look like you," I said, gesturing to Alyx's heavily darkened lids. She smiled perfect white teeth at me.

"Ow!" I said as Ariadne tried to put a pair of earrings on me while I was still twisted around to face Alyx.

"I think you need some lipstick," Skirm said.

"Am I going clubbing? Are we stopping at a dance before we go scare off a gang? What is going on?" I demanded, trying not to jostle too much and upset either Alyx's eyeliner or Ariadne's stabby earrings.

"Hush. *We* look fabulous, but you don't have the right amount of scary disaffected lady with gang ties yet," Ariadne said, adjusting my earrings. "There, now you look the part."

"We should probably do something with her hair..." Alyx said.

"No. As the boss I am declaring that the hair stays. It took me an hour to get it this way," I said, defensively patting the intricate braid. Alyx merely shrugged.

We finally made it to the street and into the heart of Olds II without any trouble. I rubbed my hands together to rid them of nerves and shaking. It partially worked. What worked somewhat better was imagining that I was a hardcore gang member, ready and prepared to strike a deal with another hardcore gang member. After a few seconds to get myself together, I opened up the car door and practically ran up the house's steps, not waiting for anyone else to follow.

"Hey!" a voice called behind me. Skirm was making his way up the steps with an irritated look on his face. "Thugs through the door first, remember?"

"The Manners aren't supposed to get here for an hour." I complained, stepping through the house's doorway.

I have made many, many mistakes in my life. Few of them have had catastrophic consequences, but some were fairly problematic. This was probably the most problematic of my mistakes, simply because I was a complete and utter idiot about everything.

Always let the thugs through the door first.

Silene was probably cringing all the way in Ascalon.

To be fair, the Manners let me make it all the way into the living room before they slammed the door behind me, separating me from my thugs. I could hear Skirm yelling and banging on the now-locked door. Even if the door wasn't locked properly, the brute behind it was almost the size of Kohinoor and just as immovable. I was thoroughly without backup or help.

I grabbed the nearest threatening object, a rusted metal pipe, and tried to fend off everyone around me with it. There were a lot of them.

"I think I've made a mistake," I said carefully. As if the pipe didn't feel meager enough, more gang members seemed to materialize from down the stairs, through the kitchen, and from any other mysteriously dark corner the house had.

They all seemed unimpressed with my bravado.

They were a smartly dressed group with neatly trimmed black vests over any sort of tank top or shirt they wanted to wear, although some of them went with just the vest, no shirt to obstruct the view of their tastefully tattooed arms. They were also all armed with a variety of weapons, include knives, bludgeons, and the odd crossbow, and one guy even had a blowgun.

"Nah, you finally did right for once," the traitorous redhead told me as he stepped forward where I could see him. Addie looked no less irritating in that fancy suit he wore. "No need for theatrics, *boss*."

I wasn't being theatrical. I was angry at everything and feeling more than a bit scared. The only real choice I had to make was if I wanted to simply spit in the traitor's face or hit it with the pipe.

May as well go down swinging.

The pipe connected with Addie's jaw with a crack, but his gang was on me before I could swing it a second time.

"Get her the—" the redhead cursed loudly and through bloodied teeth, "—out of here."

Of course, they couldn't very well let me be conscious as they dragged me into the heart of their territory. A tranquilized dart connected with my neck and I went down without so much as a scream.

Ariadne was going to be so angry.

Nineteen

I woke up with a splash of incredibly cold water to the face. I tried to yell in surprise but some of the icy liquid slid down my trachea, causing a miserable coughing fit.

"What's with this?!" a brute I could only smell shouted into my ear. I winced as he pushed my head forward, jabbing a cold finger on to the back of my neck.

"What does it look like, you dullard?" I demanded, feeling sore all over. The brute forced my head down farther, putting a strain on my shoulders and well-secured hands. I was definitely secured to a chair. At least the scratchy ropes were easier to get out of than organic swaths fused to their host beings. Not like I'd actually *need* to escape if all of this went well.

I tried to lift my head to get a good look at where I was. It looked like the living room of some sort of once-grand inorganic townhouse. The rotting wooden walls clung to their ugly metal support beams like they were lifelines. Stone was beyond that. Whoever used to live here had more than enough money to spare and no idea how to build a simple wall.

Not that the rest of the house was any simpler, but the brute shoved my head farther down before I could get a good look.

"Ah!" I yelled as he scraped the sharp side of a knife across my neck. He dabbed the blood that I knew was pooling there with what felt like gauze.

Of course, the clone graft tattoo had few nerve endings for me to actually feel with, especially since I had only had it on for a few hours, but his knife dug well past the graft.

It was a long moment before he said anything more, probably checking for any organic residue that would indicate this tattoo was an organic symbiote, not my actual skin. Bad fake tattoos were made of organic parasites not unlike Trish Abercrombie's arm or Ottoman's venom sacs that sat only a few cells thick on top of the host's skin. The problem was that when cut, these tattoos oozed both the blood of its human host and the nutrient-rich slurry that organic structures used. Usually it was only minute traces of the nutrient ooze, but that was enough to flag the tattoo as fake.

My fake tattoos were not organic components in that way. They were grafts made of clones from my own skin, with some additives to make them easier to remove and allow them to be stored away from their host body, namely myself. That meant they bonded to and bled just like my own skin, tricking any blood or DNA test that might prove they were fake. The only real way to prove my clone graft tattoos were fake was to watch me take them off later, which involved a precision cutting tool, a special solution, and a lot of anesthetics. They were almost as difficult to get off as real tattoos.

"It's real," he said in an almost panicked tone. The other Manner gang members who occupied the room murmured uncertainly. I couldn't have asked for a more perfect reaction.

Of course, uncertain whispering was a far cry from backing off a hunt, but every poisonous, mountain-moving idea had to start somewhere. Besides, it wasn't these guys that I needed to convince.

"Calm down, all of you," a surprisingly well-modulated voice declared. Footsteps rounded to the front of my head. Of course, all I could see was a pair of surprisingly small shoes.

"Finally," I said, forcing my head up, against the brute, enough to see a fantastically dressed woman who might have come up to my waist in height. Her wrinkled face was incredibly passive; the kind of dangerous passive that no doubt could intimidate even the enormous thug who was still pressing down on my head. I fought long and hard to keep any surprise from showing on my face. The Manners had not just dragged me to their local boss, they dragged me to their *head* boss. There had been a SkipCon speaker that devoted an entire talk on the rise of the Manners and speculation that this woman, Lady Emilia Clarke, was secretly their leader. She was a former do-gooding lawyer who somehow, somewhere, went very far astray, trying to set up her own rule of law through street crime and extortion.

"I get to meet the boss," I said.

"Yes, an unfortunately necessary occurrence, Miss Dunn," the Manners' boss said, waving a hand at her thug, and he released my head. With the same hand, the short woman grabbed hold of my chin with an iron grip, forcing my head one way and the other, looking over my face and neck. "You should really get that nose repaired properly before it's too late."

"I came here to make a deal, not chit chat with some old woman," I said with contempt.

"Yes, I know. You of the Seething are hardly subtle people," Lady Clarke said, gesturing to my tattoo. I could feel the blood dripping down the back of my shirt.

I've never for one second missed the money I'd spent on these fakes.

"We are a brotherhood. A family. You have done us a great dishonor by kidnapping me and interfering with my vengeance," I said angrily.

"Yes, yes, yes, I am aware of all of that. You will be returned to your clan if I am satisfied that you are who you say you are," Lady Clarke said, taking a tankard of what was probably a very stiff drink from one of her underlings. "I want to know what the Seething's interest is in the men I've clearly taken an interest in. And why you are associating with someone as sophisticated as Silene of Ascalon. You even hired a few of her thugs."

"Kohinoor said you were an old acquaintance of that—" Addie started to say as he stepped out of the corner. What was with this guy and his dramatic entrances? Lady Clarke snapped a finger and the traitorous man fell dead quiet. I was surprised he could talk at all after the run-in I had arranged with his jaw and a rusted pipe. His face was swollen to the size of a melon and already bruised black. I grinned at him a little wildly. His knuckles were almost white with anger.

"I see you are proud of your work," Lady Clarke said, seeing the wordless exchange between Addie and me. She steepled her fingers in an interested and thoughtful manner. Her voice was still dangerously passive. "Burton here is also proud of his work, and, if you don't cooperate, I'll have him rip what's left of your nose off."

It's not like I was actually willing to suffer pain for the Seething, anyway.

"I know Silene from a SkipCon a few years back," I said hurriedly as the thug's massive hand rounded my face and made a beeline for my nose. "She thought I had potential."

"As a skiptrace? Or as a foot soldier of the Seething? I tend to recall the skiptrace community not appreciating people with active gang ties," Lady Clarke leaned back in her chair, sipping on whatever liquid amber delight she was currently enjoying.

"No. The skiptracing community doesn't know of my gang ties. Neither does the law firm I supposedly work for. My job is to become a skiptrace and use the resources at my disposal to track down enemies of the Seething," I said, hoping the Manners matriarch didn't press me further. I was getting impatient and ready to get to the point.

"With a Seething tattoo on your neck?" Lady Clarke challenged. "What do you do, wear your hair down all the time? Turtleneck sweaters and high-collared shirts? What about hot summer days? I don't think so, you fraud."

Ah.

I cussed myself out while I started panicking.

I could still wiggle my way out of this. I just had to think and not take too long, looking guiltier every second.

"Fraud."

"I cover it when I need to," I defended.

"Fraud."

"No one ever gets close enough to look at my tattoo."

"Fraud."

"I will not give up the symbol of my belonging!" I yelled with a passion. "I will not give up who I am!"

Lady Clarke leaned forward, almost intrigued. She stared almost blankly at me as I shook angrily. For a moment, I *was* a soldier of the Seething. A terrible person who had earned a place of trust and respect based on the idea of subterfuge. A fraud, but not in the way Lady Clarke saw it. I would have her know just how wrong she was because at that moment, *I was.*

She held my gaze for what seemed like ever and I never wavered.

"You almost had me convinced, child," she said softly. "You almost had me believing what you say."

I set my jaw as she leaned back, confident. What did I do wrong? What was my mistake?

Keep with the role.

"It's all too preposterous. I could never believe you are so much part of the Seething and managed to get that deep into the skiptrace community," Lady Clarke gestured toward her thugs. "Skiptraces are an infection, make no doubt, but they are a suspicious bunch. Suspicion based on money for heads. They'd just as soon turn against one of their own if they thought they could get a pretty penny for it."

"You got him into Silene's camp," I said, throwing my chin toward the still-silent Addie.

"As a thug. There is a big difference," Lady Clarke said, setting her tankard down with a glassy *thunk*.

"Are you really willing to risk war with the Seething over a hunch?" I demanded, slipping further forward in the chair I was secured to, straining mightily at the rope that tied me to it, pausing in a very uncomfortable position. I could feel my arms beginning to grow numb from the tension, but I refused to give up. I would get as close to Lady Clarke as I could. I tilted my head just a little.

The Manners' boss stared at me without flinching. I wasn't sure if she could see through my deception, but I was more than willing to see it through to the end. It wasn't like I had much choice in the matter at that point. Though, even if I failed and Lady Clarke killed me right then and there, a thought I didn't relish but also didn't dwell on, Ariadne would still be able to make a living off of her parcel business.

"No, I suppose I am not," Lady Clarke finally said with a sigh. "Why do the Seething want Ottoman and his compatriot?"

"The Seething does not discuss its internal matters with outsiders," I said angrily. Although I'd really rather make headway with Lady Clarke by being less confrontational, that just wasn't how it was done in the Seething.

"Let's just say they provide an opportunity for research," Lady Clarke said. "I tell you want, there are two of them, why don't we split them. I will even let you choose which one gets, er, executed by the Seething."

"If you know they are going to be executed, then you know our claim to them is more righteous than yours," I growled. "They have committed heinous crimes against the Seething and for that they will pay."

"All you Seething do is execute people. But I think you are mistaking me for someone who cares about the Seething. You are nothing but childish fools running around your petty extortion rackets," Lady Clarke said, straightening up a little to look me in the face.

"They killed my brother!" I screamed at Lady Clarke, standing up so abruptly that the rope securing me to the chair tore. Burton, the brute who gave me a wicked-looking new neck scar, reached up and slammed me back into the chair. I bit down hard on his hand that was clamped on my shoulder. He yelled loudly, and gave the back of my head a good wallop, but Lady Clarke snapped her fingers again, preventing him from doing any more harm.

"I get the idea, child," she said tiredly. It was a long minute before she continued the conversation. I watched her carefully, searching for the moment when she decided to tell Burton to kill me. It was pretty even odds whether she would have me killed, or take me seriously and back off the Lees, but I was more concerned about the former option.

"I believe we can make a deal. I can't very well stand in the way of a Seething blood feud. Even I am not so cocky. You may have the Lees; execute them as you see fit," Lady Clarke said, rising to leave.

"How do I know you'll keep your promise and stay out of our business?" I demanded.

Lady Clarke turned back toward me.

"I run my business with a code of ethics. We are the Manners, after all, and while I am certain it is difficult for a colorful individual such as yourself to understand, our words are our guarantees," the head of the Manners said plainly.

"Why you—" I started angrily.

"And given this fact, I give you my word that someday, child, you will be lying dead at my feet. You have cost me a great deal," Lady Clarke said, walking out of the room and snapping her fingers. I yelled for effect as one of her thugs drugged me with a blow dart yet again and the whole world began to blacken.

Of course, she could still kill me, I mused as consciousness was getting more difficult to maintain.

Best not dwell on the negative.

TWENTY

I woke up slowly to a musty, mildew-y kind of smell. It took a long time before my eyes were opened *and* adjusted to the darkness, but when they finally were, I saw that the Manners had dumped me back in the house from which they'd kidnapped me. I made a quick review of my situation. The wound on my neck had stopped bleeding, thankfully, but all the change in my pockets and my knife was missing, which was no surprise. Well, the change seemed pretty petty and, if I had to guess, it was probably Addie's doing. I also wasn't particularly excited to be unarmed, but if I was going to get back on track to catch the Lees, I'd have to get out of here..

Once I was finally on my feet, I saw that the car Griffin had rented was gone. There was very little I could do to track down my entire team on foot, so I decided to head back to the hotel and regroup.

Is it even possible for one person to re*group*?

The storm that was brewing outside let out a crack the minute I stepped out the door. At the moment, more than a few people dead and alive were angry with me, but I had succeeded. The Manners, if Lady Clarke was the woman of her word she had made an effort to convince me she was, would be free to track down and re-recapture the Lees.

Of course, this house was the last building on my list and, from the reports, was the closest thing to a family home that the Lees had ever lived in. No one really knew where they came from; they just happened to appear here and stay for over a decade. I'd have to find a whole, fresh new lead to unravel and that would take some time. So I started with the best place: the Lees themselves. It was probable that, during the few weeks of close quarters Ariadne and I had spent with them, either Ottoman or Set had said something that revealed something about their whereabouts. Humans, even the terrifying and murderous ones, were creatures of habit and always returned to the same place if possible.

I began slogging my way to the nearest bus station. Of course, I didn't actually have any money for a ticket, but if I could sneak on to a living spaceship, a dead, metallic bus shouldn't be a problem.

Although, given the way I smelled, the bus driver might just refuse to let me aboard. Organic buildings never developed mildew quite to the level inorganic ones did, due to their innate microecosystems that tended to keep unwanted organisms like molds and mildews at a more balanced level. They still existed, of course, but unless the organic structure was sick in some way and their balance had been offset, mildew—

Why did that word sound familiar? *Mildew*. I stopped in my tracks for a moment, rain soaking even farther into my power red tank top.

It had a ring to it, like it was something important. Not mildew specifically, but the way it sounded. Mildew. Mill, mill...Mill Hew.

What was Mill Hew?

My brain zinged. Both Ottoman and Set had mentioned being sons of Mill Hew. I dismissed it because it, well, was coming from a raging sociopath with venom sac implants and a murderous, dead-eyed drug addict, but now the words played over and over in my head.

I had a lead.

I nearly jumped with joy. Actually, I would have, but at the exact same time an inconsiderate car splashed a tsunami of street water over my already damp form. I turned and cursed it loudly. Yeah, I'd wanted a shower, but not from water that had been sitting on the mucky stone streets of Olds II, festering with rat—

"Marcie Dunn!" The car stopped and a mass of curls leapt out. Ariadne King, in defiance of the rain, stomped toward me, each step more furious than the previous.

I opened my mouth to say something, but the irate woman just stopped and glared at me. I decided it was safer just to let her be angry first and then try to wiggle my way out of the mess I was in. She was definitely scarier than Lady Clarke.

"I am trying very hard not to smack you upside that big, thick head of yours," the princess said with a tight jaw, and one finger jabbed toward my nose. The other hand was carefully and thoroughly curled into a fist.

"I can see that," I said carefully.

"If you ever do something *stupid* like that again, I will break every bone in your body myself," Ariadne whispered harshly as she leaned closer, jabbing a long, pointed finger in my face for emphasis.

"That's perfectly fair," I said and nodded, still trying to be as carefully neutral as possible.

"You ninny!" The princess threw her arms around my neck. I returned the gesture with little hesitation. Gosh, she was tense; why was she that worried about me? I hadn't had someone this concerned about my wellbeing for years. It felt pretty good.

Ariadne ended the hug, nodding understandingly. Then, without mercy, she reached up and pinched my ear between two surprisingly strong fingers.

"Owww," I complained as she dragged me to the car. I caught a glimpse of Alyx's ghoul-like features through the car's back window and presumed that the rest of the thugs were piled into it as well.

Inside the vehicle was Skirm, bruised and not inclined to talk to me. Or even look at me. Or acknowledge that I existed. I sat as far away from his seat in the back as I could and curled up into a tight ball, trying to preserve whatever body heat I had left.

"Now what? Did your plan work? Are we free from the Manners?" the princess asked quickly, as Griffin began to take us back to the hotel.

"Yes, they think the Seething is after the Lees or, at least, they don't want to gamble that the Seething *isn't* after the Lees," I said. Alyx draped a long, black robe across my shoulders. I wrapped the thing thankfully around my shivering arms.

I marveled at the fact that the ghoul-lady wore not one but *two* robes simultaneously, so, even though I was currently bundled up in one, she still looked exactly the same as she had earlier. I was entirely curious as to how she handled hot weather.

After I had warmed up enough to think properly, I began to try to figure out the next step. Technically, the rest of this plan should go smoothly. I had a lead on the Lees and the Manners gracefully backed off of our tail and were likely to stay off for the foreseeable future.

"Wasn't that house our last lead?" Ariadne asked, glancing back to the Lee's childhood home with some concern.

"No," I said, "We have to figure out what Mill Hew is. Anyone heard of it?" I asked. Everybody shook their heads.

"It sounds like an old suburb," Skirm finally spoke, I turned to look at him. His eyes were passive.

"Old suburb?" I asked.

"There are a bunch of old inorganic settlements in the west of Olds II in the Mu district. It's mostly overrun with forest now, but they used to give these neighborhoods weird names like that," the hatted man said. "They should be on any map that's old enough. The Center of Cartography should have some."

"Okay, we'll stop there next," I said, giving Skirm an appreciative nod. He gave me one last, passive-aggressive hurricane glance before turning to stare out the window dramatically.

I sighed.

Always let the thugs through the door first.

• • •

Elated from my success with the Manners, I decided we should head straight to the Center of Cartography, which Skirm confirmed should be open by this time. Although I should have been bone-tired by this point, I was positively buzzing with excitement and a healthy dose of fear. Not even the hour-long car ride wrapped underneath Alyx's warm robe was enough to lull me to sleep, so I spent most of the time describing exactly what happened to Ariadne and the rest of the thugs. They honored me with their rapt attention, and I was thankful none of them decided to chide me on the completely reckless nature of my plan just yet.

I was waiting for some chastisement, however. It was only a matter of time.

We finally arrived at the Center of Cartography, which was exactly as dry as it sounds. The old brick-covered building was home to abhorrently creaky floorboards and shelves upon shelves upon shelves of musty, decaying maps. It didn't help that the building was semi-organic and the maps were mostly made of paper. Organic structures tended to get very humid on the inside, especially when it rains. Some of the maps had been wrapped in what looked like Centauri-made plastic sheaths, which probably prevented them from decaying too badly, but none of the maps we were looking for were quite that old.

The head cartographer was a smiling, bubbly woman who wore a magnifying glass around her neck, had copious amounts of cat hair on the hem of her long skirt, and smelled vaguely of strawberries. She spoke greatly of cartography and the Center's overly complicated organizational system as she led us to the era of maps we were looking for.

It was a *lot* more maps than I had originally anticipated. The Mu District had once been a hub for industrial growth in Olds II and so it was mapped, re-mapped, re-re-mapped at least a dozen times before it eventually declined in favor of the port-heavy Tau District. Mu District went through several major rezoning events in that time, as well as factories and laboratories opening and closing at random, and people moved closer to their jobs. All of this led to a whole aisle of shelves, an aisle that stretched lengthwise about thirty feet and upward at least ten.

"Everybody grab a map. Or eight," I commented, pulling some maps off the shelves, careful to make sure I knew where to put them back, and walked over to the nearby tables. Huge tables, meant to accommodate either multiple little maps or one ginormous one.

Surprisingly, it actually took several hours before I began to get bored. I was fairly single in that estimate as Griffin, Cabochon, and Alyx all curled up in the uncomfortable looking chairs that lined the wall, snoozing peacefully. Ariadne and Skirm had both adopted a sort of glassy-eyed stare as they sifted through each new map.

I stared at the map in front of me. It was a map on the plumbing and sewer system that ran through one of Trellis Corps-United-Consortium's iron refineries. I didn't even know why I was staring at it or how it had gotten into my pile; it wasn't even based in the Mu District. I sighed, taking a moment to observe how Trellis-United organized the sewage drains to prevent backfilling during the rainy season. I mused that all they would have had to do to fix that problem was to dig a few drainage trenches about twenty feet to the south, allowing water to drain quickly off the factory's property without filling up the sewage system.

It probably would have cost a few hundred thousand credits, but so did the fancy plumbing system they had to install.

I sighed again as the map began sliding off the table. I didn't even stop it as it vanished from view.

"Sorry," Skirm muttered from the opposite corner of the table, laying out a massive map that had nudged my map into its freefall. I grunted a mournful reply and reluctantly reached to grab the Trellis-United map.

I rolled it back up and tried to get another map to look at, but I was entirely distracted. Skirm had maintained his I'm-not-sure-you-exist routine the entire time we had been at the Center for Cartography. I figured it was because I was an idiot, allowing me to get myself captured by the Manners like that, and I figured the best idea would probably be to apologize.

The problem was, apologizing is difficult. Especially when the room was as silent as this one. Not even the bubbly-headed cartographer was around to chat everyone's ear off about the aisles dedicated solely to U.C. box stores located in the minute town of Nois, population 567.

Finally I got up the energy to apologize. I even had my mouth open to do it.

"What are you doing?" Ariadne asked, looking up at me from another table.

"What?" I asked, genuinely confused.

"You keep letting maps fall off the table. I know the head cartographer seems harmless, but seeing her wield that letter opener makes me think it's all a sham," the princess said, tone and expression serious. I blinked, looking at my new map which had managed to fall off the table like its predecessor. I stooped down to pick up the errant piece of paper and, in exaggerated motions, set it gently back onto the table. Ariadne nodded in approval.

I turned back to Skirm and opened my mouth again.

"Also I found Mill Hew," Ariadne said. I gave the princess a flat, tired expression before walking over to see what she was pointing at. There, in a fifty-year-old map, sat the words clear as day: *Mill Hew Manor*. It had been built up when the United-Consortium moved their tattoo needle factory for organic ships to the area and, after that factory closed down in favor of better-made Centauri imports, Mill Hew Manor was abandoned, left to rot and disappear from maps completely.

"Perfect," I declared, and grinned broadly. Ariadne grinned back, rolling up the map gently.

"Hey," the princess called to the head cartographer. She waved the rolled-up map in the air. "Can we borrow this?"

"No," the head cartographer said in a cheery voice, slicing through the helpless letter in her hand with an expert flick of her wrist.

I nodded understandably and grabbed a piece of paper and a pencil.

TWENTY-ONE

O ur cab finally pulled into the once-gated suburban community known as *Mill Hew Manor*. We'd had to take the train from the Center of Cartography to the southernmost end of Mu District. From there we hopped into a cab, the only one big enough to carry everyone, and instructed the cabbie to take us to Mill Hew. Of course, she didn't know where Mill Hew was, so we provided as good of a map as we could. We didn't even get lost once.

The cab crept up slowly on the suburb's broken entryway until the cabbie refused to go any farther. Stepping out onto the street made me appreciate her position all the more: the rundown, inorganic buildings were downright creepy. The houses were not precisely ugly, even if they were inorganic. Each was probably modern and cozy for their era and many even had actual, real yards made of dirt and grass. All you could hope for in an organic city was a patch of moss growing on top of each building's lumpy head.

The whole lot, however, was sorry to look at. Many of the houses were crumbling beyond repair and a few had even lost their entire roof, leaving a topless, water-stained skeleton of a building behind.

Even the air in the suburb was eerie. It was surprisingly fresh due to the massive amounts of foliage that was growing everywhere, but there was almost no sound to it. No frogs, no crickets, no breeze or rain, it was just still, like some kind of graveyard.

The community civic center positioned in the middle of everything was a decrepit wreck with a collapsed pool and the burned ruins of the pool house. Someone from the Mu District's government had placed 'No Trespassing' signs on the fence that surrounded the community center, but even those sings had to be forty years old.

"Here," Skirm finally said a word to me. He placed a good, heavy knife in my hands.

"Thanks," I whispered. He simply nodded.

I paused for half a heartbeat.

"I'm sorry for all of the trouble I caused earlier and the Lee's house," I said.

For a moment, I wasn't certain he'd actually accept my apology. His expression was almost apathetic, but then sly grin crawled across his face.

"It's alright. Aside from being a complete idiot, you're a really good boss to work for," he said. I grinned broadly.

"Hey, where do we start, boss?" Cabochon asked as the group gathered around the entrance to Mill Hew. The only problem with this lead was that it was entirely nonspecific. Yes, we knew a location that was, in some form or fashion, tied to the Lees since they themselves kept mentioning it, but we had no idea what that connection might be. I didn't know where to start looking for the twins/clones or even if they would be here.

"To the left, I guess," I said after a minute, gesturing to the dilapidated house to the left.

The house was in somewhat better condition than its neighbors, but not by much. I motioned for Alyx, Cabochon, and Skirm to circle around back while Griffin, Ariadne, and I took the front, careful not to step on any of the front porch's squeaky boards. I looked into the darkened window once I had gotten close enough. The darkness wasn't natural to the inside of the house, I quickly realized, with extremely thin lines of warm light filtering through. Someone had put a few slats of material behind the glass to make it look dark from far away. Plus, being this close to the window, I could feel a faint amount of heat radiating from inside.

Of course, I still couldn't see anything inside, so I leaned up and put my ear to the dirty panes.

There were no voices and nothing seemed to be stirring, I made a gesture to Ariadne and we moved to the door.

The princess turned the handle slowly and carefully before nudging it. The wooden construct eased open with a rusted creak coming from its hinges. I tried not to breathe too loudly.

Again, nothing stirred. I gave the thugs around back a few seconds to enter the house and scope around before I gently pushed the door open. Griffin went through the door almost immediately, eventually motioning for Ariadne and me to follow.

The room beyond was poorly lit by a tiny candle. It was furnished with furniture that could have been considered contemporary five or six decades ago. Everything was covered with a thick layer of dust, but the rooms were overall the neatest I'd seen since Meropis-C. Nothing seemed disturbed and no one seemed to be around.

After securing the rest of the rooms and confirming that the house was not, in any way, lived in, we all finally met in the kitchen, which had somehow escaped the dusty mess of the rest of the house. I couldn't decide whether to breathe easy or panic because the Lees weren't here, the last place I'd had to look for them.

Of course, this whole situation would have been a lot easier had Ottoman been an only child debtor without surgically implanted organic venom sacs.

The rest of the team was tense, but not strangely so. I was about to open my mouth for suggestions when I heard something. It was extremely faint and even the breathing of everyone around me seemed to set it off. I wasn't the only one who had heard it, however, as Alyx tilted an ear toward it. I gestured for all to be quiet as the sharp-eared ghoul and I pinpointed exactly where the sound had come from.

There it was again. Like a mouse's footstep, it came from underneath the floor. Actually, directly underneath where Ariadne was standing. Alyx shooed her off the boards and knelt down. The ghoul-lady ran two sets of very long fingers across the floor, finally wedging one between two slats. The gap was surprisingly wide for concealing a hidden passageway, but if no one was looking for it or sweeping the floor, it might have been easy to miss.

Whomever it was that caused the sound decided to show themselves. Explosively.

The floorboard shot upward with an incredible amount of force, catching Alyx in the hands before continuing up toward her chin. The ghoul-like lady was solid enough and her eyes rolled back in her head as she flew across the floor, stunned.

I made a move to kick the pouncing figure that was emerging from the floor. She, unfortunately, caught my ankle and pulled upward, forcing me to land kiester-first, without delivering a useful blow. Ariadne and Skirm, on the other hand, had better luck. While the tawny-eyed thug caught the short figure's hand, the princess slapped one of the shock pads to the intruder's other wrist. Skirm let go in a hurry as Ariadne activated the device.

Even on one of the lowest settings, the little figure seized up and fell, landing in a stupor.

"Are you okay?" I walked over to Alyx as Ariadne and Skirm secured the little interloper.

The ghoul-lady gave me a bloodied smile, making her look just a little vampiric. And I think she knew it, too.

"I've been hit by worse, katzchen," she told me. I nodded understandingly.

I turned back to the little intruder. Although I had originally presumed it was a child, and indeed this person had a very childlike body, this girl's face was worn and almost old. She had to be at least sixty if not more.

And she had a pair of gnarly-looking organic gills along her neck. It was good work, too, being almost impossible to tell where the human body ended and the organic component began. In fact, it was almost a little *too* seamless. I moved to get a closer look, Skirm holding tight to the fish-girl. The gills were not just seamlessly attached, they were also aged, with just as many wrinkles and liver spots as their owner. Now, organic components don't wrinkle or age with their human hosts. Most parasites naturally outlive their human hosts by decades due to their simplistic and usually plant-based genetic facsimile. Occasionally, there are tales of organic components being used after the death of their host, which could cause the component parasite to age faster or in pace with the host. Reusing organic parasites always came at a price, however, and that price was months and months of rejection on the part of the human host and the component itself. That left terrible lesions, swelling, and other nasty effects that ended in easily identifiable scars long after the parasite and host learned to cooperate with one another.

I didn't see any of that scarring on the fish-girl's gills or surrounding skin, which meant that she was not just merely a host to her organic gills, but they were innately a part of her. They were genetically a part of her.

There wasn't enough proof yet, but I was beginning to suspect Mill Hew's true purpose and connection to the Lees.

"Who are you?" I demanded. The little figure glared in fright. "I'm not going to hurt you."

"No," she said. "He will hurt you."

"He…?" I asked.

"In the dangerous place, down there," the girl glanced at the gaping hole in the floor.

"What is this place?" I demanded.

"This is *home*," the girl said. "This is *my* home and *our* home. You horrible—"

"Okay I get the idea," I said. "Actually I don't get the idea, but we'll let this one slide."

"Now what?" Ariadne said.

"Have someone stay with her and Alyx—" I stopped and looked over at Alyx. She seemed to be daring me to leave her behind. "Just fish-girl, definitely not Alyx. We'll go find this dangerous place."

"Griffin!" the ghoul-lady shouted. "Come stay with this little one."

I moved toward the opening in the floor. Indeed, there was falsebone-lined tunnel that led down and to the right. The exact direction to the gated community's civic center, if I was judging correctly. I wondered if the other houses had similar tunnels, and, if the tunnels met, where they eventually led.

Of course, going down into a poorly-lit tunnel and toward a so-called dangerous place is a lot easier when you team doesn't rudely shove you out of the way.

Skirm grinned at me impishly as he descended the ladder.

"I'll go first," he said in a mocking tone, "You tend to have risk-assessment issues."

"I do not!" I cried pettishly, hands on hips and everything. I quickly realized that was mightily unprofessional given the gravity of the situation, and grimaced internally.

Given there was nothing I could do but follow, I followed, clinging to the rickety ladder with a tight grip. It wasn't *that* far down, but I was not the kind of person who actually enjoyed ladders in any shape or form. Besides, this one was rotted and ancient, and it probably shouldn't be transporting anyone heavier than the little gill-sporting sprite that had introduced us to it in the first place.

I finally set my feet at the bottom, only muttering under my breath a little. The tunnel was, at least, far more well-lit than the house had been.

The tunnel itself was lined with falsebone similar to the ribcage used by the *Lilstar* to create the living area. I walked up to one of the walls for a closer look. It appeared as though this had once been an organic structure, probably around the time Mill Hew Manor was abandoned. I could still see the barest imprint of the structure's epidermis in the dirt between the ribs. The organic structure was probably used to dig the tunnel: behaving much like a worm through dirt, it snaked its way underneath the house and to who-knows-where on the other side. It was a clever system because it saved on having to dig out the tunnels by hand *and* provided an almost instant structure for human habitation.

A lot of mining operations used the same kind of organic system since all that needed to be done was plant the organic structure at one end and let it grow to maturity, stretching and digging its way in whatever direction it was led. Of course, there would always be a chance that the creature would dig in the wrong direction; in mines that didn't matter quite as much as long as the creature was going down, but a tunnel-digging operation like this would have required a lot more precision. The easiest way to keep the structure from expanding beyond where it was needed was to box it in with some kind of stone or concrete, but I didn't see any of that beyond the structure's ribcage. In fact, it seemed as though the organic structure just stopped, which meant that the previous owners might have killed it once it had grown as far as they wanted, an entirely unnecessary move that would have halted any of the other benefits the organic structure could have given them. The other option was that that they programmed the genetic facsimile to create this tunnel to be exactly as long as it was.

That second option was the most impressive. Organic structures were only as precise as their genetic facsimiles, meaning that one misplaced nucleotide during sequencing and the whole organic structure would be completely different from what it was supposed to be. The Centauri often wondered how humans got to be so good at genetics without massive computers to remember every minute detail we put into the genetic facsimiles. No one really had an answer for that, humans aren't going to let a simple thing like limited memory capacity stop us from completely manipulating the very foundations of life itself.

Skirm waited until the rest of the team made it down the ladder to head down the tunnel. Of course, he refused to let me take the lead.

Did I really have risk-assessment issues?

I sighed; that was probably musing for another time.

The tunnel went on for what felt like an entire aching mile, Skirm and me fighting subtly for the lead, with Araidne and Cabochon trying to keep close behind. Alyx seemed undaunted by the darkness, at least what I could see of her, and she darted around, sometimes cutting in front of the group, sometimes lagging behind.

Being a ghoul probably has its perks.

When the tunnel intersected with another, it was Alyx who took the lead, dashing across the opening quickly and quietly as the rest of us held back. She continued down this new spurt until we could no longer hear her footsteps. In a moment, however she returned.

"It leads back to another house, I believe," the ghoul-lady said, the swollen knot on her chin causing a slight slur. "And I found this."

Alyx handed me — not Skirm — a small bone fragment. I rolled the small piece in my hand, realizing quickly that it meant we were still continuing down the winding path of manure that was attempting to capture and retain the Lees. The fragment was, in fact, a piece of cartilage, not actual bone or falsebone. In humans, cartilage is the bendy-but-shape-holding material of the ears and noses, giving those features structure without being as inflexible as bone. More important to this situation, cartilage is also the stuff of shark skeletons, and having it around meant that someone had been playing with natural genetics.

Among other things, sharks have an innate sense of smell that rivals a dog's, and after being thrown into the organic blender a few times, that sense of smell can be adapted into all kinds of genetic sensors. For the genetic facsimiles used in the construction of organic structures or parasites, a much more blunt sensor based off of an elephant's sense of smell would do the trick. A shark-based sensor, however, was far more subtle, able to pick up even the tiniest of differences in amino acids and the overall genetic structure.

Given the highly organized and clandestine nature of this facility, it was safe to say that they were not performing any sort of legal experiments on natural genetics. This meant that more likely than not, the subjects for this lab were humans and human genetics.

"I think we found the Lees' birthplace," I said grimly, handing the princess the piece of cartilage.

"What is it?" Cabochon asked.

"This means they are manipulating genetics. *Real* genetics, not facsimiles like ships use," the princess scowled. "I think we've found a hidden illicit lab."

Cabochon grunted softly in surprise.

"I doubt they stopped at venom sacs and gills, so be prepared for some freaky stuff," I commented, readying the knife Skirm had handed me. It wasn't like I could turn around now. I was amazingly in debt in more ways than one and if I didn't get those elusive twins, I would undoubtedly end up on the wrong side of some cheap investigation novel. *The Debtor Who Tried*.

No, thank you.

I pulled the team forward, deeper into the tunnel, taking the lead despite Skirm's reluctance. I was practically stomping my feet the entire way there — quietly, of course.

The tunnel finally widened and gave us an end, directly underneath the civic center as I'd predicted, the ginormous gouge in the ceiling looking up into what used to be a fair-sized swimming pool.

The room itself was filled with both organic and inorganic medical and scientific equipment, most of which I recognized, but some of it had to be of Centauri origin. The genetic sensors were arrayed in the center of the room along with a half-dozen glass tanks filled with bulbous, semi-mummified, organic masses. The scientists would put the genetic sample into each tank and allow the sensor to give it a thorough sniff. Depending on whether or not the sensor liked what it smelled, it would sound out a variety of whistles, each signaling a different genetic defect in the sample. Of course, one sensor could only do so much, so there were multiple sensors smelling for different types of defects.

Lining the room were about ten different... well...cells, each big enough for a human or two to live in comfortably while having their genetic insides turned upside down.

I swallowed very loudly. This was definitely the dangerous place.

I motioned for the rest of the team to fan out, not too far from one another of course. Ariadne kept close to my elbow, but surprisingly wandered off toward items I hoped she was recognizing. She'd pick up a piece of old equipment or two, inspect it and put it down, all while a concerned expression drew itself on her face.

Suddenly, the hairs on the back of my neck stood up.

"Oh sh—" I began, cut off as a hand, seeming to materialize itself out of nowhere, curled around my arm. Another hand clamped my mouth shut as I tried to scream.

A fierce Ariadne swiped at the interloper, trying to put the shock pads on whatever tangible skin there was. She finally succeeded and I clenched my jaw to keep from biting my tongue off as the electricity coursed from the ruffian's body into mine.

I made it to the ground, coughing and sputtering. It looked like the rest of the team was having the same kind of trouble. Pairs of mutilated humanoids started fights with Skirm, Alyx, and Cabochon, all displaying a dazzling array of strangeness. Some were overly short, some had skin that was almost melting off their bodies, some had eyes that glowed in the low light.

Yup. Definitely an illegal genetic-manipulation lab.

The ruffian that had tried to catch hold of me had coarse, bumpy skin that flickered with a variety of natural colors. It reminded me very much of a chameleon, and made it possible for him to blend into the walls around me. He tried to stand up on disproportionately long legs and arms. His eyes were almost tear-dropped shape as he looked at me.

"Stay down," I told him coolly. I'd rather not have to fight these people. He didn't seem to mind the idea, resting his head back on the floor where he'd fallen.

I scrambled to my feet as quietly as I could, still shaking from being electrocuted. Ariadne had already crossed the room, trying to catch another person with the shock-device. I picked up the knife Skirm had given me, looking to see what the best target would be. Throwing the knife was out of the question because it was a free-for-all melee and I might hit someone on my own team. So I dove into it, flicking my knife toward one of the guys with glowing eyes. He moved almost fluidly, shifting to the side. He slapped me upside my pretty little head.

Of course, I'd pick the guy who seemed to have an unnatural affinity for fighting.

I righted myself, giving this fellow a good once-over. I might not have great eyes in the low light, but from what I could tell, this guy seemed to be part cat. I thought back to the mother cat and kittens Ariadne and I'd rescued on Myrkheim, cute, adorable, and tolerably sweet; not exactly good reference material for taking down this cat-man. At least he didn't seem to have razor-sharp claws. I took a swing at him with my knife, which he dodged easily.

For what seemed like an amazingly long and frustrating period of time, the cat-man toyed with me. I'd make a move, he'd dodge it. He'd attack, I'd try to defend and simply get slapped again. He smirked and remained content to simply harass me until I was well worn-out. It would be a while before that happened, however, because I was also getting very angry. This man was being flippant with me, not even taking my efforts with any major amount of seriousness.

Jerk. I've fought bigger.

I told myself to calm down after narrowly dodging one of his irritating, slap-based attacks. Getting angry without doing anything to fix the situation is deadly, so I observed. Cat-Man had to have a weakness of some kind; everybody did. What was it? I chanted the words over and over in my head. One good smack sent me flying halfway across the room. Ah, his patience and fun did have an end. That was good to know.

I thought over every move he had made as I recovered from the slap. His defense was almost impenetrable, up until he went on the attack. Using his height and strength against me was great, but it made him cocky. The window of opportunity that I had between his attack and him returning to the defensive was small, so I'd have to be quicker than I ever had been before.

I took a great big swipe at Cat-Man with my knife; he deflected it easily and, as I expected, returned it with another slap. This time I threw myself toward him quickly. Not so quick that he didn't start retreating immediately — he was part cat after all — but it was enough for me to shoulder his next slap and thrust my knife into his exposed side. His eyes grew big as I stared into them and he whimpered slightly. It didn't have to be a fatal wound, but it was enough to send him scurrying down the nearest hallway, leaving me and my now-bloodied knife behind.

I turned back to the rest of the fight and someone threw a cheap shot across my nose. I screamed loudly as the healing cartilage was re-shattered. One of these days I might even learn how to duck properly.

"How's that, little one?" a sickening voice cooed. Of course, I couldn't see who exactly it was, but I had enough information to figure that out. Who else took some kind of perverse pleasure in breaking my foremost facial features? I blinked back tears to look up at Ottoman, who sneered.

"Where's Set?" I asked, trying not to sniffle. I started to stand up slowly, only to have a run-in between Ottoman's boot and my stomach. I gasped as the air escaped my lungs at startling speeds. I curled sideways, trying to breathe again, and Ottoman followed, poised to kick me again.

So I slammed the knife I still held into his thinly shoed foot. The blade went through boot, flesh, and floor, pinning the murderous Lee in place. Ottoman yelled in surprise, giving me a moment to stand back up.

He reached down for the knife, but not before I caught his head, slamming it down onto my knee. He began to fall backward in reaction, but couldn't quite catch himself with one foot still immobile. Ottoman's head fell with a loud thud onto the floor and for a moment I almost figured he was dead.

Unfortunately, while I'd witnessed his still-breathing form, Set had not.

"You promised he would *live!*" the other twin/clone came out of nowhere and screamed. Before I could react, he caught me by the throat, shoving me backwards until I was up against the wall. He held me by the neck with his right hand, using his left one to jam a blade into my right hand, pinning it to the wall in much the same motion I'd used to incapacitate Ottoman.

Karma was a...*pig*.

I gasped and sputtered, panic filling my mind as I tried to pry open the addict's grip. My eyes widened in terror as I watched Set squeeze the life out of me. His face had the sharpest and most keenly bent-on-death expression I had ever seen on a living being. Setesh was not a human, he was a weapon, a genetic monster, and while Ottoman was bad, Set was the one who'd set up their reputation. He was the murderer who loved it, who relished the idea of killing over and over again. But somehow he'd known that was wrong, somewhere along the road he'd decided to empty his brain with drugs instead of continuing to kill.

I tried to squeak out a few words, trying to plead to whatever part of him hated what he'd become, but all that came of it was a few garbled noises.

Set pressed harder with both hands, and my vision grew spotty.

I would die because I was a bumbling idiot, I mused.

Of course, I couldn't even do that properly.

A blur of a human came up to Set, the overly task-saturated psychopath not noticing that something was wrong until Ariadne had already begun her punch. The princess's hand connected solidly with the side of Set's skull, rendering the psychopath instantly dazed and releasing me from my doom.

I sputtered loudly as I fell to my knees, hand still skewered to the wall.

"Marcie!" Ariadne called after she'd made sure Set was unconscious. I gestured to my hand as I coughed. The princess carefully removed the excruciating hand/knife combo from the wall, leaving the blade in place to staunch the bleeding.

I took stock of the rest of the room. It appeared that our team won, although both Alyx and I were in need of some serious medical intervention, as the ghoul-lady held a bloodied towel to her side. It must not have been a serious wound, however, since she was still standing upright and smiling her ghoul-like smile. Ottoman and Setesh were both incapacitated and safe to bind, along with one or two of the other genetic experiments, including the grey-skinned chameleon and little fish-girl from earlier who Griffin brought down at Cabochon's behest. Secure in the idea that Alyx, Ariadne, Skirm, and I could handle the highly incapacitated mutants, Griffin and Cabochon headed back to the first house to get back up and find paramedics.

"I don't wanna be a skiptrace," I whispered hoarsely.

"Oh, don't give me that." Ariadne said, sporting a new busted lip, as she ripped the knife out of my hand without warning. I yelped in pain as she wrapped the wound in a swath of fabric.

So I waited impatiently for the paramedics to arrive.

Twenty-Two

"**N**eed help with that?" I asked Ariadne as she struggled with our substantial stack of Receipts of Capture. The folders threatened to slide off of one another onto the damp ground.

"Count how many usable hands you have right now," she muttered, almost tripping over her own feet.

"One," I muttered, looking down at my bandaged hand as if I could still see the knife sticking out of it.

"Use it to open the door," the princess said, panting.

I sighed loudly, but pressed the iris' access scale. We were both bandaged, healing, and in possession of a sizable Receipt of Capture from the Old II's police department, where we'd delivered the Lees and all their illicit genetic experiment compatriots, too. While the chief of police couldn't let us in on all the details, she hinted that we'd unearthed one of the biggest and oldest illegal genetic manipulation laboratories in the area.

My hope that this unruly stack of captures would please Aristotle had gradually turned to irritation that the lawyer had sent us into the mess in the first place. I didn't feel like this was any sort of test to prove I was worthy of the skiptrace license; it felt more like the room was full of idiots. What I did hope was that I could curb my tongue.

"Come," Aristotle's voice wafted from behind the door. The organic membrane retracted, revealing an unchanged room with the lawyer seated behind his desk. He looked up at us for a moment without recognition. Once he finally did realize who we were, his eyes went big and he started pleading.

"You're really alive," he exclaimed, standing up in surprise.

"Yeah, about that," I said as Ariadne slammed the receipt onto the lawyer's desk. "We really, really shouldn't be."

"I know; once you left I heard all about the Lees. I can't describe how sorry I am." Aristotle was beginning to sweat. Despite his nervous demeanor, he sounded genuine. He reached into his desk for a checkbook and began scribbling into it. "That was a horrible mistake."

"Did Silene of Ascalon contact you?" I demanded.

"Yes, yes, and I have taken her up on the offer of keeping my records up-to-date," the lawyer said, handing me a check. "Here is the total bounty for all the quarries you took into custody. Plus I am willing to foot the bill for whatever healthcare you need for mission-related injuries."

I looked at the check, scrutinizing it before handing it to Ariadne. I watched the shamed lawyer in front of me as he looked me in the eye sincerely.

I might even get a little cosmetic surgery for my nose.

"I'm sure you ladies want to get on with finding a new lawyer. I can officially mark your license as up for representation," he said. I looked at Ariadne.

"Are we really going to fire him over a messed-up file?" I asked the princess. She tugged at the check thoughtfully. In all honesty, we really didn't have much of an option. While we had uncovered a massive conspiracy, it was unlikely any lawyer would be willing to risk hiring two beat-up sprites such as ourselves. I also happened to know that Aristotle's company was not known for its mistakes, and was already suffering great losses, what with only four working skiptraces — and that counted Ariadne and me.

"I don't really think so. As long as he pays to get your nose patched up properly," Ariadne said.

"And pays for a new wardrobe for you," I commented.

"You guys know the definition for idiot is to repeat the same thing over and over expecting a different result?" Aristotle said.

"You said you'd take Silene's offer, so *technically* it won't be repeating the same thing over," I shrugged. "You'll be better prepared."

Aristotle sighed, but it sounded largely in relief.

"Come and see me for a new mission whenever you want it," he said, sticking his hand out to shake. After Ariadne and I took turns shaking it, we strode out the door.

Bonus Scene

How Humans Discovered Pluripotent Cells

Time: A little over 70 years ago
Location: Station Eden-3, in heliocentric orbit between Mercury and Venus

Human engineer Culman Andrews let out a long, slow sigh.

He was greatly enjoying the process of turning the organic Eden-3 into the system's biggest cyborg by combining human living technology with Centauri machineries. The whole station smelled in equal parts of warmed-over wheat - a common scent for plant-based organic structures - and of the plastics and metals brought in from the Proxima Centauri system. Eden-3 was a sort-of testing ground to truly push the limits of what human and Centauri collaboration could accomplish and Andrews was at the very heart of it.

So far, though, it mostly involved staring at the Centauri-invented electricity-based screens for inordinate amounts of time. Andrews looked back at his screen, but unfocused his eyes and let the numbers and diagrams it projected get comfortably fuzzy. He couldn't understand how his Centauri

351

compatriot - short-ish, grey telepath named Whiffle - was able to watch these screens for so long without needing any sort of break. Maybe it was his flat, dark eyes or some kind of implant that eased the visual stress of staring for so long.

After a moment of rumination, Andrews finally refocused his eyes and set back to his task, noted the dust that was beginning to collect on the top of his monitor. He reached up and began to wipe the dust off, slicing his finger along the sharp metal edge of the screen's casing.

"OW!" he yelled, retracting his hand and inspecting the damaged finger. It was bleeding quite a bit as Andrews looked around for something to use as a bandage.

Are you injured? Whiffle said without any outward sign of communication. The Centauri telepathy was still weird to Andrews, but he was getting used to it.

A little, Andrews said/thought, still looking for a makeshift bandage. Without warning, Whiffle reached over and grabbed Andrew's injured hand. Taking off his argon-providing mask, the Centauri exposed his small mouth and gave Andrews' wound a good lick, then returned the mask to his face and went back to work as if nothing happened.

Andrews looked at the saliva-covered appendage with a barely veiled mixture of horror, revulsion, and uncertainty. He wasn't necessarily disgusted at Whiffle - Andrews always tried to remain open to alien customs - but as a human, Andrews didn't see any benefit to what had happened.

Uh, thanks? He thought to the Centauri carefully wiping the spittle onto his coveralls.

Tsk, tsk you didn't let it sit long enough. Whiffle made the strange clicking sound Centauri do when they're irritated.

Pardon? Andrews asked as Whiffle once again took his injured hand and licked the wound.

You're just like a baby, making other people lick your wounds. Whiffle sighed. *Don't your human mothers teach you to lick your own wounds?*

"Teach me what?" Andrews said aloud without thinking. "Humans don't lick their wounds, at least not literally."

Then how do you heal? Whiffled asked with almost affronted curiosity.

"We put a bandage on like normal," Andrews said.

That's the exact opposite of normal. Does your saliva not heal you? Whiffled asked. Andrews shook his head.

"No its actually unsani—" the human glanced at his finger. He yelped aloud and stumbled out of his seat, falling less-than-gracefully on the organic floor. The formerly wounded appendage was looking mostly whole and uninjured. He rubbed it repeatedly in disbelief. There wasn't even any pain or scarring.

You really are idiots, Whiffle laid his pronouncement across the whole of humanity.

"Is this why you've been licking the organic walls?" Andrews asked.

After our current discussion, I'm very concerned about the fact that it took you this long to ask why I was doing that, Whiffle folded his arms.

"Good point," Andrews said, still looking at his finger. "We should probably tell the medical about staff this."

Whiffle shrugged and turned back to his screen.

Author Biography

Honestly, this book is probably way more interesting than anything I could write about myself in an author's biography. Does the book tell you my favorite ice cream flavor (mint with brownies)? Well, no. Does it tell you if I'm a dog or cat person (actually I prefer fish, but cats are cool)? No, not really. Does it tell you that I grew up at the end of civilization and that I'm actually faxing all of my books through time to be published thousands of years before I'm even born? Duh, of course not. That would be silly. And would result in my immediate arrest by the local Temporal Enforcement Authorities (TEA).

By the way, do you hear sirens? No? Huh. Those must just be on my end.